AS THE EARL LIKES

ROGUE RULES
BOOK FOUR

DARCY BURKE

Zealous Quill Press

For the amazing people I've met at Dave Matthews Band shows over the (many) years, particularly at the Gorge. You're the best of what's around. #iykyk

AS THE EARL LIKES

Heir to a dukedom, Clive Halifax, Earl of Shefford, is weary
of fixing his father's scandalous messes and watching his
mother suffer for them. Sheff vows to live as the Lothario
everyone believes him to be, never to wed. However, his
parents will not stop insisting he marry, so he chooses the
most inappropriate bride he can find and pays her to be his
fake betrothed for the remainder of the Season.

Josephine Harker lives at the edge of Society with a mother
who runs a gaming club and an artist father who flits about
the ton. She just wants the ability to choose her own path
instead of what society dictates—or what her parents think is
best for her. When Shefford, a notorious rake, proposes a
faux engagement along with a substantial sum, she cannot
refuse.

Dangerously captivated by one another from the outset, their
attraction explodes into a searing passion they can't deny.
But the last thing Jo wants is to risk her heart on a rogue who

can't see he's much more than his reputation—or that there is such a thing as true love.

Don't miss the rest of the *Rogue Rules*!

Do you want to hear all the latest about me and my books? Sign up at <u>Reader Club newsletter</u> for members-only bonus content, advance notice of pre-orders, insider scoop, as well as contests and giveaways!

Care to share your love for my books with like-minded readers? Want to hang with me and see pictures of my cats (who doesn't!)? Then don't miss my exclusive Facebook groups!

Darcy's Duchesses for historical readers
Burke's Book Lovers for contemporary readers

Want more historical romance? Do you like your historical romance filled with passion and red hot chemistry? Join me and my author friends in the Facebook group, Historical Harlots, for exclusive giveaways, chat with amazing HistRom authors, and more!

THE ROGUE RULES

Never be alone with a rogue.
Never flirt with a rogue.
Never give a rogue a chance.
Never doubt a rogue's reputation.
Never believe a rogue's pledge of love or devotion.
Never trust a rogue to change.
Never allow a rogue to see your heart.
Ruin the rogue before he can ruin you.

CHAPTER 1

May 1816, London

"Shefford, this reluctance to marry has gone on long enough."

Clive Halifax, twelfth Earl of Shefford and heir to the Duke of Henlow, closed his eyes and tipped his head back slightly. He counted to three, then lowered his head, opened his eyes, and leveled his bored gaze at his mother.

"It isn't so much reluctance as refusal." Sheff gave her a bland smile. "It will continue for the foreseeable future." He moved to the tray atop a cabinet that held a helpful supply of wine and liquor. This was his father's house, and there would never be a lack of such fortification. After splashing port into a glass, Sheff turned.

The Duchess of Henlow, standing in the center of the drawing room, nearly growled in frustration, her blue eyes flashing. Though she was a small, very thin woman, her presence could fill a room. "It's bad enough your sister hasn't wed yet. She's now seen as having impossibly high standards. Her position on the Marriage Mart has fallen far below that of other young ladies of less stature and breeding. It's unconscionable!"

"Oh, yes, it's just a *scandal* that Minerva doesn't want to wed herself to a philanderer or a drunkard. Her standards are *absolutely* too high." Sheff kept from rolling his eyes, but the urge was strong.

His mother narrowed her eyes at him. "Don't take that sarcastic tone with me. Your sister is being altogether too demanding. No man is perfect."

"He doesn't have to be. He just needs to be perfect for *her*," Sheff said softly. He lifted his glass in a toast before taking a drink.

"Pfft. I never credited you for a romantic," the duchess said. She stared at him a moment, her ire seeming to ease. "I didn't think you or your sister would be like that. Not after… Well, not with what you've been privy to."

She meant the awful example of matrimony she and their father had set, not that it was her fault. Sheff knew it was entirely his father's. Just as Sheff expected to be the same kind of husband. Some men weren't meant for an eternal love.

Or love at all.

"This is precisely why you shouldn't expect or demand marriage from either me or Min. Our sense of it is rather warped."

His mother's gaze hardened once more. "You've a duty to the dukedom. And your sister isn't going to be some hopeless spinster. It's bad enough she's aligned with one."

The duchess referred to Min's companion, Ellis Danger-field, an orphan they'd welcomed into their household when she was nine years old—at his father's insistence. Their mother had never been particularly warm toward Ellis, but that was to be expected given Ellis was just one of the duke's many illegitimate children.

Or so Sheff believed. No one had ever said, and he'd never asked. It was just something he took as truth. Why else would the duke take in the child of a family friend who'd died? He'd never possessed one sentimental thought, as far as Sheff could tell.

That wasn't exactly true. If it were, the duke would never have accepted Ellis. Someday, Sheff would like to know definitively that Ellis was his father's daughter, but they never discussed the duke's indiscretions outside of when they were happening. In those moments of crisis, Sheff was typically required to clean up his father's mess to protect the duke's reputation, though Sheff didn't do it for him. He did it for the family—for his mother and especially for Min. Then, they were never mentioned again. And the duke's past peccadilloes were certainly never resurrected.

"Mama, I'm sure you don't mean to disparage dear Ellis," Sheff said. "She has been a sister to Min and me."

The duchess pursed her lips, her expression disgruntled. "I have no concern for her whatsoever except for how she reflects on and influences your actual sister."

Sheff exhaled. "I don't think she bears any reflection on Min, nor does she exert influence. Min has a mind of her own, which I should think you would know." He sipped his port and glanced at the clock. They were due to leave for the ball at Northumberland House shortly. Which meant Min and Ellis would enter at any moment. They might even be eavesdropping outside the door. That made him smile. It would serve his mother right to be overheard in her judgment.

"Of course I know that," the duchess snapped. "But the two of them together...it's concerning. Min *must* wed this

Season. I fear she will be relegated to spinsterhood if she does not."

Sheff considered arguing, particularly since it would keep the conversation away from him, where it had started. But he was saved from doing so by the arrival of his sister and Ellis.

Min looked beautiful as always, her dark hair coiled into an elegant, complicated style of curls and braids adorned with pearls and a tall peacock feather. Her gown was a shimmering teal blue with purple ribbon decorating the flounces at her hem.

Ellis, by contrast, wore a simple peach-colored gown with a minimum of lace at the bodice and hem. Her blonde hair was styled and decorated without fuss, a single ivory ribbon wound through the curls.

"I am sure I heard the word 'spinsterhood' just before we entered," Min said, looking at the duchess. "Were you referring to me or to Ellis?"

Sheff didn't give their mother the chance to prevaricate. "Both of you, really. Come, we should go."

The sooner they arrived, the sooner he could leave. He often escorted his mother, Min, and Ellis to events, stayed a short but acceptable amount of time, then took himself off to one of his clubs. He was already considering where he might go. The Phoenix Club to drink fine whisky? Perhaps the Siren's Call to play a hand of cards or two. Ultimately, he would likely end up at the Rogue's Den, where his favorite courtesan would greet him with a seductive smile.

However, it appeared Min was not ready to let the matter of spinsterhood drop. She narrowed her eyes at their mother, looking nearly like the duchess had when she'd scolded Sheff a bit ago. "Spinsterhood is not akin to hanging, Mother. If that is how I am meant to spend my life, so be it. I will choose being alone if that will bring me the most happiness."

"It will not," the duchess said firmly.

"Can you really say that?" Min asked quietly. "Would you not be happier if you weren't leg shackled to Father?"

Their mother sucked in a breath. She did not hesitate before answering. "I would *not*. Where would I be? Alone at my parents' estate in Dorset. Reading the same books over and over, and probably herding cats."

"That sounds rather lovely," Ellis murmured.

Sheff swallowed a grin. Ellis rarely spoke around their mother, and she certainly didn't take an adversarial point of view. He was glad she did just then.

Min was too, for she sent an approving smile toward Ellis. "Yes, it does. Anyway, Mother, I'm not in danger of anything horrible. I am quite content with my life as it is for now, and I'm not concerned about the future. So you shouldn't be either. Why not pester Sheff instead?" She sent him a look, then mouthed an apology.

Now, Sheff did roll his eyes. "How do you think our conversation started?" He finished the port and set the glass down on the tray. "Time to go."

He started toward the door, gesturing for the younger ladies to precede them. Then he offered his arm to the duchess.

She set her gloved hand on his sleeve. "Would you please just find a wife? Any wife will do at this point. Then your father will stop bothering me about what I'm doing to ensure you do."

That was the truth, then. She was seeking to put a barrier between herself and her loathsome husband. Sheff not only didn't blame her, he felt badly that his actions had caused her to be the focus of any of his father's attention, let alone his anger.

"I will consider it," he said in a low tone that made him feel as hollow as his intention. He would not find a wife. Not even *any* wife. But he would say anything to end the haranguing.

Would he also *do* anything?

An idea began to form. It was daring. Perhaps even foolhardy, but it would give him a much-needed reprieve. If they believed he was betrothed, their persistent harassment would end. But he couldn't *actually* betroth himself, not unless he intended to marry, which he absolutely did not.

Was there a woman who might help him? Someone who would agree to a betrothal—but no marriage? Finding her might be a challenge, but Sheff was always up for that.

She wouldn't be someone on the Marriage Mart, for such a young lady would never agree to the scheme. That meant finding someone perhaps older or less "appropriate." He suddenly realized this plan could have the added benefit of horrifying his parents. That would serve them right after their years-long campaign to see him trapped in marriage.

He would consider this most sincerely. But was he desperate enough to make it happen?

~

After staying a dutiful hour at Northumberland House, Sheff departed in a hack bound for the Siren's Call. He might play cards, or perhaps he'd just have an ale. He could not stop thinking about the plan that had been formulating in his head all evening. And there was no better place to continue his contemplation than the Siren's Call.

He seated himself at the table in the corner where he and his friends usually sat. One or more of them might turn up, but it was early yet, not even eleven.

His mind turned to the matter at hand: marriage. More accurately, stopping his parents' incessant demands that he wed.

If he were betrothed, he could put an end to their harassment, both of him *and* Min. Perhaps then he and his sister could breathe easier and live the lives they chose instead of what their parents or Society demanded.

But could Sheff really avoid that? He'd successfully kept himself from serving in the House of Commons, but that wasn't something his father bothered him about. Why would he when the duke could hardly be moved to tend to his own duties in the Lords? If he went to Westminster more than once a month Sheff would be surprised.

Someday, perhaps sooner rather than later, if his father didn't ease his indulgences, Sheff would inherit the dukedom. Then it would be his responsibility to serve in the Lords. Even if he paid only a modicum of attention, he'd do better than his father.

Though, he planned to do more than that. He also knew one of his friends in particular, the Baron Droxford, would ensure he did. No one took his duty more seriously than Droxford.

"If it isn't the Earl of Shefford." Josephine Harker, daughter of the owner of the Siren's Call, approached his table with a sway of her hips and a quirk of her lush mouth. "You don't have ale yet?"

"Becky's been busy." Sheff inclined his head toward the redhead balancing a tray of ale as she made her way to a table. "Are you short a serving maid tonight?"

Jo's dark brows pitched over her hazel eyes. What would have been an expression of consternation on someone else was an arresting look of contemplation on Jo's striking features, as if her mind churned faster than even she could keep up with. But then she was inordinately clever. "No, but I don't know where Agnes has gone. I hadn't realized she was missing until you just said something. Damn."

"Is that a problem?" Sheff asked. "Perhaps she's taking care of a personal matter."

Snapping her gaze to his, Jo smirked. "I'm surprised you would think of such a thing."

Sheff wasn't sure if he ought to be offended or amused. "Why?"

Jo lifted a shoulder, which was covered by the slightly puffed sleeve of her otherwise austere blue gown. "Because you are a rogue with little consideration for the fairer sex."

Touching his chest in mock affront, Sheff sucked in a breath. "I have *great* consideration for the fairer sex. Some would argue too much," he added with a comical leer that prompted her to laugh, which had been his goal. Straightening his expression, he added, "I also have a sister and an almost sister, and I know that sometimes a lady just needs a moment—or ten—alone."

"How shockingly astute of you," Jo murmured with an appreciative nod. "And now you must excuse me so I may look for Agnes. I'm sure Becky will be along directly with your ale. She knows what you like."

"I am an open book, I'm afraid."

"Come now, Sheff, even you must have secrets," Jo said with an almost flirtatious edge, but that was the relationship they shared—not quite flirting with one another, but not entirely platonic either. "I know you do." She sent him a taunting look, daring him to ask what she imagined them to be.

But she was gone before he could ask.

A moment later, Becky brought him his ale, and they chatted for a few minutes. When she departed, Sheff took a drink as he contemplated whether he wanted to visit the cardroom.

Deciding he may as well, Sheff stood just as Jo returned. She strode straight for him, her face dark with concern.

"Come with me," she said without preamble before taking his hand and tugging him from the large common room.

Sheff had no choice but to leave his ale on the table as she pulled him through an arched doorway. There were stairs leading up and down. She released his hand and took the ascending staircase. As Sheff trailed behind, he wondered at the tingling sensation shooting from his palm and alerting his body to the fact that Jo was an exceptionally alluring woman. Who'd touched him.

Jerking his focus to whatever problem was at hand, he asked, "What is happening?"

"I've found Agnes." Jo looked back at Sheff over her shoulder as they reached the first-floor landing. "She was not taking care of a personal matter, at least not to do with her." She continued up the next flight to the second floor.

Jo opened a door into a small chamber. Moving through the space, she entered a narrow corridor. "We rent rooms here to some of the employees. Agnes has been living here since she was hired three months ago."

They were going to Agnes's lodgings, and she was not dealing with a personal matter.

Sheff reached out and snagged Jo's elbow, drawing her to stop. "Why did you want *me* to come up here?"

Facing him, Jo pursed her lips. "I suppose it's better if I prepare you before we just walk in. Agnes was…entertaining a gentleman. He has, unfortunately, become ill, and Agnes was afraid to leave him."

A cold certainty settled into Sheff's middle. "This gentleman wouldn't be the Duke of Henlow, would he?"

Why else would Jo ask for his help specifically? What's more, this was precisely the sort of activity Sheff's father would engage in on a Thursday evening. Hell, any evening.

"Yes," Jo replied. Her tone was short, succinct, but her gaze was soft, caring.

"Has he done this here before?" Sheff asked. Over the past few years, he'd had to rescue his father from countless similar situations, but never from the Siren's Call. Most often, it was from some opera singer's bed or one of many brothels he liked to visit.

Jo nodded. "It's been a while, nearly a year, I'd say. My mother tossed him out that time and told him not to come back. I don't think he has—until tonight."

Sheff blew out a breath and muttered, "Lovely." It seemed Jo *did* know Sheff's secrets. Or one of them anyway. Summoning a bland, humorless smile, he gestured for her to continue along the corridor. "Shall we?"

Turning on her heel, Jo led him to the room at the end on the left. The duke lay face down on the floor next to Agnes's narrow bed, wearing his shirt and breeches, which had been loosened. The rest of his clothing, including his boots, were strewn about the small bedchamber.

Agnes sat on the edge of the bed, a blanket drawn around her shift-clad form. Tears streamed down her cheeks as she shook. Upon seeing Sheff, she bolted to her feet, barely missing his father sprawled on the floor. His low snores filled the tight space.

"I'm so sorry. I was just trying to be hospitable. Him being a duke and all," Agnes blathered. She sniffed and wiped the edge of her blanket over her nose. The lift of her arm exposed more of her shift, and Sheff noted a splash of sick on the garment.

He closed his eyes and tamped down the disgust coiling within him. He counted to three before opening his eyes again, his shame and fury buried once more.

"Did anything happen between you before he fell unconscious?" Jo asked.

Agnes stared at her. "I…yes." She looked down at the floor. "But we did not have intercourse."

Relief coursed through Sheff. He appreciated small triumphs.

"Still, if my mother finds out, you'll be looking for a new job," Jo said.

Sheff snapped his gaze to her. "Don't let that happen. This isn't Agnes's fault. My father is a master manipulator. Furthermore, he *is* a duke. What young woman has the gumption to turn her back on him? Besides you," he added.

"It isn't my decision." Jo sent poor Agnes a sympathetic glance. "My mother has no patience for serving maids who dawdle with customers. It is a condition of employment and made very clear at the outset."

Agnes's crying started anew. "I know. I'm so ashamed." Sobs racked her frame.

"Come away now," Jo said, holding her arm out. "You can go to my chamber downstairs and get cleaned up while his lordship manages the duke."

"Wait," Sheff said. "Agnes, it's imperative you say *nothing* of this to *anyone*. Can you promise me that? This is vital." Rumors of the duke's transgressions were numerous and sometimes obscene, but Sheff did his best to quiet them.

Agnes nodded.

Jo gave her a pointed look. "Do listen to his lordship. If you manage to retain your position here, it will be in jeopardy if you gossip."

"I understand. I am terribly sorry. I didn't mean to cause trouble." Agnes's voice hitched, and she began to cry again. She quickly dashed from the chamber.

"Poor girl." Sheff frowned at his father's snoring form. "I can't comprehend how she—and others like her are—are swept away by him."

"As you pointed out a few minutes ago, he's a duke," Jo said sardonically. "That is enough to turn many heads. And he's not unattractive. Speaking objectively," she added.

Yes, he was a not-unattractive duke with more charm than he deserved. "Can you bring coffee? I'll need that to rouse him from his stupor, at least long enough for me to get him dressed and into a hack. Once he's home, the footmen can carry him upstairs."

"I take it that is not an unusual occurrence. How unfortunate that you must involve members of your household."

"They are discreet. If they aren't, they are soon dismissed."

She looked at Sheff with sympathy. "I didn't realize the situation was that bad. I mean, I knew he had a reputation for debauchery, but it sounds as though you manage regular misbehavior."

"Honestly, tonight's situation is far from the worst I've dealt with." Why was he telling her this? "Never mind. Forget I said that." He wiped a hand over his brow.

"What the devil is going on in here?" Jo's mother, Jewel Harker, stepped into the small chamber, one hand on her hip. She possessed the same wide, expressive mouth as her daughter, but her hair was a lighter brown and now lined with gray. Her eyes were smaller and her chin broader. She was a striking woman, her figure curved and enticing in all the right places. Noticing such things about any woman he encountered was one of many reasons Sheff knew he was a scoundrel at his core.

Jewel looked down at Sheff's father and scoffed. "Is that bloody Henlow? He's not allowed here." Her gaze snapped to Sheff. "Given your presence, it must be him." Finally, she fixed her attention on her daughter. "Explain."

Exhaling, Jo detailed what they knew or had deduced—that Agnes had been persuaded by the duke to bring him here, that they had not engaged in intercourse, that he'd been ill. Then he'd lost consciousness.

"Make sure she's gone tomorrow," Jewel said. She glowered at the duke. "And toss him out now."

Before Sheff could advocate for Agnes, Jo spoke. "Mama, Agnes knows she made a mistake. Henlow took advantage." She glanced toward Sheff.

"Yes," Sheff quickly agreed. "He preys on impressionable young women."

Jewel snorted. "I bloody well know that. I was once an impressionable young woman." She moved closer to Sheff's father and sneered down at him. For a moment, Sheff thought she might spit on him. And Sheff wasn't sure if he'd care.

Then he realized what she'd said. He saw that Jo was staring at her mother.

"Mama, you and the duke…?"

"Me and half of London." Jewel shifted her attention to Sheff. "Honestly, I'm surprised he doesn't have the pox. Or does he by now?"

If he did, Sheff was not aware of it. God, what would Sheff even do if that were the case? The man was unstoppable.

"To my knowledge, he does not," Sheff said tightly. "I will remove him from the premises as quickly as possible." How he wished he had his coach and driver. Or at least the driver.

"Good." Jewel pinned him with a dark stare. "And make sure he doesn't return, else I will make sure all of London knows he couldn't fornicate with a pretty, young maid and then tossed up his accounts all over her."

The duke wouldn't like that, nor would Sheff because of how it would reflect on the rest of them. Protecting his mother and Min was the reason Sheff worked so hard to keep the duke out of serious trouble. "I will do my best," Sheff promised. Though, trying to control the duke's actions was akin to trying to stop a waterfall.

Jewel started to turn, but Jo touched her arm. "Mama, please give Agnes another chance. I'll make sure she follows the rules."

Blowing out a breath, Jewel narrowed her eyes at Jo. "You're going to have to harden that heart of yours, my girl, if you're going to run this place someday. Fine, Agnes is your responsibility. If she blunders again, it's on you. And she's working in the kitchen and cleaning up after we close every night for a fortnight."

"Thank you, Mama." After Jewel left, Jo faced Sheff. "How can I help?"

"I appreciate you advocating for Agnes. My father has ruined situations for enough young women," he added quietly. Moving toward the duke, Sheff wrinkled his nose as the scent of vomit grew stronger. "You don't have to help me, though if you want to bring me cleaning supplies, I'll wash the floor." Sheff could see there was sick on the wood pooling from underneath his father's midsection.

"Nonsense, you're heir to a dukedom." She blinked at him. "Do you even know how to wash a floor?"

"Yes, actually. This is not my father's first disaster with drink," he said wryly.

One of her brows gently arched. "I'll be back shortly."

Sheff heard her leave and close the door. He crouched down and poked at the duke, whose only reaction was to snore more loudly.

Over the next several minutes, Sheff managed to bring the duke's breeches into the appropriate position and button the fall. He'd had to roll his father over, and now Sheff worked to haul him up to sit against a dresser.

Jo returned with a bucket, mop, and some toweling. She took care of the floor while Sheff wiped up the duke's face and shirtfront. When he was finished, Jo took the soiled cloth from him. Their fingers touched, and Sheff felt a shocking arc of desire, which he'd been well on his way to earlier when she'd grabbed his hand. What a bloody inappropriate time to experience that.

And why now? He'd known Jo for a while. He found her attractive and fun and enjoyed flirting with her. But he'd never considered her for bed sport. He wasn't quite as bad as his father—he only dallied with widows and courtesans. And it had been a long while since he'd spent time with a widow.

"Shall we get him downstairs?" Jo asked. "We can go all the way to the basement and take him through the scullery up into the alley. No one will see you leave. But first, he needs coffee. I asked Becky to have some sent up and left outside the door."

"Excellent." He met her gaze with appreciation. "Thank you. For everything."

With a nod, she turned and went to the corridor, returning with a small tray bearing a pot and a cup. She poured the coffee and picked up the cup. "Are we tipping this down his gullet?"

"Eventually." Sheff took the cup from her, and again their hands grazed one another. He looked at her, but her gaze was directed elsewhere.

Hell, this was no time for him to be distracted even if he hated these situations the duke created. Sheff put the cup beneath his father's nose. "Wake up!"

The duke snuffled and jerked. His nose twitched. He mumbled something.

"That's it," Sheff said cajolingly. "Wake up now. Time to go. You've had your fun." Though it pained him to speak pleasantly, he'd learned through experience that this was the best way to achieve the desired result—the duke's cooperation.

Thankfully, he didn't resist tonight, which wasn't always the case. The duke sipped the coffee. then blinked his eyes open. "Give me some love now, my gel." His lips curved into a smile, and Sheff had to stop himself from spilling coffee on the man to jolt him fully awake.

"There's no woman, Father," Sheff said flatly. "Just you unconscious after being ill. You need to get yourself up and out of this chamber."

Nodding, the duke took another drink of coffee, then allowed Sheff to get him dressed, though they didn't bother with the cravat, and his coat wasn't buttoned.

"Where's my hat?" the duke slurred.

"Here." Jo handed it to Sheff, who jammed it, none too gently, onto his father's head.

"Ow!" The duke glared at him.

Sheff pulled the duke to his feet, holding him by the arm as he swayed.

The duke's gaze locked on Jo. "She's not the same gel, but she'll do." He smiled at her, his lips parted.

Sheff jerked his father toward the door. "She is not available. Perhaps you aren't aware that you are at the Siren's Call, where you are *not* permitted. We need to leave. Now."

"She can come with us." The duke tossed her a suggestive grin, then tripped over the threshold as Sheff tried to pull him out to the corridor.

Jo darted to help keep the duke on his feet.

"That's more like it," the duke said, hunched over, reaching for Jo. His hand grazed her breast, and Jo twisted. She bent her knees and jammed her elbow into the duke's loins.

Sheff watched as his father doubled over and crumpled to the floor. Instead of helping the man who'd deserved what he'd just received, Sheff looked at Jo with sheer admiration. "Bloody brilliant."

"I know how to protect myself from revolting men. Come, let's get him downstairs."

"You don't have to help, not after that." He could hardly believe she was offering. Jo was a remarkable woman.

She was also not on the Marriage Mart. And she was precisely the type of woman who would shock his parents. Additionally, she was quite capable of handling herself with them and in Society, as far as Sheff could tell.

The scheme of a faux betrothal rose in his mind. The perfect candidate was standing right in front of him.

He locked his eyes with hers. "Marry me, Jo."

The duke groaned. Then he heaved.

"No, you are not to be sick again!" Sheff hoisted him up and steered him down the corridor. "I'll call on you tomorrow," he said over his shoulder, thinking tonight's disaster had turned out rather well.

There was a first time for everything.

CHAPTER 2

The following afternoon, Jo paced the sitting room of the lodgings she shared with her mother, which occupied the entire first floor over the Siren's Call. It consisted of this room, a dining room, their bedchambers, a bathing chamber, and a study lined with bookcases where her mother worked. That had been Jo's favorite room growing up. As her mother had sat at her desk balancing accounts or drafting bills, Jo had sprawled upon the settee and devoured every book in the room. Then her mother had added more. And more. That was why the walls were lined with cases.

Pausing, Jo put her hand to her temple. Had the Earl of Shefford actually proposed marriage to her last night?

He had to have been joking. And yet he'd said he would call today. It was after noon, and he hadn't yet. She supposed it wouldn't have been appropriate to do so before now. How she loathed Society's rules.

Walking to the windows that overlooked the street below, she looked for his coach. Of course it wasn't there. He wasn't coming.

"Josephine," her mother called from the study, which adjoined the sitting room.

Jo walked into the study where her mother sat at her desk, her head bent. "What happened with the duke last night? I trust he was expelled with no undue difficulty?" She looked up at Jo expectantly.

"Yes." Jo wasn't going to tell her about Sheff's ridiculous question. It had been a jest. Or a flirtation. They did that with one another. She couldn't deny he was attractive, with his thick brown hair that waved just perfectly from his forehead and his blue eyes that shone with amusement. Last night, however, they'd been dark and intense. She'd never seen him quite like he'd been last night. But then, she'd never witnessed him cleaning up his father's mess, which it seemed he did often.

Jo wanted to ask her mother about her past with the duke but wasn't sure how to phrase it. She didn't normally struggle to find words or nose her way into someone's business, but her mother was different. She was the only person who intimidated Jo.

"What is it?" her mother asked with a sigh. "I can tell you want to ask me something. I'll wager it's about what I said last night."

"About the Duke of Henlow, yes."

Tossing her pen on the desk and sitting back in her chair, Jo's mother chuckled. "It's not a captivating tale. I was young and stupid, and he was incredibly handsome and seductive. And he was a duke. Or heir to a dukedom. I forget if he'd inherited yet."

"You were intimate with him?"

"Once. I don't think either of us was that impressed, but we were young." She narrowed her eyes briefly at Jo. "His son is even more attractive. Are you and he intimate?"

"No," Jo said quickly. "We are friendly, nothing more. It

was sheer luck that he was downstairs when I found Agnes with His Grace."

"His Disgrace, you mean." Jo's mother shook her head. "I do feel sorry for his wife. How awful to be leg shackled to one such as him."

Jo perched on the settee. "I'm surprised to hear you say that. You've never let the bonds of marriage impede you. Why should she?"

Her mother laughed again. "That is true. However, I am not held to the same standards as the Duchess of Henlow." She sobered and sat forward in her chair, pinning Jo with a serious stare. "I would advise you not to wed. Unless you absolutely feel you must have a child. In that case, it's prob-ably best if you do, though you can certainly do as I have done and live a separate life."

"Is that why you married my father?" Jo asked. "So you could have a child?"

"Not entirely. I certainly didn't make the decision in that order. I was with child and realized I needed to marry him if I wanted it to be legitimate."

"It…you mean me."

"No, I lost that child," her mother said softly.

Jo had never known that. "Why didn't you ever tell me?"

Her mother shrugged, but there was a hint of regret in the motion. "It was a sad time. I didn't realize how badly I wanted to be a mother until I wasn't going to be one. Then I set out to change that, and I was lucky to have you."

"Papa has always told me that you loved each other once." Though, he had also never mentioned the child they'd lost. "You don't speak of that."

"We did love one another, but only for a short time. Then I was content to be a mother, and he was delighted to take a mistress." Her mother straightened. "Enough of that claptrap.

I called you in here to speak to you about the future of the Siren's Call."

Had something happened? Jo oversaw the employees and spent more time at the club than her mother did these days, but her mother was still the owner and proprietress and would be for a good many years to come. "That almost sounds ominous."

Jo couldn't help feeling a touch of anxiety, for while she was committed to the club, she did not possess her mother's passionate attachment. Why would she? Her mother had built the club from nothing with hard work and a vision for the future. Jo, however, wasn't sure she shared that vision for her own future.

"I think I may wish to retire sooner than planned," her mother said, causing Jo's pulse to jump. "Marcel has leased a lovely cottage in Weston, of all places." She laughed—almost gaily, which never failed to jolt Jo. Her mother exhibited a giddy sweetness whenever she was with or spoke of Marcel.

"But you don't live together now, and you prefer it that way," Jo said slowly. Her mother and Marcel had been together five years, but they maintained separate residences—on purpose.

Her mother shrugged faintly. "I may still prefer that, but I did tell him I would try to share the cottage. He says it's plenty large enough for us to not see each other at all for days on end if we choose."

That sounded larger than a cottage, but what did Jo know? "What if you don't like it?"

"I will have to find my own cottage, I suppose."

Jo stared at her. This was not the ambitious woman she'd known, who'd worked tirelessly to build a hugely successful enterprise. "You're leaving London?"

"Just for a few months each year—for now. I'd say in five years, I'll move to Weston permanently, assuming I like it. I honestly don't know if I will. The idea of living near the sea is intriguing, but I've never lived outside London. I fear I won't know what to do with quiet and fresh air." She laughed again. Sobering, she cocked her head. "Or perhaps just three years. Five seems a long time."

Jo was glad she'd been sitting down to receive this news. She'd long known her mother had planned for her to take over the Siren's Call—she'd known forever, in fact. But Jo wasn't sure she was destined to run a gaming club. She enjoyed attending literary salons and orations about science and nature and art. Her mother didn't share the same cerebral pursuits, which wasn't to say her mother wasn't intelligent. Jewel Harker was the cleverest woman Jo knew. And she had an appreciation for art. How could she not when her lover was an accomplished portraitist?

"I'm surprised to hear this," Jo admitted. She'd thought she had more time to decide whether she really wanted to follow her mother's path. Or perhaps she was hoping for more time to *want* to do that. Her mother worked so hard, so tirelessly, and Jo didn't feel the same passion for owning a club.

"I'm surprised to be saying it, in truth." She gave Jo a warm smile. "You're ready for this, my dear. In fact, I'd like you to start managing the ledgers next week."

The bell indicating someone had come to the door to their lodgings sounded. Their housekeeper, Mrs. Rand, would no doubt answer it, but Jo wished she could use it as an excuse to end this conversation.

"This is a great deal to take in," Jo said.

"I know. Which is why we'll wait to start your transition until next week. And it's not as if I'm going anywhere yet. We won't leave for Weston until the middle of July."

That was less than three months from now. Jo would be alone here. Who would watch over things on the evenings she wished to be elsewhere? She spent most Monday nights at one literary salon or another.

Before she could ask whom her mother had in mind to assist Jo—for she couldn't mean to abandon her without any support—Mrs. Rand stepped over the threshold of the study. "Miss Harker, the Earl of Shefford is here to see you."

Jo rose, so glad for the interruption that it took her a moment to recollect why he might be calling. To discuss marriage. She swallowed an urge to laugh.

"Shefford?" Jo's mother asked, her brow arched high. "Was there a problem with his father last night?"

"No, not really." Jo surmised the duke was just a problem in general. Last night had seemed typical. She couldn't help but feel sorry for Sheff. "Excuse me, Mama."

"Close the door so I'm not disturbed," her mother said as Jo made her way out.

Jo made sure the door latched, particularly since she'd no desire for her mother to overhear whatever the earl had to say.

Shefford stood just inside the sitting room, his hat in his hands, his gaze moving about the room until settling on her. "Good afternoon, Jo."

She walked to where he was, preferring they sat on this side of the room, as far away from her mother's study as possible. "Afternoon, Sheff. I'm surprised to see you."

"Are you?" He also appeared surprised. "I told you I would call."

A bead of panic wriggled up her spine. "I didn't think you were serious. Let us take a walk." Jo really didn't want her mother overhearing anything. She gestured for him to precede her into the entrance hall, where she grabbed her hat and gloves from a small table.

The earl waited while she donned her accessories. "After

you," he said politely, inclining his head toward the stairs that led down to the ground floor entrance.

Jo hastened down the stairs and opened the door, stepping out onto Coventry Street. Shefford closed the door and then offered her his arm.

She stared at it, not sure what to do. To be seen walking arm in arm down the street with the Earl of Shefford would be to invite all manner of speculation, curiosity, and…judgment.

Pursing her lips, she started toward Piccadilly without taking his arm.

"Is something wrong?" he asked, hastening to keep up with her long strides.

Jo realized she didn't need to walk that fast. She wasn't running from anyone or anything. "I don't know why you've called today. We see one another at the Siren's Call. That is the extent of our acquaintance. This is very strange."

"Haven't you just recently become friendly with my sister and her group of friends?"

"What does that have to do with you?" She sent him a sideways glance, realizing she was unaccountably irritated. Because she was nervous. He couldn't actually have meant what he'd said last night.

"I only mean to suggest that our social circles now intersect, so perhaps our acquaintance is deepening." He flashed her a smile that made her toes curl.

Why? They'd never done that before in his presence.

He'd never proposed to her before.

"You're going to need to come to the reason for your call today," Jo said, flexing her hands as she walked.

"I told you I would last night," he repeated. "Right after I asked you to marry me. I've come to set forth the arrangements. If you're amenable."

Jo tripped.

Sheff caught her, not that she'd been in danger of falling. She pushed at him and stepped back. "You didn't have to do that."

He blinked at her, seeming surprised at her reaction. "I couldn't let you fall."

"I am not going to marry you." There, she'd managed to get the words out. Why was she behaving in this manner? She was normally coolheaded, calm, and extremely rational. Apparently, a marriage proposal was just the thing to send her reeling.

She hadn't expected that, but then, no one had asked her to marry them before.

"I don't want you to *actually* marry me," he said with a chuckle. "I misspoke somewhat last night. My apologies. I am in search of a pretend bride, and you are, without question, the perfect candidate."

Relief coursed through her. She laughed, lifting her hand to her chest. "Thank God. I thought you were asking me to be your wife, and I couldn't conceive of *why* you would do such a thing." She lowered her hand and started walking again but at a more sedate pace.

"I would never," he said, falling into step beside her. "I think you know I am a confirmed bachelor."

"Well, perhaps you are unaware that I am also determined to remain unwed."

"I'd suspected that, but hearing you say so makes you even more qualified to serve as my make-believe betrothed." He sounded almost giddy.

Jo smiled. "What ridiculous plan have you concocted and why?"

"Given your attentive ear, I'm sure you know that my parents have long badgered me about marrying."

"You've moaned about it on several occasions." Jo heard a

great many things at the Siren's Call, and Sheff had made no secret of his parents' desire for him to wed.

He laughed. "Just so. Misery does love company. This season, their fervor has risen to a near-deafening crescendo. I simply cannot tolerate another day of their harassment."

"You poor thing. So, your plan is to pretend to be betrothed? How does that solve anything?"

"It means they will leave me alone, at least for the remainder of the Season. It also means my father, in particular, will mind his own business, which he largely prefers anyway, and stop bothering me and my mother about this issue." He caught her eye for a quick moment. "Is it too much to want some peace for a couple of months?"

"Only a couple of months? Won't they be right back to pestering you?"

"Perhaps. Or they may feel sorry for me for some time after you cry off."

Jo stopped then and faced him. "I am not going to pretend to be betrothed to you, nor am I going to cry off." She'd be squarely in Society's sights then, and she'd be ruined forever. Not that she wasn't somewhat tarnished already as the daughter of the owner of a gaming hell who openly consorted with a man who wasn't her husband. Not to mention Jo's father, the charming gadfly whom everyone liked but who was not truly accepted into Polite Society.

It wasn't that *she* cared what Society thought. It was that she didn't want certain doors closed to her because of what Society thought. Reputations mattered, and so far, she had a decent one, even if she wasn't accepted in the upper levels of the ton. She didn't want that anyway.

His face had fallen when she'd denied his request. Now he was actually pouting. "But, Jo, I need you. You are too perfect."

"Why?"

"Because you can survive crying off. You will decide I am unfit to be your husband—and rightly so. You'll be lauded for possessing such sense."

"Except that I will first be denigrated for lacking sense when I agree to be your countess," she said wryly.

He lifted a shoulder. "Perhaps, but I will sweep you off your feet, and everyone will find that romantic."

Jo chuckled as she shook her head. "You're not making any sense. I will be praised for agreeing to be your wife *and* for deciding we don't suit after all. I think you've perhaps gone daft, Sheff."

"The ton doesn't make sense," he said. "You can't disagree with that."

No, she could not. She'd seen the upper ten thousand support someone and then not, only to support them again. And the reasons for doing so were ridiculous. Not to mention, there were plenty of people who actually behaved badly, but because of their rank, their behavior was overlooked. Sheff's father was a prime example of that.

"You've overlooked one important factor," she said plainly. "I don't want to be engaged to anyone, not even if it isn't real. And I especially don't want to be betrothed to someone like you. I'd have to acquire an entirely new wardrobe so that I could attend balls and fêtes and alfresco suppers, *and* I'd have to promenade about Hyde Park like a preening bird. *No, thank you.*"

He exhaled. "How much do you want?"

She blinked at him. "For a new wardrobe? Nothing. I don't want a new wardrobe." In truth, a small part of her would love the ability to choose clothing without thinking of cost or usefulness. But she would never admit that, especially to a man such as Sheff.

"Not just the wardrobe, though you are right that one

would be required. I will pay you to masquerade as my betrothed. Would five hundred pounds be sufficient?"

If they'd been walking, Jo would have tripped again. And this time, she would have fallen for certain.

Five hundred pounds.

Five *hundred* pounds.

Five hundred *pounds*.

The number was so massive in Jo's mind that she could barely fathom it. The things she could do with that sum of money… It was more than she could imagine.

No, it wasn't. She knew precisely what she would do with that money. She would decide her own future. She could more seriously entertain the idea of not taking over the Siren's Call.

Excitement pulsed through her. She had to move. There was too much energy and emotion inside her. She continued along Piccadilly.

"You're considering it," Sheff noted as he walked alongside her.

"How can I not? That's a staggering sum." She stopped abruptly and turned to face him. "You'd pay that much?"

"And a new wardrobe, don't forget." His gaze was pleading, and Jo had to admit he looked rather adorable.

"What else?" Jo asked. "I mean, what do you require? How long will this scheme continue? What do you expect of me?"

"Once you are properly attired—not that there is anything wrong with your clothing, but you know what I mean."

Yes, Jo did know. "My wardrobe is not that of a young lady who would marry the heir to a dukedom." Because Jo wasn't ever going to marry, let alone the bloody heir to a dukedom.

"Just so. Rest assured, you will have full control over the wardrobe. I trust that you will know what to procure."

The fact was that Jo *didn't* know. She had an idea, but thinking of it was overwhelming. There were different costumes for every kind of activity. Plus accessories. And how would she wear her hair? She and her mother had a maid who sometimes helped them with their hair and clothing, but primarily, she took care of their bedchambers and their wardrobe. Frannie was not a ladies' maid.

But Jo knew whom she could ask. "Will you mind if your sister and her friends help me?"

"Not at all," he said jovially. "In fact, I recommend you seek their assistance. However, you cannot tell them our betrothal isn't real. I can't risk one of them slipping up and exposing the truth. I also don't want to ask them to lie."

"But you're asking me to," Jo said wryly. Lying to her new friends would be difficult. She didn't really want to do it. She didn't really want to do any of it. But *five hundred pounds*. It was a life-changing sum.

"I'm *paying* you to," he said meaningfully, his gaze filled with hope.

She could not ignore the substantial sum he'd offered. "How long are we to keep up this farce?"

"Until the end of the Season." He cocked his head briefly. "We'll set a wedding date for the autumn or winter."

"Won't your parents insist on a June wedding?"

He gave a slight nod. "They may try, but we'll tell them you've always had your heart set on a fur-trimmed gown and cloak."

She put a hand on her hip and stared at him. "Have you thought of every detail?"

"I'm trying to," he said with a grin.

"What sorts of events will I need to attend?" This was not only important with regard to the wardrobe she needed. She needed to prepare herself.

He sobered. "First, there will be a betrothal ball."

A ball. Where *she* would be the focus of everyone's attention.

"You do know how to dance, don't you?" he asked.

"Yes." Though she rarely had occasion to do so, and when she did, it was a raucous reel or a line. She'd almost no experience with sedate dancing, and she'd never waltzed. "Though I don't waltz."

"That's fine. We should be able to avoid doing that. Unless you want to learn? It's not difficult compared with other dances, provided you can move in time to the music."

Jo thought of one of her new friends, the brand-new Viscountess Somerton. She could waltz—apparently—and Jo knew her to be absolutely incapable of discerning the time of music.

"If it's the same to you, I'd just as soon not bother dancing at all, if possible." It was too…exposing. Everyone would be watching them. And wondering why he was betrothed to someone like her.

Her resolve faltered. What was she thinking?

She nearly balked. But five hundred pounds!

"We won't be able to keep from dancing entirely, especially at our betrothal ball, but I'll do my best to keep it to a minimum. Do you have any other requirements?"

"You didn't finish telling me what events I need to go to. I presume I have to attend at least a few events before you even announce the betrothal, else we will have to tell everyone that we met at the Siren's Call."

"We did meet at the Siren's Call," he said with a frustrating chortle.

"Are you going to be serious about this? You are planning to fool your family, friends, and the entire ton."

He coughed, straightening his features. "I am serious. My apologies. I am just so happy—a relieved kind of happy—that you are going to help me. I can't tell you what a load this will be off my mind for the next couple of months."

"You are willing to undertake a great deal and pay a large sum for what amounts to a temporary alleviation of your frustration." She studied him closely, trying to see past his façade, for she'd always known there was more to Sheff than met the eye. "What do you really hope to gain?"

"Peace." He answered quickly and firmly, with a soft but urgent tone that made her want that for him. "You don't need to attend any events. What about the Phoenix Club? Isn't your mother a member?"

"Yes, and as it happens, I will be at the assembly there tonight. Your sister talked me into going."

"That is even better," Sheff said, his blue eyes gleaming in the afternoon sun. "We will dance and promenade, and I will call on you tomorrow to propose marriage."

"The Season's fastest courtship," Jo muttered. She took her hand from her hip and let it fall to her side. "That is how it begins. How does this end?"

"As I said, you'll cry off because you just *can't* marry a rogue. No one will blame you. In fact, I could do something scandalous so that you really don't have any choice. You will be cheered and supported."

"And you will be vilified." Just like his father. Sheff couldn't want that. She'd seen how his father's behavior affected him. And now she wondered if that was part of the secrets about himself that he kept buried.

Sheff shrugged. "I'll be a duke someday. My reputation will recover."

Sadly, he was right. There would always be someone willing to suffer horrid behavior for the sake of a title and wealth. And here Jo was considering a scheme she did not want to participate in for the reward of money. Alas, she was not going to be a duke someday. She had to make choices for her own security and happiness.

"When will you give me no choice but to end our betrothal?" she asked drily.

"I should say the end of summer. There will also be much less likelihood of lasting gossip. The Season is over, and we don't even need to be in London. I usually spend part of August near Weston at my father's seaside estate."

Weston? Jo could probably visit her mother, provided they had someone to watch the Siren's Call. "Oddly enough, my mother will be there this summer. I could visit at the same time."

"I hadn't considered that you would need to be there. You could hear about my misbehavior from your friends—they are in Weston for the entire month of August—via letter." He smiled and nodded. "Though, if you have occasion to be in Weston, that could work quite well."

"I'll have to see if that fits into my plans." If there was no one to manage the Siren's Call, she couldn't leave London. Did she really want to travel all the way to Weston to pretend to have her heart broken? That sounded rather dismal. The letter idea was far superior.

"You must do whatever is most convenient for you," Sheff said. "If you do decide to come to Weston, I shall pay your expenses. It's only fair."

She supposed that was true.

He gave her a hopeful look. "Are we agreed, then? I can provide you with a banknote tonight at the ball, if you like. Two hundred and fifty pounds now and two hundred and fifty pounds when we are finished. If that is agreeable to you."

It was the smart thing for him to do. He was offering her a huge sum and should protect his investment. "Yes, though if I agree to this scheme, I will see it through to the bitter end."

"I don't doubt it." His mouth lifted in a thoroughly roguish smile.

"I have one more requirement."

"Name it."

"No kissing or any other romantic overtures, even for the sake of looking as though we are in love."

"You must let me kiss your hand, at least."

"Fine. Make that two more requirements. I may add other requirements as I see fit." She was worried she wasn't thinking of everything just now. This was a monumental decision—not just because it would dictate her life for the next two months, but because her life was about to change. There would be difficult conversations with her mother, both about this betrothal and whether Jo actually wanted to assume management and ownership of the Siren's Call.

"Done," he said eagerly, holding out his hand. "Are we agreed?"

Jo hesitated the barest moment before clasping his gloved hand in hers. "We are."

Everything had shifted. Her mother wanted her to take over the club sooner than Jo had expected. Jo had to face the fact that she really didn't want to take over the club. Sheff's offer gave her the freedom to do what she wished—she had only to tell her mother. And that would be difficult.

It might also be premature. She needed to think this through. But for the first time, she could do so knowing there was another path for her if she wanted to take it.

None of that considered how Jo's actual life was about to change for the rest of the Season. She would be surveyed, discussed, judged. Her insides roiled at what she was about to subject herself to.

She dearly hoped she hadn't just made the biggest mistake of her life.

CHAPTER 3

*A*rriving at the Phoenix Club that night, Sheff went directly to the first-floor members' den to have a drink with his friends before going downstairs to the ball. He typically did so—attended a ball—with a sense of disgruntlement, but for the first time ever, he was actually looking forward to it. Because he had a plan that would ensure he could enjoy the rest of the Season without being pestered by his parents and without the specter of the Marriage Mart haunting him everywhere he went.

He hadn't been sure Jo would accept his offer. She'd been very hesitant—until he'd offered her five hundred pounds. He was going to suggest three hundred, but once he realized she wasn't leaping at the chance to help him, he'd elevated the offer. And it would be worth every shilling, even though it was only a temporary reprieve. By next Season, he'd likely be right back where he was, with his parents badgering him to take a wife.

Or not. A great deal could happen between now and then, such as his parents realizing and acknowledging that no amount of harassment would force him to take a wife.

Indeed, their behavior had the opposite effect. Their demands had not once swayed him on the point of marriage. Rather, they'd driven him to be even more steadfast in his resolve to remain unwed.

He also had good reason to cling to bachelorhood. He would not subject a family to his nature, which was, unfortunately, too much like his father's. And Sheff feared it would only grow worse over time, as his father's behavior had done.

The rational part of Sheff's brain told him that he was not as bad as his father, for he at least possessed self-awareness. But what if that changed? What if Sheff was powerless to stop that or even see it? Sometimes, watching his father act, he rather thought the duke suffered from a disease. That even if he wanted to change his ways, he could not.

That scared Sheff more than anything.

"Evening, Shefford." The owner of the Phoenix Club, Lord Lucien Westbrook, stood near the entrance to the members' den. "Will you be joining the ball tonight?"

"I will, after a bit of fortification."

"A wise move considering the scheme the patronesses have planned," Lord Lucien said with a faint grimace.

The Phoenix Club had a group of lady patronesses, much like Almack's. However, the Phoenix Club patronesses weren't stuffy or judgmental. Indeed, one was the manager of the club, Lady Evangeline Blakemore, who'd been a courtesan in her former life.

"What's that?" Sheff asked.

"They are trying their hand at matchmaking by randomly pairing dancing partners. I did tell them I think it's a risk, but they assured me it would all be in good fun."

"Will you be participating?" Sheff asked.

"Heavens, no," Lord Lucien replied. "I am, happily, already matched." His eyes glinted with a joy one only saw in those who believed themselves to be in love.

Sheff recognized the look because a number of his friends had recently fallen. Time would reveal how long they remained that way. Sheff did not think it would be forever. Romantic love was fleeting at best.

"Since you have the ear of the patronesses, I would appreciate if they would pair me with Miss Josephine Harker." Sheff wanted to be sure he danced with her this evening.

Lord Lucien's dark brows shot up. "Have you set your sights on someone at last?"

Sheff wanted to deny it, to reiterate that he would never wed, but that was not the point of this endeavor. Everyone must think he'd finally succumbed—at least for now. At some point, he would have to do something to prompt Jo's rejection of him. Though it would be necessary, he realized the thought of that turned his stomach. He would not humiliate her. He couldn't. He could ruin himself without adversely affecting her.

"Jo is someone with whom I am able to be myself," Sheff said, shocked to find that was actually true. Mostly. He had to keep some things secret. Even she would be horrified to learn how roguish he really was, how like his father he could be.

"I like Jo—and her mother—a great deal," Lord Lucien said. "Don't let anyone deter you from what you want. Or whom you love," he added softly before moving on to a new topic. "Evie found a delicious whisky from the Highlands that just arrived today if you want to give it a try."

"I do, indeed." Sheff went into the members' den and immediately saw his friend the Marquess of Keele seated at a table on the side of the room. Joining him there, Sheff bid him good evening. "Is that the new whisky?" Sheff asked, inclining his head toward the glass of golden liquid in Keele's hand.

"It is. Can't imagine it will last long unless Lord Lucien is rationing it." Keele gestured toward the opposite chair with his free hand. "Sit and have a splash. I assume you're here for the ball."

"Why would you assume that?" Sheff asked. "I am no more interested in marriage than you are." Too late, he realized that was the wrong thing to say in light of his plan to propose marriage very soon. He couldn't forget the scheme he was launching or the role he was playing within it. He needed to be careful not to ruin this ruse before it even began.

"Because regardless of what you say, a small part of you still considers the possibility that you will wed. You have to—there's a dukedom at stake."

"Your marquessate is somehow less important?" Sheff noted wryly.

Keele chuckled. "It's still a mess, so yes. Leaving it to someone in this state would be cruel." He'd inherited a severely indebted estate along with his title several years ago and spent nearly every waking moment trying to repair the damage, even marrying a woman whose family was in trade —a very successful one—to fill the empty coffers. However, she'd died two years ago. Keele had just ventured out into Society in the last month or so.

A footman stopped at their table, and Sheff requested a glass of the whisky, though, glancing at the clock, he supposed he ought to be quick. He'd no idea when Jo would arrive, but probably soon if she hadn't already.

Sheff thought of what Keele had said, that a small part of him would consider marriage. Keele was wrong, but Sheff couldn't argue that point. Not on the verge of his scheme.

Keele sipped his whisky and closed his eyes in brief appreciation. "Still can't believe Somerton wed. Perhaps you'll be next, for matrimony seems to be spreading amongst your set." He smirked. "Like a disease."

Dammit, Keele wasn't wrong. Sheff had lost Bane, Wellesbourne, Droxford, and now Somerton. Keele and Price were all that were left, and Keele wasn't even really part of their set. Their set being the group of gentlemen who gathered in Weston every August for a week or so of masculine pursuits. Though, that wasn't quite the same anymore since Wellesbourne had married eighteen months ago. Last August, their fun had been interrupted when Droxford had shockingly proposed marriage to his now wife. And now Somerton had gone and wed Price's sister.

Sheff was leaving Bane out. He'd been the first to ruin things when he'd been caught in a compromising position with a young lady and then refused to wed her because he was already betrothed to someone else. That had been news to Sheff, who'd thought he was Bane's closest friend. Sheff hadn't seen him since he'd gone north to marry his bride, and they'd recently received news that his wife had died giving birth to their daughter, who had also not survived. Dammit, now Sheff was feeling melancholy.

The footman brought Sheff's whisky. Raising his glass, Sheff offered a toast. "To good friends, even when they fall prey to the parson's trap."

Keele lifted his glass. "It's not so bad when you find the right person," he said quietly. "But you must be prepared for the possibility that it won't last." He finished his whisky and waved his glass for the footman to refill it, which happened a moment later.

Amen to that, Sheff thought as he sipped the rich liquor, its smoky flavor coating his tongue. While he enjoyed it, there were other varieties he preferred more. Setting his glass down, he said, "You should come to Weston with us this August. As you noted, my set is dwindling."

"Your father has an estate there, does he not?" Keele asked.

"Yes. The stables are excellent. We do a great deal of riding, and the countryside is beautiful, as is the beach. Have you ever ridden a horse across the sand?"

"I have not," Keele replied. "I don't like to take time away from my work here in London. As it is, I only go to Westlands for a month in September." He referred to his estate between Birmingham and Manchester. "I don't think I could spare more time away, especially someplace that is nowhere near London or Westlands."

"Has anyone ever told you that you're dull?" Sheff asked with a laugh.

"Often. And I'm quite content with that description."

Sheff recalled when he hadn't been. They'd been at Oxford together, and though they'd been in different colleges, Sheff had known him. More accurately, he'd known *of* him. Keele was an excellent horseman and a cunning pugilist. He'd also possessed a rakish reputation, just like Sheff and his friends. Rather, his friends before they'd traded roguery for matrimony.

Evan Price approached their table as if Sheff's thoughts of horsemanship and pugilism had summoned him. Sheff knew no greater sportsman than Price, whose younger sister had married their friend, the now formerly infamous rake, the Viscount Somerton last month.

Since there wasn't a third chair, Evan dragged one over from another table. "New whisky tonight?" he asked eagerly.

"Yes." Sheff slid his glass across the table toward Price. "Finish mine. I need to go downstairs."

Price was a couple of years younger than Sheff and possessed incredibly dark eyes and a nearly tan complexion due to his Welsh heritage. He blinked at Sheff. "*Why?* Don't you know the assembly tonight is an ill-conceived matchmaking scheme?"

"We all know you've no interest in that," Keele said to Sheff with a chuckle.

Sheff wanted to agree, but he had a role to play. Instead, he forced a closed-mouthed smile. "Sometimes duty cannot be ignored."

"Very glad I don't have to produce an heir for a title," Price said as a shudder twitched his shoulders. He picked up Sheff's whisky and took a drink. "Ah, marvelous."

Standing, Sheff looked down his nose at them. "I'm off to the ball. Have a good evening, cowards." He departed to the sound of their laughter.

Feeling disgruntled, he made his way downstairs. Why was he so bothered? Because he was about to surrender to expectation and take a wife. Even though it was pretend, everyone would believe it was real, and they'd jeer at the rogue who'd finally fallen. Just like his friends.

The disease was spreading.

No, Sheff wasn't going to let that happen. This was a faux betrothal.

Music met his ears along with the buzz of conversation before he stepped through the curtains from the men's side of the Phoenix Club into the ballroom. Spanning the width of the building, the ballroom sat at the back, with multiple doors to the divided garden—there were men's and ladies' sides just as with the interior. On Tuesday nights, the women were invited to join the men on the men's side; however the men were never invited to the ladies' side. On Fridays, when there were assemblies, the entire ballroom and both gardens were open to all.

Sheff scanned the bustling ballroom to see if Jo had arrived. As an unmarried woman, she was not a member, but her mother was, and Jo was allowed to attend the Friday night assemblies if a family member belonged to the club. Typically, they arrived in the company of that family member, though Sheff didn't think he'd ever seen Jewel Harker at one of the club balls. He had, however, run into her on the occasional Tuesday when she drank whisky with Lord Lucien—probably—in the men's library.

So, in whose company would Jo arrive tonight?

The dance floor was on the men's side of the ballroom. Sheff moved closer to see if she was, perchance, dancing. And there she was.

Gowned in dark coral, her sable hair dressed with coral-encrusted combs, she danced in a square with Edwin Cleveland, who, at the moment, was laughing. Indeed, he looked most engaged with his partner. Jo was smiling, her demeanor somehow more feminine than he was used to when he saw her at the Siren's Call. He supposed that made sense because that was her place of work while this ball was a social occasion.

It occurred to him then that he could cause a massive stir in the social order by taking a wife with an occupation. Except he wasn't taking a wife, he was only pretending to. Still, the effect of their betrothal, fake or not, would be significant.

Lord Lucien had mentioned the manager of the Phoenix Club, Lady Evangeline. She'd been employed when she'd married Lord Gregory Blakemore, who was currently heir apparent to the Marquessate of Witley because his older brother had not yet produced an heir. Yes, there'd been a stir when they'd wed, but that was perhaps more due to Lady Evangeline's prior life as a courtesan than the fact that she had a job.

Sheff watched Jo laugh at something Cleveland said and felt a shocking stab of jealousy. She was quite stunning when she laughed. And though Sheff had provoked her to do so on many occasions, it hadn't been in this environment. He shook the thought from his head. Why should that matter?

They were business partners at this point. He was paying her to complete an assignment.

The dance concluded, and there was to be a brief respite in the dancing. Good, for then he could speak with Jo before they were paired off again for the next set. Sheff made his way to where she was leaving the dance floor with Cleveland.

Jo's gaze met Sheff's as she took her hand from Cleveland's arm. "Good evening, Lord Shefford." She dipped into a curtsey.

"Good evening, Miss Harker." Sheff felt strange not calling her Jo.

"Evening, Shefford," Cleveland said. He was a friendly sort but sometimes reserved. Perhaps that was why Sheff had been jolted by watching them laugh together while they danced.

"Evening, Cleveland. You were fortunate to be paired with Miss Harker for this set."

"I was indeed." Cleveland chuckled. "Not sure if this scheme will last the entire ball. I already witnessed people trying to avoid their assigned partners—mutually, I will add."

"How does the assignment of partners work?" Sheff asked.

Jo's lips pressed together, and one brow arched in a wry expression. "It's not a very smooth scheme. A footwoman or footman gives you a piece of paper with the name of your partner for the next set. I think it's proving difficult because, in some cases, they are assigning people who aren't yet here. Or perhaps they have no intention of even coming. So, they're having to make adjustments, and there are delays between sets, which is why I think they've inserted a 'brief respite' between this and the next." Jo laughed. "They need to reorganize."

"That sounds complicated," Sheff said.

At that moment, a liveried footwoman—the ladies' side of the club only employed women—delivered folded pieces of parchment to Jo and to Sheff.

They opened them simultaneously.

Jo's eyes rounded briefly, almost comically. "What a surprise. I'm to dance with Shefford for the next set."

"That is a surprise indeed," Sheff said, tucking the paper into his pocket. "I wonder if we might take a promenade until then. That way, I won't lose you."

"Of course," Jo replied.

Cleveland took his leave, and Sheff offered his arm to Jo. He guided her toward the perimeter of the ballroom. "Refreshments or night air?"

"Refreshment and then night air," she said, pulling him gently toward the other side of the ballroom where there were tables bearing ratafia, lemonade, and even champagne. Jo selected champagne, and Sheff did the same. Then he escorted her outside to the ladies' side of the garden.

Jo took her hand from his arm as she sipped her champagne. "Lovely," she murmured. "Though I hate knowing there is all manner of rare liquor upstairs in the men's side and I can't have any of it."

"The same beverages are available on the ladies' side." Sheff noted the flash of surprise in her expression. "Did you not know that?"

"I did not. I've only been here a handful of times, and I've not been upstairs."

Sheff inclined his head. "You should make a point of it tonight. They just received a new whisky from the Highlands today. It's not quite my taste, but you might enjoy it."

Her eyes lit with interest. "I've yet to meet a whisky I didn't like."

"So noted." Sheff reached into his pocket and removed an envelope. Inside was a banknote for two hundred and fifty pounds. He handed it to her. "You can purchase a great deal of it with this."

Pausing, she grasped the envelope, her gaze fixing on it for a moment before she slipped it into the side of her gown. Presumably she had a pocket. "Thank you," she murmured.

"You seemed hesitant to agree to this scheme," Sheff said, continuing to walk away from the building. "Are you certain you wish to do this?" He held his breath. There would be no one better to complete this task. She was clever, charming, and she could weather whatever the ton would say or do.

She'd moved with him and didn't stop to answer his question. "If I'm honest, not entirely. However, you've made me an offer I can't refuse." She slid him a sly smile that made his toes curl inexplicably.

No, not inexplicably. Jo was a beautiful woman, and they were alone in a dark garden. Furthermore, he was a scoundrel of the highest order. He'd already identified a half dozen places in the garden to which he could whisk her and steal a kiss.

Not that he would. He was not allowed to do that, per their arrangement. And he would follow her requirements to the letter.

He watched her profile as they walked along the path toward the back of the walled garden. "You *could* refuse. I don't want you to feel pressured."

She gave him a cool look. "I won't ever agree to something I don't want to do. I appreciate your concern, though."

"I realize this will be challenging for you, but I never would have asked if I didn't think you would be up to the task." He wanted to make her laugh, at least a little, as she'd done with Cleveland. "The new wardrobe is reason enough to agree, isn't it?"

No laugh, but her lips lifted in a brief smile. "It is enticing. However, I am a businesswoman with an eye toward expense, so you may be assured I will not spend your entire fortune on gowns and shoes and gloves." She looked over at him. "Perhaps I should pay for the items; then you can reimburse me. That seems easiest and won't draw any undue interest." She took a drink of her champagne, and Sheff was drawn to the press of her plump lower lip against the rim of the glass.

"It's not unusual for a man to pay for his wife's trousseau."

"Especially when the man is a wealthy heir to a dukedom and the woman is working class?" There was an edge to her voice that made him wonder if this truly made her uncomfortable.

"The difference in our classes means nothing to me," Sheff said with great conviction.

"And yet, you didn't ask a nobleman's daughter to participate in your scheme."

They'd reached the back of the garden and now turned to the left to make a circuit on the path that ran parallel to the wall. Shrubs and trees separated the path from the wall.

Sheff sipped his champagne and sent her a sideways glance. "Perhaps I did."

"Did you?" she asked in surprise.

"No," he replied with a sheepish laugh. "I'd only conceived of the idea last evening before I took my mother and sister to Northumberland House. Then I saw you at the Siren's Call. Watching how you handled the situation with my father, I realized you were the perfect candidate."

"You must admit part of what makes me 'perfect' is that I don't need to maintain a place in Society when this is finished."

"All right, that *does* recommend you. If you want to back out, I won't be angry." Frustrated, but not angry.

"No, we shook hands, and to me, that makes this an

agreement of honor. I will be your betrothed. Do you still plan to propose tomorrow?"

He waggled his brows at her. "Since my plan is to fall deeply in love with you tonight, I think I must."

She laughed, and a warmth spread inside Sheff as he saw the woman from the dance floor.

The dance floor!

"Hell and the devil. Is that the music starting?" Sheff asked before tossing back the rest of his champagne.

"I believe so." Jo tipped the contents of her glass down her throat. "Ready."

Sheff stared at her, thinking she really was perfect. "Let's dance."

CHAPTER 4

*I*t was a bloody waltz.

After dropping their glasses on a footman's tray upon reentering the ballroom, Jo and Sheff rushed to the dance floor. Jo frowned.

"I'll guide you," Sheff said. "Do you know where to put your hands?"

"I can see what everyone else is doing." Why had she never learned to waltz? Jo put her hand on his shoulder and clasped his other hand. "I've no idea what to do with my feet."

"Count with the music. One, two, three."

Jo stepped on his foot. "Damn. Sorry."

"It's all right. Stamp away." He grinned at her though she was scowling.

"You'd better not be laughing at me," she warned.

"I am *not*. But what would you do if I were?" he asked saucily.

She stepped on his foot again, but this time on purpose and with greater vigor. Blinking innocently, she said, "I'm so sorry, my lord."

He laughed louder. "I deserved that. You're doing well. I'd say you're naturally inclined to move with the music."

"I don't know if that's true, but permit me to concentrate for a moment." She focused on her feet and the music and counting steps in her head. *This isn't terribly difficult,* she thought. Relaxing, she became aware of Sheff's hand on her back, of the gentle but firm way he clasped her hand, of how much closer the waltz brought them than any other dance. She felt an odd pull toward him, and she didn't like it. Though, since she was going to have to pretend to be smitten with him, perhaps it was for the best that she was at least attracted to him.

How had she never noticed that before?

Because you've never danced with him before.

Jo decided her policy of dance avoidance was a good one and would be reinstated at the earliest possible moment.

"You're doing beautifully," he murmured. The rich timbre of his voice wrapped her in a seductive warmth. When was this dance going to *end*?

Recalling what he'd told her about being able to drink whisky upstairs, Jo resolved to make her way there when the dance was over. Aside from sampling fine liquor, she would hide from further dancing. She'd look for her friends and see if anyone wanted to join her.

"You're a natural waltzer," he said.

"That does not mean I want to repeat the endeavor."

"I know I said we would avoid it, but it may be that we must do so again." He gave her a sympathetic look, and at this proximity, she could make out the depth of blue in his eyes. They were darkest at the center and faded to a lighter blue at the rim of the iris. And his lashes were ridiculously long for a man. "Now that I think about it, I'm certain my mother will arrange for us to dance a waltz at our betrothal ball."

Jo resisted the urge to groan. A ball in their honor *and* a waltz. Could anything make this ruse worse?

"I trust your parents will be in attendance," he said. "I do think their public support would be good for the overall scheme."

Yes, something could make it *far* worse.

"I am not sure you know what you are asking for." Jo couldn't remember the last time her parents were together. At least ten years ago, probably longer. "My parents rarely speak."

"I didn't realize their relationship was contentious."

Jo grimaced. "It's nonexistent. My mother has had a lover for five years, and my father moves from lover to lover like a bee searching for an elusive perfect pollen."

Sheff's eyes rounded. "I had no idea."

"Why would you? Their behavior is not of interest to the ton, though it will be when our betrothal is announced." She locked her gaze with his as they continued to twirl, somewhat effortlessly, to her surprise, around the floor. "You may wish to change your mind."

He shook his head. "I don't want to. Besides, I've already paid you. And we shook hands. We are committed."

Jo rolled her eyes. "I won't be angry if you do."

"Do *you* want me to? It occurred to me I've been shortsighted with regard to how this betrothal will affect you. I don't want you to be miserable, Jo, especially not to help me." He seemed genuinely concerned.

She appreciated his words more than she would have anticipated. "I'm glad you understand," she said softly. Then she raised her chin and tossed her head. "I don't think I shall care what others say." He was paying her enough money to not give a thousand figs to care. "However, you must be prepared for people to find me wholly unsuitable. Though, I suppose that is one reason you chose me." She smiled.

"It is indeed. Will you need to tell your parents the truth about the betrothal?" His brow creased. "We didn't discuss them. I apologize for that."

"I should take my mother into my confidence, else she will be angry. She will keep the secret. My father, however, should probably believe we are actually engaged to be married. He is not very good at being confidential. In fact, he has never met a piece of gossip he didn't love to chew."

Sheff's dark brows arched briefly. "I see. Well, I shall leave it to your discretion. Only tell me what I must do. Should I call on your father to ask for permission to wed you?"

Jo laughed. "He would adore that."

"Have you any idea where he might be this evening? I'd like to call on you tomorrow to officially ask for your hand."

It was possible that Jo's mother would take offense to her father being asked for permission to wed their daughter since she had raised Jo almost entirely by herself. However, once Jo explained to her mother that this was entirely fake, she would understand.

Jo would tell her of Sheff's plan later. Or in the morning, since by the time Jo returned to the Siren's Call this evening, it was likely that her mother would have retired with Marcel —either to her suite or to his house near Soho Square. It had been a few days since they were together, so Jo expected they would seek each other's company tonight.

As to her father's whereabouts this evening, he could be any number of places... "I'm not sure where you may find my father," she said. She gave Sheff a list of her father's favorite haunts. "Wait, it is the first Friday of the month. He is likely at Lord Gerard's soiree."

Sheff's eyes narrowed slightly. "I've heard of those. Rather eccentric occasions, aren't they?"

"I have never been. It is one of the few social events to which my father refuses to take me. He says they are too close to debauchery." She arched a brow at Sheff. "I'm surprised you've never been."

"I've never received an invitation." He wrinkled his nose. "Nor would I want one, as I believe my father attends once in a while."

"Then I understand why you would avoid it." She sent him a look of caution. "Do be careful tonight. You know how susceptible you are to debauchery. And you need to be on your best behavior now that you are betrothed—or at least nearly so."

A smile teased his lips. "You know me too well. I will exercise great prudence—tonight and for the duration of our ruse. Until I inevitably trip up and you have no choice but to protect your heart and toss me aside." He hung his head in mock defeat.

Jo stepped on his foot again. "My apologies, my lord," she murmured with a mischievous smile.

Sheff sniggered as the music drew to a close. They released one another, and Jo was shocked and perhaps a little dismayed at how much she'd enjoyed dancing with him.

"I will see you on the morrow, my fair Josephine." He gave her a gallant bow.

Jo sank into a curtsey and gave him a sweet smile. "Never call me that again. Only my mother calls me by my full name. Shall I call you *Clive*?"

"Noted, and you could, but I likely wouldn't respond. No one has ever called me that. I have been Shefford or Sheff since the nursery." He offered her his arm and led her from the dance floor. "Though perhaps you calling me by my given name would be a charming endearment that would captivate Society."

Taking her hand from his arm, she lifted a shoulder. "I'll consider it. I'm not sure you can be anything but Sheff to me."

"Have a pleasant remainder of your evening," he said.

"Don't forget to behave. I'm for the ladies' library and whisky." Jo took herself off and went in search of her friend Tamsin Deverell, Lady Droxford, with whom she'd come to the club tonight. Tamsin was now a member in her own right. It was one of the few perks of being married, Jo supposed.

Jo found Tamsin seated against the wall on the ladies' side of the ballroom with another of their friends, Ellis Danger-field. "Ellis, you aren't dancing?"

"No," Ellis replied. At twenty-five, she was a few months younger than Jo and apparently just as content to be unwed. "They don't match spinsters."

"I was matched," Jo said. "Twice. With Mr. Edwin Cleve-land and Sheff."

"You had to dance with my brother?" Lady Minerva, or Min, as they all called her, came up behind Jo as Ellis and Tamsin stood.

"A waltz," Jo replied. She had to stop herself before making a sarcastic comment. It wouldn't make sense for her to poke fun at Sheff if they were supposedly falling in love. A wave of agitation rolled through her. How was she going to lie to her friends? She'd only just made them recently. She'd never had close girlfriends before. And she liked having them. An unsettling feeling settled into her belly.

"Have you ever waltzed before?" Tamsin asked in her lilting Cornish accent, her naturally round blue-green eyes fixed on Jo.

"No. I did catch on fairly quickly, much to my surprise."

"Don't tell Gwen, not that she is here tonight. I am not sure when she and Somerton will venture forth from their newly wedded cocoon of rapture." Min made a face, then laughed. "You know I am delighted for them."

"We all are, but we can still poke fun at their bliss," Jo replied.

"I will not," Tamsin said primly.

"Only because you are in the throes of the same," Ellis said with a hint of a smile. "And it's lovely. We only speak in jest."

Tamsin nodded. "I know. Also, because Somerton is my cousin, and I am thrilled to see him so happy and in love. Our grandmother is overjoyed to see him settled at last." She looked to Min. "How was your dance with Mr. Wilton?"

Min made a sound of disgust in her throat. "He kept talking about how surprised he was that Gwen and Somerton are wed. Then he tried to insinuate that there was a reason they had to marry. I informed him that it was simply Cupid at work. Then I stepped on his foot."

They all tittered. Jo wondered why she hadn't noticed Min on the dance floor. Probably because she'd been too focused on learning the dance. Or she'd been too fixated on her partner.

"This matchmaking scheme for dancing is rather clumsy, isn't it?" Tamsin asked. "They seem to be having trouble finding people, and the matches seem almost haphazard."

Jo nodded in agreement. She was somewhat surprised she'd been paired with Sheff. But he'd likely arranged it.

"I don't think I can manage another dance," Min said with a shudder.

"Then let's not," Jo suggested. With a nod toward the door, she led them from the ballroom into an antechamber. "I understand we can drink the same liquor they serve on the men's side upstairs. And I heard there is a new whisky that arrived today. Who wants to join me?"

"I do," the other three said in near unison.

Ellis and Tamsin started toward the stairs, and Jo and Min followed.

"I'm sorry you had to dance with Sheff," Min said. "Was he a terrible flirt?"

"He was his usual self, which I find amusing. Generally." Damn, that did not sound like a woman who'd begun to see someone in a different light, namely a romantic one. "I actually enjoyed the waltz…immensely." Jo added the last part to aid her cause. "Because of Sheff, which I suppose is surprising." That much was true. He had taught her rather effortlessly, and she had enjoyed it, even if "immensely" was a slight exaggeration.

Min looked at her askance. "I was expecting a sardonic response."

Jo shrugged. "Your brother displayed excellent behavior. Perhaps I am merely trying to honor that." She winced inwardly. None of this sounded believable.

Too late, Jo realized she should not have made that comment earlier about poking fun at wedded bliss. Not if she was to about to become one of their number. Supposedly. Blast, this was harder than she'd anticipated. Min's skeptical stare as they reached the first floor didn't help Jo's confidence that she'd be able to convince anyone that she was in love with one of England's most notorious rogues.

Rogues!

How could she have forgotten the rogue rules? Her new friends had created a list of rules for avoiding rogues so that none of them fell prey to scoundrels who would either ruin them or break their hearts—or both, which had been the case for one of them.

The ruin of Pandora Barclay by the Earl of Banemore had prompted them to make the rules in the first place. And so far, three of the friends had fallen for rogues in spite of them. Although, Jo wasn't sure if Tamsin's husband qualified as a rogue. He possessed a somewhat surly nature, but Jo could see the warmth beneath his hard exterior. She could not, however, detect even a hint of roguishness about him. Tamsin assured her it was there—buried deep inside him.

As they walked to the library, Jo ran through the rules in her mind:

Never be alone with a rogue.

Never flirt with a rogue.

Never give a rogue a chance.

Never doubt a rogue's reputation.

Never believe a rogue's pledge of love or devotion.

Never trust a rogue to change.

Never allow a rogue to see your heart.

Ruin the rogue before he can ruin you.

Jo had already broken several of those, and not with Sheff. Did that mean she characterized her former lovers, of which there had been exactly two, as rogues? They were perhaps roguish, but they were not notorious for their behavior as Sheff was.

And she'd broken two of the rogue rules with him. They'd definitely flirted, even if it was just silliness between them, and she'd been alone with him when they'd gone to take care of his father last night. Actually, since his father had been there, they hadn't really been alone. But they had been alone that afternoon in her sitting room briefly, before she'd taken him to walk outside. And while they weren't alone on a busy street, they also hadn't had a chaperone, which was probably the spirit behind the rule.

All that aside, she not only had to convince her friends that she'd fallen in love with Sheff, but that she'd fallen in love with a *rogue*. She glanced at Min and knew that convincing her would be the hardest.

As much as Jo wanted to try the whisky, she ought to have gone home. Now she was going to have to spend time acting just different enough so that her impending betrothal would not seem as though it had come from nowhere.

Perhaps she'd just remain quiet and drink several glasses.

They sat at a table near the center of the room. Several other tables were occupied.

"It seems as though there are quite a few ladies here," Tamsin observed.

"Refugees," Ellis said with a smirk.

"Can you blame them?" Min asked. "Rather, can you blame *us*?" She looked toward Jo with a commiserative chuckle.

In that moment, Jo realized she'd already somehow crossed into the land of make-believe. Since when did she go to balls and sit with her good friends, the daughter of a duke and a baroness? There was also the viscountess, who was not present, not to mention the duchess whom Jo had met at Gwen's wedding celebration dinner earlier in the week. That was where she'd met the ruined member of their group, Pandora, who was visiting her sister and newborn nephew for a time but not participating in Society.

Why was Jo participating in Society? She'd floated around the periphery in her father's company and at various literary salons, but a Phoenix Club ball was another level. And she was about to climb even higher. She ought to feel a sense of dread, but if she were honest, there was a faint sense of anticipation. To be able to move amid Society would give her entrée to all the salons and access to even more artistic and scientific minds. But would she be welcome?

A sense of unease grasped at her throat. When the footwoman arrived, she barely managed to ask for the Highland whisky.

"All right, Jo?" Ellis, who'd also requested the whisky, asked.

Jo summoned a smile. "Just parched."

Again, Min sent Jo a look of mild suspicion. How on earth was Jo ever going to fool her?

~

*S*heff departed his coach in front of Lord Gerard's fine stucco-faced terrace in Portman Square. The front door was ajar, and the sounds of music and conversation drifted out into the cool spring night.

After informing his coachman that he wouldn't be terribly long, Sheff went to the partially open door. He stood there a brief moment before it swept wide open, and a liveried footman admitted him. The footman closed the door firmly behind Sheff.

Unsure how to proceed—Sheff was, after all, invading a soiree to which he hadn't been invited—he handed his card to the footman.

"Shefford?" Mrs. Ackley-Dewitt, a widow in her late thirties, approached him from the staircase hall with a surprised smile. "I didn't know you attended Gerard's parties."

"This is my first one," he said, his gaze moving briefly over Mrs. Ackley-Dewitt. The bodice of her gown dipped rather low, and Sheff wondered if one of her nipples might make an appearance. He'd seen them before, though it had been three or so years.

Her hand fluttered near her breast, and she gave him a suggestive look. "Shall I show you upstairs?"

After what Jo had told him about Gerard's soirees, Sheff wasn't sure how to take Mrs. Ackley-Dewitt's invitation. She could just be offering to escort him to the heart of the soiree, or she could be trying to entice him into a dark corner to engage in something wicked.

"I'd very much like to pay my respects to Lord Gerard," Sheff said. *And to find Rowland Harker.*

"Then you must attend him in the drawing room," she said with a laugh. Clasping Sheff's arm, she pulled him toward the stairs.

They passed several couples conversing and one doing more than that. He was talking while she was massaging the front of his breeches. Were there no dark corners in which to conduct such acts? Sheff was by no means a prude, but even he didn't indulge in public exhibition. Perhaps that was a special aspect of Gerard's soirees.

They passed more people at the top of the stairs as they made their way to the drawing room at the front of the house. The buzz of conversation was louder here, as was the music. A quartet played in the corner while the room was stuffed with people talking, laughing, dancing, and paying court to their host. At least, Sheff assumed it was Lord Gerard seated between the front windows, his chair sitting atop a small dais. He lounged with one leg curled over an arm of the chair and was flanked by a man and a woman. The man was speaking with someone else while the woman appeared to be feeding Gerard from a tray.

Sheff felt certain he'd walked into a party that even Dionysus would have found hedonistic. He scanned the very crowded room in search of Jo's father. He wasn't entirely sure that he knew what Harker looked like.

Turning to Mrs. Ackley-Dewitt, he asked, "Have you seen Mr. Rowland Harker this evening? I am hoping to speak with him."

Her eyes rounded. "*Are* you? I did not know you enjoyed that sort of diversion."

What on earth was she talking about? "I wish to speak with him on a private matter."

"I'm sure you do," she said with a suggestive look followed by a gleeful laugh. "Here I thought you were entirely dedicated to the pleasure of women."

Sheff began to understand. "I am seeking Harker purely for a conversation."

"I see." Mrs. Ackley-Dewitt slid her hand farther up Sheff's arm. "That bodes well for me, then, doesn't it?"

Though Sheff didn't wish to be rude, he also didn't want to flirt with the widow, lest she think he was interested. And he was not. "I really must speak with Harker."

"There he is," she said, gesturing toward a corner where a group of men and women were clustered in a seating area. "In the bright orange waistcoat on the settee."

"Ho, there, is that Lord Shefford gracing us with his presence?" a voice boomed over the drawing room, halting both music and conversation.

Sheff froze as heads turned toward him. He was rarely uncomfortable, but at this moment, he felt distinctly uneasy as the focal point of what was surely a pleasure party.

"Welcome, Shefford!" The voice belonged to the host, Lord Gerard. In his fifties with a balding pate but egregiously long, gray sideburns, Gerard was dressed in a flowing gown with an open collar that made him look as if he were perhaps trying to personify Dionysus.

Sheff detached himself from Mrs. Ackley-Dewitt and made his way to Gerard's throne, for that was what it appeared to be. "Good evening, Lord Gerard. I do hope you don't mind my being here."

"Not at all. I would have invited you long before now, but your father is a frequent guest, and it seemed strange to extend you an invitation. However, your father isn't here tonight." Gerard smiled, his lips parting to reveal a rather crooked upper row of teeth. "At least not yet."

God, Sheff did not want to run into his father here. He needed to conduct his business with Jo's father and leave as quickly as possible. "I've come in search of Rowland Harker. I see him there in the corner. If I can just speak with him a moment, I'll be on my way."

Gerard pouted. "Don't rush off. There is much to entice

you here." He gestured about the room. Thankfully, people had gone back to their conversations and other activities instead of gaping at Sheff.

"I'll consider that," Sheff said, growing anxious. In truth, this was the type of event that *would* entice him, but knowing his father was often a guest ensured that Sheff wanted to be anywhere else.

"Have a glass of wine at least." Gerard snapped his fingers, and a footman with a tray appeared.

There were several varieties of wine available. Sheff selected a golden-colored one, which he assumed to be a Madeira. Lifting the glass from the tray, he motioned it toward his host. "Thank you for your kind hospitality, Gerard."

"Do take full advantage, Shefford," Gerard said with a throaty laugh before accepting a nut of some kind from the woman feeding him. He sucked the nut and her fingertips into his mouth.

Sheff turned and hastened toward Harker's corner, taking a fortifying drink of wine on his way.

The group of people with Harker were dressed normally —mostly. A few of the men were missing certain items, such as their coat or cravat. And the women were all dressed in a revealing fashion, as Mrs. Ackley-Dewitt had been. One of them sat pressed against Harker on a settee, her hand splayed across his thigh.

It was not difficult to see, at least physically, why Harker was surrounded by admirers. He possessed a generous smile, expressive eyes, and lustrous dark blond hair, which was somewhat of a rarity for a man in his fifties. He wore a bright orange silk waistcoat, and his cravat was a dark ivory. He was not wearing a coat, nor did he need one to mask a thick middle, for he was still quite trim.

Sheff recalled what Mrs. Ackley-Dewitt had told him.

He'd presumed Jo's father perhaps preferred male company, but the proximity of the woman's hand to his loins seemed to indicate he was accepting of whoever wished to give him attention.

"Good evening, Harker," Sheff said. "Might I steal a few moments of your time?"

"Certainly." Harker glanced about their seating area. "I apologize there is nowhere to sit."

"Actually, if you wouldn't mind taking a brief respite from your…companions, I would appreciate conducting our conversation in a more private and quiet space."

The woman next to Harker whispered in his ear, and her hand moved farther up his thigh until her fingers were touching his groin.

Harker patted her arm. "I'll be back before you know it, my dear. And I promise you will have me all to yourself in a while."

Extricating himself from the possessive woman at his side, Harker stood. He moved from the seating area, and they left the drawing room. The corridor was still not particularly conducive to a private conversation about marriage.

"This way," Harker said, leading him downstairs. "I can't imagine what you'd want to speak to me about. Have we even officially met?"

"We have not," Sheff replied as they reached the ground floor.

Harker took him into the dining room, of all places. It was devoid of people. "This is where people come if they need a respite from everything—and everyone."

"But there is no one here," Sheff noted.

"Hardly ever," Harker said with a laugh, moving into the room and turning to face Sheff. "People don't come to these parties for a respite. Still, Gerard tries to provide a welcoming space to all."

"That is most benevolent of him." Sheff straightened his shoulders. "I shan't take too much of your time."

Harker nodded. "I imagine you'd like to partake of the party's offerings." His gaze fell to the glass in Sheff's hand. "Damn, I should have brought wine too."

Sheff had forgotten he was even holding it. Setting it down on the table, he faced Jo's father. "Jo told me I could find you here tonight."

Harker's brow furrowed. "You are acquainted with my daughter?"

"Yes. I just danced with her at the Phoenix Club ball, in fact."

Harker's face lit with joy. "Oh, splendid! I'm so glad she went. She can be so hesitant to attend events like that. Now that I think about it, you probably also know her from the Siren's Call. I imagine you are a frequent visitor."

"I am, in fact. I have come to know your daughter well and find we have much in common."

"Do you?" Harker's features smoothed. "And you danced with her?"

"Yes." Sheff needed to proceed to the heart of the matter and be on his way. "Tomorrow, I should like to call on her to propose marriage. However, I wanted to secure your approval first."

"Bloody hell!" Harker slapped his palm against the table. "You wish to marry Jo? *My* Jo?"

"I'm rather hoping she'll become *my* Jo," Sheff said, surprised to find he actually felt a thread of possession, even if it was only pretend.

Harker's eyes narrowed. "She is in favor of this?"

"She is."

Pursing his lips, Harker was silent for a long moment. Deep creases furrowed along his brow. "Forgive me, Shefford, but your reputation does not recommend you for the state of matrimony. It is understood that you avoid the parson's trap and that you enjoy the company of a variety of women. That is not the sort of man I would want for my daughter."

Sheff blinked. There was a distinct irony to this *married* man, who would shortly join a woman for any number of sexual exploits, questioning Sheff's behavior. "I have fallen in love with your daughter and look forward to demonstrating my fidelity."

"Bah!" Harker waved his hand through the air. "You'll try to be loyal, but men like us are not capable of limiting our attentions to one woman. I'm sure your father has told you that."

He had not, but actions spoke much louder than words, and Sheff was well aware that the duke was not made for monogamy. Nor was Sheff.

Harker continued, "Still, I understand your need to do your duty, and the thought of my Jo as a future duchess is rather intoxicating." He grinned, then quickly sobered. One eye narrowed skeptically. "She feels the same about you and has indicated she will accept your suit?"

"She has." Sheff found lying about their relationship distasteful, and that surprised him. It wasn't as if Jo hadn't agreed to every aspect.

"I must speak with her first," Harker said, straightening his spine. "You plan to call on her tomorrow? I'll arrive before you and speak with her. If she tells me she wants to marry you, I'll give my approval."

Why was this so bloody difficult? Sheff never imagined a fake betrothal would require this much work. He'd write Jo a note and drop it off at the Siren's Call so she could be prepared for her father's visit.

"An excellent plan," Sheff said with a forced smile. "Thank

you for your time." He started to turn, but Harker stopped him with a question.

"You really do love her?"

Sheff met the man's gaze. "With all my heart."

Harker smiled widely, his joy evident. "I'm so pleased. This is truly a marvelous development. Surprising, but marvelous indeed."

Sheff feared the man would not be able to contain his excitement when he returned upstairs. "You must keep this private until I propose tomorrow. Can you promise me you'll do that?"

"Of course." Harker waved his hand again. "You can trust me to keep a secret."

Except that Sheff knew the opposite to be true. He had to expect that a portion of London would be talking about his engagement tomorrow.

He'd need to speak with his parents as soon as possible after meeting with Jo. He'd write notes to them too, requesting a meeting. Addressing them together filled him with an anxious dread, but he'd rather suffer their reactions at one time than separately. They could manage to be in the same room together for a brief period. Especially if it meant their son was finally betrothed.

"Thank you," Sheff said. Then he turned and started out of the dining room.

Harker followed him. "You really aren't going back up to the party?"

"No." Sheff continued toward the entrance hall.

"Perhaps my daughter really has set you on a new path," Harker said. "Love can change a person. It did me."

Sheff bid the man good night. As he left the hedonistic soiree, he contemplated what the man had said and dismissed it entirely.

Love changed nothing for those who couldn't feel it.

CHAPTER 5

*J*o woke up to a note from Sheff telling her that he'd tracked her father down at Lord Gerard's soiree, and that he had not yet given his approval for their marriage. That would come, Sheff had explained, after her father called on her today and ensured *she* wanted to wed.

Now Jo not only had to tell her mother about the betrothal scheme with Sheff, but also that her estranged husband would be calling. It was nearly enough to make Jo want to take the money Sheff had already given her and flee London.

Instead, she knocked on the study door, knowing her mother was inside working, having returned from Marcel's house a few hours earlier. Jo took a deep breath as her mother bade her enter.

Jo's mother sat in the chair at her desk with her eyes closed and waved a fan with considerable vigor over her face and chest. The windows had been thrown open, and the overall temperature of the room was quite cool. Jo concluded that her mother was having another one of her "heat intolerances," which had started a year or so ago.

Jo was especially sorry to bother her mother after she was already discomfited. "Pardon me for interrupting, Mama, but I've an important matter to discuss with you."

"I do hope Weston will be cooler in the summer than London," Jo's mother said, opening her eyes. "Marcel assures me there will be a lovely ocean breeze."

"That sounds restorative," Jo said, going to sit in the chair situated next to her mother's desk.

Her mother straightened in her chair, but continued to ply her fan as she addressed Jo. "What is your important matter?"

Jo had rehearsed what to say—she did this often when she wanted to discuss something important or when she wanted to remember certain points she wished to make—but at the moment, she was struggling to recall how to begin. "I'm going to accept a marriage proposal."

Brows drawing together tightly and lips pursing, Jo's mother stopped waving the fan as she spoke. "Who has proposed?"

"He hasn't yet, but he will be here shortly. There is a caveat, however." Jo smoothed her hands over her lap. "This will be a fake betrothal for the remainder of the Season."

Her mother employed the fan once more. "Explain."

"I'm going to assist Shefford. His parents won't let him alone with regard to taking a wife, so he'd like to put an end to their haranguing."

"Of course it would be Shefford," her mother muttered. "A temporary, fake betrothal will stop nothing. I credited him with being smarter than that."

"He thinks it could have a lasting effect, and anyway, that doesn't concern me. He's asked for my help and will be compensating my efforts."

Her mother's brown, sculpted brows now shot up. "You should have started with that part, for that is the most important and explains right away why you have agreed to such nonsense. How much?"

Jo was not surprised that her mother would want the financial details. She'd considered lying so that her mother wouldn't try to manage any of it, but she'd only ever lied to her mother once. She'd been nine years old, and she'd lied about taking in a kitten. Her mother had been furious and banished Jo to her room for a week. When Jo had been allowed out, she'd discovered that her mother had fallen in love with the kitten and so she'd stayed, a beloved member of their household until her passing two years ago.

"Five hundred pounds." Jo enjoyed the gleam of approval that entered her mother's gaze.

"Well done. I am impressed with your enterprising spirit. That is an excellent investment sum for your future. You needn't ever wed now, not that you needed to in the first place given the income from the club. But this provides you with even more security." She smiled. "How do you feel?"

"Liberated." Not only did Jo not have to wed, she didn't have to take over the Siren's Call if she didn't want to. It occurred to her that she was, in a way, lying to her mother by not discussing her reservations about assuming ownership of the club, but Jo hadn't firmly decided. Until then, there was no need to broach what would surely be a contentious conversation.

"Excellent." Her mother's smile broadened. "There is no better way for a woman to feel. Shefford is coming today to pretend to propose? Am I supposed to also pretend?"

"Yes, he is coming, and no, you needn't pretend—to him. He knows I've told you the truth. However, you are the only person who knows. Everyone else will think this is a real engagement and that we are in love."

Jo's mother laughed, her fan stopping in midair. "That anyone would believe either you or the Earl of Shefford would fall in love illustrates how gullible people can be. But I suppose we will see how it plays out. There will be speculation—and judgment—because of his reputation and your standing, or lack thereof. I'm sure you're prepared for that. Enduring it will be worth five hundred pounds."

"That is what I decided too," Jo said, though she still felt slightly uneasy. There was no predicting what would happen once she attended a ball. Perhaps she'd be given the cut direct. "There is one other thing." Jo braced herself. Her mother wouldn't be angry, but she would feel inconvenienced, and she disliked that intensely.

"From your tone, I can sense that I will not be enthused. I think I can surmise that this involves your father. It's only reasonable to think that the two of us will need to publicly endorse the betrothal, probably in person." She wrinkled her nose. "But he won't know the truth?"

"No. In fact, Sheff tracked him down last night and sought his approval for the betrothal."

Her mother interrupted. "At Lord Gerard's Friday soiree?"

"Yes. How did you know?"

"Some people seem to think I want to know what your father is doing," Jo's mother replied with a shrug. "But even if they didn't, Gerard's soirees are precisely where I would expect to find him on the first Friday evening of the month."

"I see," Jo said, more curious than ever about Lord Gerard's soirees. Perhaps Sheff would enlighten her. "Papa did not immediately offer his endorsement. He is coming here to ensure it is what I want before he grants it."

Her mother had started fanning herself again, but now stopped and frowned. "Your father is coming here. Today?"

"Shortly, I would imagine."

Blowing out a breath, Jo's mother began to fan herself zealously. "This is a great deal of effort for a fake engagement. Why is Shefford even bothering to come?"

"I suppose he thought he should be seen calling the day after we danced at the Phoenix Club." Jo hadn't asked. This was his scheme, and she would do what he planned. Though, she'd let him know if there was anything that troubled her. She'd retained the right to set rules, after all.

Laughing again, her mother slowed the movement of the fan. "*Seen* calling here? We don't live in Grosvenor Square. I won't quibble over the details of this farce, not when he's paying you that much. I'll set an appointment for you with the solicitor so you can discuss investment options."

"Er, thank you." Jo appreciated the help, but she also wouldn't mind doing things for herself. The word *liberated* had been her true feeling, and it meant something for her to be independent.

Her mother frowned. "I do want to make sure this ruse doesn't interfere with your responsibilities at the club. You will be doing more, not less, over the next few months, and you can't be gadding about town most nights of the week."

"Nor do I want to." Jo would prefer to keep her temporary involvement in the upper echelon of Society to a minimum.

Her mother scrutinized her for a moment. "Is that true? I understand you enjoy your Monday literary salons, but of late, you've been gone other nights of the week with your new set of friends, which includes Sheff's sister. You can't very well run the Siren's Call *and* commit to such events."

No, she could not. In the long term, anyway. Jo would have to choose. Though, she noticed her mother did not say so. She, of course, would assume that Jo would run the Siren's Call. That was the expectation.

Voices carried from the sitting room, and Jo recognized

her father's as one of them. The other was their housekeeper, Mrs. Rand.

Jo stood, feeling slightly nervous as she couldn't exactly recall the last time her parents had been together.

Rising from her chair, Jo's mother snapped her fan closed. "You are smart not to tell your father the truth," she whispered. "The secret would be all over London by tomorrow."

She preceded Jo from the study into the sitting room. Jo's father stood near one of the front windows. Turning to face them, he bowed.

"Julia, you are stunning as always," he said to Jo's mother, using her given name, which Jo thought only Marcel used to address her. Hearing her father say it was strange, but then so was this entire meeting.

"You never change, Rowland," Jo's mother said. She looked to Mrs. Rand and quietly said, "No tea, thank you." The housekeeper departed into the entrance hall.

Jo went to buss her father's cheek. "It's good to see you, Papa."

"You don't seem surprised to see me," he noted with a wry expression.

"Sheff wrote to me that you were coming," Jo replied. "I informed Mama."

Her father lifted his hands. He used them often when he spoke. It was part of his enthusiastic animation. "Perhaps I should have sent word ahead. My apologies." He shifted his attention to Jo and smiled. "Now, tell me about you and the Earl of Shefford. I had no idea he was courting you." He ushered her to join him on the settee.

Jo glanced toward her mother, who was watching them with mild amusement. She did not move to sit.

"I am surprised you would marry Shefford, of all people," her father said.

Knowing she would hear this sentiment a great deal, Jo

had prepared for it. "We've been friends for a while now—from the Siren's Call. Sometimes friendships bloom into something more."

"That is so true," her father replied with a nod. "And sometimes the opposite happens. Love cools to friendship." He sent a wistful smile toward Jo's mother, who'd crossed her arms. She didn't look impatient, exactly, but she did not look as though she wanted to linger.

Jo wanted to ask if her parents were actually friends. She hadn't thought so. If they were, why did they avoid one another? Couldn't they have spent holidays together if they were friendly? Or at least Jo's birthday?

Sadness wasn't something Jo felt with regard to her parents, but at the moment, a shocking melancholy swept over her.

"You're in love with one another, then?" Jo's father asked, thankfully yanking her from maudlin thoughts.

"Yes," Jo said with a bright smile. She hoped that would convince him as opposed to her gushing effusively about her fake betrothed.

"When is the wedding?" he asked.

"We haven't discussed specific dates, but not until the autumn or winter."

Her father frowned. "Why not sooner? A June wedding would be lovely, even if this spring has been positively miserable. The sun must come out eventually!" He laughed.

The weather had been cool and rainy, but that was, of course, not the reason for their delayed nuptials. "I'm not sure I want to marry in the midst of the Season, Papa." That seemed as good a reason as any. Certainly better than Sheff's —that she wanted a fur-trimmed cloak or whatever he'd said.

"I also asked if they could perchance wait," Jo's mother interjected, drawing Jo's attention. She gave Jo a slight nod, as if to communicate that she was there to help with the ruse.

"I'll be traveling to Weston for a good portion of the summer."

Except she wouldn't be leaving until July. Still, it was a lovely excuse, and Jo appreciated her mother offering it.

Jo's father angled his body toward his wife. "Weston? With Marcel?"

Her mother nodded. "He's taken a cottage there."

He goggled at her. "You're leaving London for more than a few days? I am flabbergasted."

"Sometimes change is good," Jo's mother said evenly. "Or even necessary." Her eyes narrowed just slightly as she looked at Jo's father, and Jo thought there must be some unspoken communication going on.

Jo's father turned his focus back to Jo. "For the remainder of the Season, we will do our best to support you. I know it won't be easy for you to be scrutinized as you absolutely will be." He gave her a sympathetic smile and patted her hand.

"There will be a betrothal ball," Jo said, looking from her father to her mother and back again. "It would be good if we could all arrive together—just that one time. You can leave whenever you like." She darted a glance toward her mother and caught the slight curl of her lip. Jo wasn't sure if her mother's distaste was due to having to spend time with her husband or that she'd have to attend a high society event. Not just attend, but be at the center of it.

Her father sucked in a breath. "Oh, this is going to require an entirely new wardrobe, my dear. Why did I not come to that conclusion much sooner?" He looked to his wife. "You must set an appointment with a modiste. Not any modiste—a French one. I can find out who is the most popular this Season."

"Marcel's sister will be more than adequate," Jo's mother said, referring to the woman who currently made their clothing. "She is French."

Shaking his head vehemently, Jo's father said, "Absolutely not. Jo must look like a future duchess, for she is one. I mean no offense to Marcel's sister, but Jo must be outfitted by someone the ton patronizes. She cannot afford to invite any more scorn than her position already will."

Jo flinched inwardly, though he wasn't wrong. Looking at her mother, Jo could see that she knew it too.

Exhaling, her mother said, "Then you find someone appropriate."

He moved his hands about in front of him as he slowly spoke. "Well…that is…I'm afraid I can't contribute much to a wardrobe." He sent a faint grimace toward Jo. She was not surprised to hear that he didn't have money. He never seemed to have much, but then he also never seemed to be struggling. How would Jo even know? She'd always lived with her mother.

"I wouldn't expect you to," her mother said. "We will manage." She sent Jo a pointed look, and Jo presumed her mother expected that Sheff's payment would cover the expense. Later, Jo would inform her that he was, in fact, paying for her new wardrobe outside of the five hundred pounds. Her mother would be even more impressed with how Jo would benefit from this arrangement.

The bell from the front door sounded, announcing the arrival of, presumably, Sheff. Mrs. Rand passed by the doorway and went down the stairs to the front door.

"That must be your groom," Jo's father said with a gleeful smile. "I must say, I am delighted to see you've done so well, my girl. I worried your mother had convinced you not to wed." He arched a brow at his wife, and Jo sensed a pulse of tension between them. She did not want them to do or say anything untoward while Sheff was here.

Voices drifted up the stairwell along with footfalls. Mrs. Rand appeared in the doorway and stepped aside for Sheff to move past her. "The Earl of Shefford," she announced before retreating.

"Good afternoon," Sheff said brightly, a dazzling smile lighting his features. He moved into the sitting room and bowed to Jo's mother. "Always a pleasure to see you, Mrs. Harker."

"I confess I'm surprised to see you in *this* capacity, my lord," she said with a hint of bemusement.

"Yes, well, no one is more surprised than I to have been swept completely off my feet by your daughter." His gaze met Jo's with a heat that almost convinced *her* he was truly enamored of her.

"Absolutely splendid," Jo's father said, standing. "I must shake my future son-in-law's hand. I forgot to do that last night when you ran me to ground at Gerard's."

Jo caught her mother's slight grimace at the mention of Gerard. She watched as her father eagerly pumped Sheff's hand. Sheff had barely managed to remove his glove.

"We have your approval, then?" Sheff asked.

"Certainly. But you've yet to actually propose." Her father moved to the side and watched expectantly.

"You can't want Shefford to kneel down in front of us?" Jo's mother asked, incredulous.

"Why not?" Jo's father asked, sounding mildly affronted. "You know I am a romantic in my heart."

"Yes, I do." Jo's mother's tone held more than a bit of irony.

Sheff met Jo's gaze with a silent question. In response, Jo lifted a shoulder. They might as well become accustomed to performing.

She stood and moved away from the seating area. Sheff seemed to understand and joined her.

"We can pretend they aren't there," she said. Then, much

more quietly so her parents couldn't hear: "We need to master the art of performance."

"Indeed," he murmured before taking her hand. His fingers were warm against hers.

He knelt before her and pulled something from his pocket. Something that sparkled. Did he have a *ring*?

"My dearest Jo," he said, his lips curved into a seductive smile that, together with the touch of his hand in hers, sent heat curling through her. "You make me happier than I ever knew I could be. I cannot imagine the days of my life without you in them. Please be my wife, my countess, and someday my duchess."

"And the mother of your children!" Jo's father added, rather ruining what was a very lovely fake proposal.

"Yes, that too," Sheff said with a glint in his eye and a quirk of his lips that said he was trying not to laugh.

Jo had to press her lips together to contain her own humor. "Yes, I will marry you."

Sheff slid the ring onto her finger. A large, stunning sapphire shone up at Jo from her left hand. The weight of the ring was odd. Its beauty was breathtaking.

Rising, Sheff lifted her hand to his mouth and pressed a kiss to the back.

"Don't be shy, my boy," Jo's father said. "You must seal an engagement with a kiss, and we won't even watch."

Jo darted a glance and saw that indeed her father had turned away from them. Her mother looked…bored. But she also turned her head.

"They aren't watching," Jo whispered. "You don't have to kiss me."

"I know that is our agreement. How about if I just barely touch your cheek." He looked askance, and the edge of his mouth ticked down. "Your father is, in fact, watching now."

Blast! "Fine. Kiss me." Her mother was right. This was too much effort for a fake engagement.

Sheff leaned his head toward hers and brushed his lips against her tightly closed mouth.

Dear God.

Jo was not prepared for the rush of heat that pulsed in her core, just from his merest touch. His lips were warm and firm. They moved gently over hers, coaxing her to relax. Her entire body had clenched in preparation for his kiss. Only for it be extraordinary.

She couldn't help kissing him back. Her body knew what to do when she was kissed, when she was…aroused.

Then he was gone, his head lifting from hers.

She dared to look into his eyes. She caught the barest flash of surprise. Had he been as moved as she was?

This would not do. The no-kissing rule would be reinstated forthwith, and it would be absolute.

"Let me see the ring!" Jo's father exclaimed, shattering the seductive aura Jo had found herself in—and none too soon.

Her father came toward them, and Jo held up her hand. "It's a sapphire," she said unnecessarily. "Isn't it?" she glanced at Sheff, but didn't want to look at him. Especially his lips. She could still feel them against hers.

"Yes. It belonged to my grandmother, the dowager duchess," Sheff said. "She died last year."

Jo would be very careful with it. Indeed, she was almost afraid to wear it, not when none of this was real.

"It's spectacular," Jo's father said, taking her hand. He gave her a squeeze before releasing her. "I'm delighted for you both. I shall look forward to the betrothal ball. Do let me know the details as soon as you can. I must make sure I look like the almost father-in-law of the heir to a dukedom." He laughed joyously. "And see what you can do about moving the wedding up. Jo would look so beautiful with summer flowers in her hair."

"I'm afraid that won't be possible," Sheff replied evenly.

"The wedding will be lovely whenever it is," Jo's mother said.

"Indeed, it will." Jo's father bid them all good day before bussing Jo's cheek and departing.

No one said anything until they heard the front door close at the base of the stairwell.

Jo's mother shook her head. "Your father is going to be devastated when this wedding doesn't happen." She directed her attention to Sheff. "This is a very odd scheme. I fail to see how it will help you in the end. You will still have to wed as dukes must."

Sheff smiled, his gaze sly. "Rules are only meant to be broken by you?"

"Saucy," Jo's mother said as she laughed. "Touché."

"We can count on your discretion?" Sheff asked.

"Yes, and I will help as I can—within reason." She turned to Jo, her features softening slightly. "Be gentle with your father when you tell him the truth. He possesses a sensitive nature."

Jo knew that, of course. She did not like having to deceive him, but there was simply no other choice.

"Mama, I forgot to mention that Sheff is also paying for my new wardrobe."

"And I'm happy to do it," Sheff said affably. "Jo is doing me a great favor."

Jo's mother speared him with a probing stare. "You will look after my daughter. I won't see her hurt in any way as a result of your roguery. I suggest you engage in a period of celibacy for the duration of this farce."

He clasped his hands behind his back. "I will, ah, take that under advisement."

Jo didn't believe he would.

Her mother left the sitting room, going through the entrance hall, either to her suite or perhaps downstairs to the club.

A sudden wave of exhaustion swept over Jo. She drooped and wiped her hand over her brow. Forgetting there was now a ring on her finger, she scratched her skin with the raised jewel. "Ow."

"What did you do?" Sheff moved closer, which she didn't particularly want. She'd barely recovered from the shocking intimacy of their kiss.

"I forgot about this ring and scratched my forehead. Is it bleeding?"

He fixed his gaze on her brow, his expression intent. "No, it's just red." Lifting his hand, he rubbed his thumb over where her flesh stung. "I did not mean to provide you with a weapon. You don't have to wear it all the time. But I had to give you something."

"Couldn't you just have purchased a paste jewel? What if something happens to your grandmother's ring while it's in my possession?"

"Nothing is going to happen to it," he said with a faint smile. "I have complete faith in you. What self-respecting gentleman puts a paste betrothal ring on a lady's finger?"

She gave him a sardonic look. "What self-respecting gentleman pays that lady to pretend to be his betrothed?"

"This one," he said with a laugh.

Jo moved away from him, eager to put distance between them. Her pulse was still moving a little more quickly than she would like. Today had simply been a great deal to manage. Both her parents together and this faux proposal.

Not to mention a stirring kiss.

No, she didn't want to mention that at all. Not even in the confines of her own thoughts.

"Have you told your parents yet?" she asked, moving back toward the seating area, not that she had any intention of sitting. She didn't want him to stay, for she had work to do and she probably ought to visit a modiste. But whom?

Sheff followed her, but didn't come too close. "I haven't spoken to them, but I will in a short while. I've requested their presence for a meeting. I confess I'm a bit apprehensive about seeing them together, but I would rather share the news once. This also ensures that neither is upset that the other found out first." He rolled his eyes.

"Managing parents can be a challenge," Jo said with a commiserative nod. "I can't recall the last time mine were together. That made me anxious about today, though it seemed to have gone well."

"I should say so, at least from my perspective. Your father appears to be quite delighted, while your mother is more reserved. I suppose that is to be expected since she knows the truth of the matter, and he does not."

"Even if she didn't, she would still be more reserved than my father." Jo cocked her head. "How was your meeting with him last night? Did you manage to avoid debauchery?"

He laughed. "Yes, though there was plenty of opportunity. It was unlike any soiree I've ever attended."

"Do you plan to attend another in the future?" She assumed it was precisely the type of entertainment he enjoyed, especially since he didn't seem to want to discuss it with her.

"Not as long as my father is invited. Gerard said that is why I haven't ever received an invitation—he didn't think I'd want to come. And he was right. I suppose I must be on my way." He started to turn, then stopped himself. "Oh, if I may suggest a modiste—Madame Demarest is one of the most popular this Season. If you'd like, I can have my mother arrange for you to have a fitting on Monday."

"Your mother?"

"I am fairly certain she will want to accompany you." He grimaced, then gave her an apologetic look, his brow furrowing in a way that was actually quite endearing. "Is that all right? It didn't seem as though your mother wanted to go with you."

"My mother would likely say she is too busy. That does not bother me." Indeed, Jo had been managing her own clothing for nearly a decade. Having someone else help her decide would be awkward. "Will your mother hope to choose everything for me?"

"I honestly don't know. Perhaps Min should go too."

"It would be nice to have Min and Ellis there." Even if that meant more time lying to them. On second thought, perhaps Jo would be fine without them.

"Oh, not Ellis. My mother wouldn't invite her. But she'd be delighted to have Min along. Just tell me what you prefer."

Jo wanted to ask why Ellis, who was absolutely lovely, wouldn't be included, but she didn't want to pry. He also needed to be on his way to meet with his parents. "I will go along with whatever is easiest. You should probably get on. You've an appointment to keep."

He exhaled. "Yes. Wish me luck." He flashed her a smile. "I'll stop in at the Siren's Call this evening to let you know how it went."

"If you wish." Jo wanted to tell him not to bother, for she rather thought she'd seen quite enough of him for one day. They would be spending a great deal of time together in the coming weeks, and she didn't need to look at his mouth or recall his lips on hers any more than was necessary.

Sheff gave her a courtly bow. "Until later, my dearest." He chuckled before leaving.

Jo put her hand to her mouth, her fingertips pressing gently against her lips. Then she turned her hand and surveyed the oval sapphire weighted against her finger. For something that was entirely make-believe, today's charade had felt far too real.

CHAPTER 6

As Sheff paced the library where he was shortly due to meet with his parents, he wasn't thinking of the impending interview. He couldn't seem to stop thinking about kissing Jo.

He'd felt an undeniable and profound connection, sharp and sizzling like electricity, but also deep and persistent. It was as though he could still feel the imprint of her lips on his.

Apparently, he'd been too many days without the embrace of a woman. He'd rectify that this evening and pay a visit to the Rogue's Den.

Jo's mother's suggestion came back to him, that he ought to abstain from sexual congress for the duration of their fake betrothal. He'd somehow managed not to gape at her in horror.

"Shefford, my darling."

Sheff turned to see his mother glide into the room, her hair impeccably arranged with her gray streaks somehow looking as though they'd been placed specifically to enhance the style. She wore a pale green dress, and a simple gold cross adorned her neck.

"Good afternoon, Mama."

"I confess my curiosity is quite piqued that you asked me to meet you at a specific time." A smile teased her lips, and Sheff hated that his father's arrival was about to ruin her mood.

However, before he could tell her that his father would also join them, the duke strode into the library. His gaze fell on the duchess. He pursed his lips but said nothing as he went straight to the liquor cabinet and poured a glass of wine.

"Afternoon, Sheff," he said gruffly.

"Why is he here?" Mama asked, her eyes darkening.

"I live here," Papa replied as he turned to face her, a bored expression flattening his features.

"Hardly." Mama sniffed and turned so that she faced Sheff. "You asked us both here?"

"I did. I'm pleased to announce my betrothal."

His father had just taken a drink of wine and was now coughing whereas his mother gasped. One hand flew to her throat as she gaped at him, her blue eyes wide with shock.

"You'd better not be bamming us," his father said after he'd recovered himself. He cast a glance toward the duchess, a single furrow marring his brow. Was he...concerned about her? About how she might feel if Sheff was tricking them?

No. Of course not.

"Sheff would never," the duchess said almost breathlessly.

A pang of guilt gripped Sheff and squeezed him tightly. But then he thought of the incessant haranguing, of the countless uncomfortable conversations with her in which she'd browbeat him about his duty and how he *must* wed. And that he needed to be a good husband—kind, understanding, and, above all, discreet.

It was an impossible situation. He would disappoint her by remaining unwed, and he would disappoint her by utterly failing as a husband.

"I truly have a betrothed," Sheff said, pushing the guilt to the back of his mind. "Even now, she is wearing Grandmama's ring." He glanced at his father, who blinked in surprise.

"She would like that," the duke said somewhat somberly before sipping his wine.

"Aren't you going to tell us who she is?" Mama asked, her voice slightly shrill. "I can't begin to imagine. This is a shocking development. You weren't even courting anyone, as far as I know."

"I was not. However, I have known this lady for a while now. We are friends. I danced with her at the Phoenix Club ball last night, and something had changed between us. I realized—and she did too—that we could perhaps be more than friends. I think that is why I haven't wanted to wed before now," Sheff said, warming to his tale. "Apparently, I needed a strong foundation with someone before I felt ready to propose marriage."

Something about the words, though they were a complete fabrication, rang true somewhere deep inside Sheff. If he were ever to wed, *and he would not*, friendship seemed as good a basis as any. A friend would not expect love.

His mother and father stared at him blankly.

"Who is it?" his mother prodded, her expression eager.

"Miss Josephine Harker."

"Damn me," the duke breathed.

The duchess scrunched her face, her mouth drawing into a frown. "Who?"

"Her mother owns the Siren's Call," the duke replied. "It's a gaming hell."

The color drained from the duchess's face. "A *what?*"

"It's not a gaming hell, Mama," Sheff said, throwing his

father a perturbed glower. "It's a club, and a very nice one. Jo's mother opened it close to twenty years ago, I think."

"That's about right," the duke said with a nod. He drank more of his wine. "But good heavens, Sheff, couldn't you have chosen someone from your own class?"

They were reacting exactly as he'd expected and hoped. Though, for some reason, their obvious disapproval rankled. Jo was a fine woman.

Except, you chose her precisely because they wouldn't like her and would be less likely to press for a rush to the altar.

The reminder sounding in his brain settled his agitation a bit. This was proceeding just as planned, and he needed to remember that.

The duchess gripped the back of a chair before moving stiltedly to sit in it. Or, more accurately, collapse onto it. Her face was still pale. She clasped her hands tightly in her lap.

"Her mother owns a gaming hell," she whispered. She shook her head slowly. "No, no. This cannot be." Lifting her gaze to Sheff's, she actually looked as though she might cry. "You must rescind your offer. It's not too late."

Sheff clung to his patience. This was all part of the scheme. But what if he were truly in love with Jo? He gritted his teeth. He had not expected to be annoyed by the very reaction he'd sought to provoke.

Taking a deep breath, he said, "Mama, I trust you will come to welcome Jo warmly. She is exceedingly clever, well-mannered, and she will be an excellent countess."

"But she isn't even part of Society," the duchess said, sounding as though she'd just heard the worst news possible. "And her parentage..." Her voice trailed off as her face became even paler.

"At least he's marrying someone," his father said. "You can whip her into shape, I'm sure, Alice."

Sheff's mother sent her husband a glare before addressing

Sheff once more. "This will ruin the family." She threw her hands up and clenched her jaw.

"It will not," Sheff ground out. "Jo is wonderful. You aren't even giving her a chance. She will exceed every one of your expectations." He took another deep breath to try to calm his surprising anger. "The matter is settled. I have already secured her father's permission, and, as I said, Jo is already wearing Grandmama's ring." He almost mentioned the presumptive betrothal ball, but if his mother didn't want to have one, wouldn't that be for the best?

The duke frowned at his now-empty wineglass before moving his focus to Sheff. "There is no chance you'll change your mind?"

"No."

"We must have a betrothal ball," the duchess said bitterly. She looked at Sheff expectantly. "I don't suppose your gaming-hell betrothed could plan and execute a ball?"

"Since she manages a busy club with seemingly little effort, I imagine she could." That was perhaps the truest thing he'd said yet.

The duchess gripped the arm of her chair, her knuckles going white. "She *works* at this gaming hell?"

"Yes." Sheff felt no guilt at duping his parents, especially his mother, given her reaction. He loved her, but she'd been completely unreasonable on the subject of his marriage. Her reaction today was even worse. "Mama, was I supposed to permit you to choose a wife of whom you approve?"

His father snorted, and Sheff was fairly certain he was trying not to laugh.

"Don't be ridiculous," the duchess said, sniffing. "But you cannot fault me for wanting you to wed someone who is your social equal."

That was most important to her, which Sheff ought to have known. Hearing her say it, however, hit him. He now realized that what he'd been seeking wasn't a reprieve from their demands, but a reprieve from *them*. An odd sense of exhaustion settled over him. Why did everything in this family have to be so fraught, so bloody difficult?

"I am sorry you are unhappy with my choice of bride," Sheff said, stiffening his spine and adopting his most noble tone. "However, I am going to marry Jo and I encourage you to find it within yourselves to be happy about it. Or at least not distraught. I am getting *married*. That is what you wanted."

"He's right," the duke said. "Congratulations, Sheff. I hope you will be very happy. *Truly*." He sounded as if he actually meant it.

The duchess stood. Some color had returned to her face, but her features looked as if they'd been carved from ice. "I will need time to acclimate myself to this…situation." Then she strode from the room.

"I didn't know she could walk that fast," the duke muttered, moving back to the liquor cabinet to deposit his empty glass on the tray. Turning to face Sheff, he smoothed the lapel of his coat. "Ignore her. She's always been demanding and unforgiving."

Unforgiving? Was she going to be angry with Sheff forever? "You say that because she will never forgive you for your behavior. I am not you." Except parts of him were.

"No, you are not, thank goodness. Your mother possesses deep convictions. She also applies different sets of morals and expectations to everyone. It's bloody confusing." He massaged his brow.

It seemed as though his father might say more, but when he did not, Sheff asked, "What, exactly, is confusing?"

"Never mind. Forget I said anything." He gave Sheff a half smile. "Your mother winds me up like an automaton. I'm happy for you, my boy. Jo seems a delightful young woman, not that I know her very well. If she's anything like her mother, you've found an excellent helpmate—strong, capable, and likely to make sure you don't cause a scandal." He chuckled as he left the library.

Sheff frowned after him. Was his father trying to say that his wife—Sheff's mother—wasn't able to prevent him from causing a scandal? As if it were her fault.

"That is precisely the expression I would expect to see on your face after meeting with Mama and Papa," Min said as she walked into the library. "Percy said you were in here with them. Did they give you a deadline for marriage?"

"On the contrary, I requested the meeting so I could inform them that I am betrothed."

Min narrowed her eyes at him. Skepticism radiated from her as she set her hands on her hips. "*You* are betrothed?"

He nodded. "As of today."

"Who was foolish enough to say yes? Or is there a scandal that hasn't broken yet?" She cocked her head. "You were at the Phoenix Club for a while last evening, but if something had happened there, I would have heard about it already."

"There isn't a scandal. Nor will there be." That was perhaps the greatest lie he'd told yet. He just hoped it would be a minor scandal, particularly since the dissolution of the betrothal would happen outside of the Season and outside London. Most of all, he would ensure the scandal was entirely about him. Jo would be unscathed.

"You aren't telling me her name," Min said, her features still cloaked with doubt. "What's wrong with her?"

"Nothing is wrong with her. In fact, I think you'll approve, unlike our mother. It's Jo."

Now Min's expression changed to one that resembled their mother's reaction to Sheff's choice of bride. There was shock and even a bit of horror. "*Jo?* As in my friend whose mother owns the Siren's Call? Jo who hasn't set foot in a proper Society event in…forever?"

"I would argue that a Phoenix Club assembly is plenty proper. But I am not concerned about any of that."

"Clearly, else you would not have proposed." Min crossed her arms over her chest and moved closer to him. "Why Jo? I can't imagine you've fallen in love with one another in the last five minutes."

"We danced last night, and it was most revealing."

"Bah. I spent the rest of the evening with her, and she was not a woman enamored."

"I believe she likes to keep her emotions close." Sheff had no idea if that was true, but it was a good excuse for both of them to use through this ruse.

Min studied him a long moment, her brow furrowed as she seemed to consider what he said. "Jo doesn't want to marry. How did you convince her?"

"I don't want to marry either, so perhaps that makes us perfect for one another," he replied smugly.

Min shook her head. "Something doesn't smell right about this. I happen to like Jo very much. If you hurt her in any way—"

Sheff cut her off. "I won't." He'd expected Min to express disbelief, but this level of skepticism was more than he'd anticipated. Perhaps that was because he'd failed to take Min's friendship with Jo into account. Sheff would speak to Jo about expressing her feelings in such a way that Min wouldn't question their betrothal.

But honestly, did it matter if they were in love or had never planned to wed? Sheff was expected to wed—his wishes be damned—and what young lady would say no to marrying the heir to a dukedom? Even a young lady who didn't wish to wed.

Put like that, Sheff wondered if they ought to just wed

anyway and agree to lead separate lives. Both their parents did it. Why not them?

Because Sheff didn't even want that much of a commitment to someone. He wanted absolutely zero chance of disappointing a spouse.

Min was still watching him with concern, prompting him to consider just telling her the truth. Except then, she'd have to hide it from their parents. And from Ellis. Or he could just tell Ellis too. But Sheff didn't want many people knowing. It would increase the risk of the secret becoming known, and that would be damaging—especially to Jo.

"You say you won't hurt her, but you're a terrible rogue," Min said. "And she knows that!" Min uncrossed her arms and made an exasperated sound in her throat. "Rest assured, I shall learn the truth of this scheme."

Before he could think of how to respond, such as pleading with her not to tell their parents when she discovered it, Min sailed from the room.

Sheff was now doubting the wisdom of his plan. Perhaps they should call it off.

Then he'd be right back where he started.

$\sim$

After spending a couple of hours cleaning and tidying the cardroom downstairs in the club, Jo was having tea in the seating area in her bedchamber. The work in the cardroom hadn't really been necessary because one of the employees would take care of it when they came to work, but Jo had needed to *do* something. Her mind was too active with thoughts of this fake betrothal, her parents, Sheff's meeting with his parents, and, perhaps most of all, Sheff and that stupid kiss.

She just needed to stop thinking about it. They had a rule

—that she'd made—about no kissing, and they would stick to it. There was no need to even recall they'd kissed in the first place.

Mrs. Rand popped her head into the room; the door hadn't been closed. She did not look like a typical housekeeper in that she utterly disdained house caps. Instead, she wore a small, rather smart hat that she pinned into her blond hair. Her blue eyes fixed on Jo. "You've more callers. I suppose because you're betrothed now."

Her features were austere—small eyes, sharp chin, and thin lips. She did not ever smile widely, but Jo suspected that was due to her teeth. Jo had only ever glimpsed them once or twice, but they were rather crooked. Despite Mrs. Rand's generally stern expression, she was a wonderful woman, and to Jo, she was family.

"I suppose so," Jo said, though she couldn't imagine who would be calling now. She might have guessed Sheff had returned. He'd said he'd see her tonight at the Siren's Call, but perhaps his plans had changed. Except, Mrs. Rand had said callers, plural. "Who is it?"

"Lady Minerva Halifax and Miss Ellis Dangerfield. They gave me a card." Mrs. Rand's mouth quirked into a slight smile as she pushed the door open wider. "Very highborn."

"Min is my betrothed's sister, so yes."

Mrs. Rand wrinkled her nose. "Your fake betrothed? Your mother told me the truth of things. I won't breathe a word, except to Frannie."

Jo wasn't surprised her mother had confided in Mrs. Rand nor that the housekeeper would tell the most important person in her life. "I would have told you. It's not as if you would believe I would marry an earl."

"Why would you trade one enclosure for another?" Mrs. Rand asked with a chuckle. "Though I believe the life you want lies somewhere between the two. At some point, you are going to have to tell your mother that."

Sucking in a breath, Jo was surprised now. How had Mrs. Rand discerned that? Jo hadn't ever said anything about wanting to do anything other than take her mother's place at the Siren's Call. "My mother doesn't suspect that, does she?"

Mrs. Rand shook her head. "No, which is why you will have to tell her. I know it won't be easy, but she will understand. She won't want you to commit to something you don't really want, not when she fought so hard to have a life she treasures."

"Then why is she going to the seaside for the summer?" Jo was still baffled by this turn of events.

"I'm not sure she knows," Mrs. Rand replied with a shrug. "Don't keep your guests waiting. Shall I bring tea?" She glanced toward Jo's tray. "Perhaps not."

"I'll ask if they want any, but for now, no." Jo stood, and Mrs. Rand moved to pick up the tray. "Thank you. I would have taken it to the kitchen." Jo had prepared it herself, as she often did, and she nearly always returned the tray downstairs.

"I know you would," Mrs. Rand said with a nod. "But you've got to pretend to be betrothed. Off with you."

Jo made her way to the sitting room, where Min and Ellis were already seated. Min wore a very determined look. Presumably, she'd heard about the betrothal.

"I can surmise why you're calling," Jo said as she sat down in a chair opposite their settee.

Min's gaze dipped to Jo's hand. "He gave you our grandmother's ring?"

"Yes." Jo glanced down at her bejeweled finger. Why had she forgotten to take the ring off? She should not have worn it while tidying. She should only wear it when she went out in Society, which would hopefully be a small amount of time.

The urge to strip it off now was great, especially if her friend had issue with Jo having it. "Is that a problem?"

"It's surprising," Min said, exhaling. "All this is most shocking. I don't for one moment think you and Sheff have fallen madly in love after one dance at the Phoenix Club. You've known each other for some time."

A few years at least, Jo reasoned. And they should have expected that Min wouldn't be fooled into thinking this was an ordinary betrothal.

"Min thinks it's a marriage of convenience," Ellis said, sending Min a patient look that told Jo she'd heard a great deal from Min on this subject. That was not surprising, as Min was always one to offer an opinion.

Min pursed her lips. "It has to be. Nothing else makes sense."

Jo hadn't known Min terribly long, just a few weeks, really, but they'd become friends. It seemed Min was upset. "Are you angry?" Jo asked.

"No," Min replied quickly, but her lashes fluttered, and she looked away briefly. "Perhaps a little…hurt. If you were developing a tendre for my brother, why wouldn't I know?" She met Jo's gaze, and Jo felt a snag of guilt. She'd known it would be difficult to lie to her new friends. She hadn't realized how much it would sting.

Jo decided she couldn't be completely dishonest, especially not when Min knew better. "Yes, it's a marriage of convenience, but you mustn't tell anyone. Sheff wants everyone to think it's a love match." He hadn't used those words, but he also hadn't said they were marrying for convenience. Perhaps they should have discussed things in greater detail.

Min's shoulders relaxed, and her features softened. "Well, that makes much more sense, though I'm still perplexed as to why either of you are doing this. Neither of you wants to wed."

"Want and need are not the same thing," Jo said. "Your brother has a duty, and I'm sure you know how your parents have become increasingly demanding that he wed."

"So, he chose to marry you, someone of whom they would almost certainly disapprove? Why not choose one of the many young ladies from our social circle?" Min's expression was apologetic. "I hope you know I mean no offense."

"I do. And I did suggest that, but Sheff doesn't want to marry any of those young ladies." That was true. Otherwise, he would. Jo would not reveal that the betrothal itself was a ruse. She'd made a deal with Sheff. Hopefully, he would understand that letting Min think they were marrying for convenience was necessary.

"I suspect your brother chose Jo because they are friends," Ellis said. "If you are going to wed out of necessity, why not choose someone you know and at least more than tolerate?"

"Yes, exactly that," Jo said, grateful for Ellis's wisdom. And help, even if she didn't realize she was helping.

"I suppose that makes sense. You are certainly a far preferable sister-in-law than any of the young ladies on the Marriage Mart," Min said with a smile. "But why did you agree?"

"I'll have security and a measure of independence," Jo said, which was true. The money Sheff was paying her would provide both.

Min's brow formed gentle pleats. "Don't you already have that with the Siren's Call? You have an entire future with a successful enterprise. Though, I suppose you won't have that anymore. The Countess of Shefford can't run a gaming club."

Ellis gave Jo an encouraging smile. "We must presume that is a trade Jo is willing to make."

Min's eyes narrowed shrewdly, and Jo braced herself for another question. "What about an heir?"

"Min!" Ellis glared at her. "Stop sticking your nose into this. We are Jo's friends, but some things are too personal."

Jo was especially grateful for Ellis's defense. She didn't want to discuss that, not even as a hypothetical situation.

"It is precisely because I am her friend that I am concerned," Min said. She looked at Jo. "What about his rakish behavior? It won't upset you to be married to someone with his reputation?"

It was hard for Jo not to think of her own parents. They weren't together as a married couple, and they weren't unhappy apart. Society was the one with the problem, not them. "Not particularly," Jo said, hoping the next several weeks weren't rife with conversations like these. "I'm not breaking any rogue rules, in fact." Except she had been alone with him, and that was even before the betrothal when she'd helped him with his father. Rather, he'd helped her since the duke had been unconscious in her home and place of business.

"Do we need to keep the truth of the reason behind the marriage from Tamsin and Gwen?" Ellis asked. "We see them quite often, though I imagine Gwen will be spending more time at home with her new husband."

"We do need to keep the real reason a secret, but I trust them to do so," Jo said. "I will tell them."

Min seemed to relax even more. "I'm glad. I would not want to lie to them."

Again, Jo felt a stab of guilt. She didn't like lying to Min. "I hope you're not unhappy with this news, Min. Sheff and I are pleased with the arrangement. And we will be sisters," she added with a light laugh.

"That is true, and as I said before, I could not imagine a better one. What can I do to help?"

"Sheff said your mother will set an appointment with Madame Demarest for a new wardrobe befitting my new role. He suggested you could come along, and I would like that very much."

Min's eyes gleamed with anticipation. "I will speak to my mother. We'll go Monday afternoon."

"You're certain the modiste will be available so soon?" That was only the day after tomorrow.

"Madame Demarest always makes time for my mother and me." Min frowned slightly. "I must say, I would rather Mama not come with us. I imagine she is disappointed in Sheff's choice of bride. Sorry to say that." She looked at Jo with sympathy.

"Disappointed may be an understatement," Ellis said softly. "Min, you must do what you can to support Jo."

"I will," Min vowed. "I will try to prevent Mama joining us." She winked at Jo. "Now, we must be off. There's another ball tonight, though I am rather tired after the Phoenix Club last night and Northumberland House the night before."

Jo was exhausted just hearing of that schedule. She would need to tell Sheff that she wouldn't go to more than two Society events each week. She couldn't abandon the Siren's Call. And yet, if she did not, Society would judge her harshly. She hadn't thought of that either. More and more, she realized this was perhaps a foolish scheme.

Except the money and the promise of a future *she* chose was too tempting to refuse.

As Min and Ellis made their way to the entrance hall, Jo accompanied them. Ellis briefly touched Jo's forearm. Her clear blue eyes met Jo's with warm admiration. "I understand wanting to secure your future—through whatever means necessary. It is reasonable and smart."

"Thank you," Jo murmured.

Still, she hated lying to them and looked forward to when this was all behind her.

CHAPTER 7

t was just after ten when Sheff arrived at the Siren's Call. He'd barely stayed at the ball to which he'd conveyed his mother, Min, and Ellis because he'd been immediately besieged by people asking if he was really betrothed. His mother had appeared downcast, which was frustrating. The ton would be buzzing loud enough about him choosing Jo as his wife. And now his mother was going to fuel the blaze with her obvious disapproval.

Before leaving, he'd asked her to please act as if she were happy, that to do otherwise would invite gossip. That had provoked a response, and she'd summoned an expression that could, perhaps, be mistaken for smiling.

He now knew that his happiness didn't figure into any of this. His parents' insistence that he wed had never had anything to do with Sheff finding the other half of his soul or a joy that would brighten all the days of his life. No, there was no discussion of romantic claptrap or even contentment. Ever.

Marriage was a business transaction, and Sheff had invested poorly, according to his mother. His father hadn't been terribly pleased either, but he'd at least accepted it. Probably only because he preferred to focus on his own enjoyments.

Perhaps this love-deprived environment had fed Sheff's belief that he wasn't capable of the emotion. How would he even know?

Becky, the jovial Scottish serving maid with blazing red hair, greeted Sheff with a tankard of ale as he sat at his usual table. "You're here early tonight. If you're looking for Jo, I think she's hiding."

Sheff had lifted his mug to take a drink, but stopped before doing so. "Why?"

"After the sixth or seventh guest asked her about your betrothal, she must have decided she'd had enough. I think she's organizing chips or perhaps cards in the storage cupboard."

"Where can I find that?" Sheff stood, ale still in hand.

"Er, I don't think that's a place you can go," Becky said, her brow creasing as she appeared somewhat confused.

"Nonsense. I'm Jo's betrothed, and I must speak with her. I don't want her to come out here if she's uncomfortable." Though she was going to have to tolerate people's questions and stares—and murmured judgments.

Sheff should be telling himself that. Hadn't he just fled a ball for the same reason Jo was hiding in a closet?

"Please, Becky," he tried again with a smile. "Where can I find her?"

Becky directed him to a door behind the stairs. "Don't tell her I told you where she is."

Sheff nodded before hastening from the common room and finding the cupboard. He knocked once before opening the door and stepping inside.

The small space was lit with two lanterns that allowed him to easily peruse the contents. Shelves crammed with decks of cards, bins of dice and chips, tablecloths and other linens lined three of the walls. There were also glasses and other serving items. A small table sat in the center. Jo stood on the other side of it, organizing decks of cards.

She'd looked up when he walked in and now her gaze burned into his. Or perhaps it only felt that way because they seemed oddly bright.

"How did you find me?" she asked.

"I guessed."

She made a noise in her throat. "Becky must have told you. It's fine. I was expecting you, though not this early. Did something happen?"

"I deposited my mother, sister, and Ellis at the ball and came here." He sipped his ale.

"You didn't stay at all?"

Sheff set his tankard on the table. "For a few minutes. Now that I am betrothed, there is no reason for me to linger."

Her eyes lit even brighter as her lips curved up. "Does that mean we don't have to attend any Society events?"

"Er, no. I'm afraid we must." But why, really? Someday when he was the duke, he'd have to use social events to forge important relationships, and some would argue he ought to do that now. But Sheff hadn't ever bothered to do that. He didn't serve in Parliament, and he hadn't been looking for an advantageous marriage.

"Min called on me this afternoon," Jo said as she continued to sort the cards on the table. "She was not convinced we were making a love match."

Sheff recalled Min's reaction to learning of their betrothal. "No, I didn't think she was. How did you respond?"

"I decided there was no point in trying to persuade her we'd fallen madly in love during the span of a waltz. She asked if we were marrying for convenience, and I thought that was as good an explanation as any." She gave him a tentative look. "I hope that's all right."

"I had contemplated whether to let Min in on the scheme." Sheff blew out a breath. "I just worry that my mother will find out—not because Min will tell her on purpose, but perhaps something would slip." He picked up his ale and took a long drink.

Jo went back to sorting the cards, and Sheff watched her stack them by number and face. "Can I assume your mother didn't respond well to your news?"

"She did not. My father wasn't terribly enthused either, but he accepted my choice." Sheff saw that Jo's brow was still dimpled. Was that due to concentrating on the sorting, which likely didn't require much concentration, or distress from this situation he'd created?

"Do you want to call it off?" he asked.

Jo snapped her gaze to his. "I didn't say that. This is just more challenging than I anticipated. I'm sorry that I told your sister this is a marriage of convenience, but I dislike lying to her. And to Ellis. And to my other friends. Don't worry, though; they won't reveal the truth."

"It's fine that they think that—good, even." Sheff crossed his arms over his chest. "This seemed like such a brilliant plan. My parents would leave me alone. Marriage-minded mamas and their daughters would move on from me. When you cry off, people would be inclined to avoid me for quite some time. I failed to think deeply enough about the present ramifications, particularly to you. Perhaps I should double your fee."

Her eyes rounded. "That would be excessive. Especially with the wardrobe." Her forehead smoothed. "Is it really that terrible? Putting up with the demands? Why don't you just remove yourself to the far reaches of Scotland or somewhere?"

He chuckled. "That has occurred to me. I do like Edinburgh. Have you ever been?"

She shook her head.

"You'd like it, I think. There is Society, of course, but it's much smaller and it seems easier to move between classes. There are so many wonderful pubs and gathering places. And the countryside is ruggedly beautiful. It's unlike anything you can imagine."

"Sounds intriguing." She stacked a five on the pile of fives.

"Draw a card," he said. "If it's an odd number, we'll call this off. If it's even, we'll continue."

"What if it's a face card?"

He smiled. "I'll double your fee."

Jo arched a brow and drew the next card, turning it over on the table in front of him as if she were the dealer in the cardroom. His grandmother's sapphire sparkled on her finger, and the sight of it there gave him a shocking rush of possession. It was a delectable sensation, though he had no real claim to her.

There was also something undeniably seductive about the stretch of her arm and the play of her finger against the card. Perhaps he imagined her reaching for him. The notion was rather enticing.

The number eight looked back at them from the table.

"We continue," Jo said.

"Are you sure we should leave it up to a card?" He wanted to be sure she was all right with moving forward, even if they had already agreed on it.

She shrugged. "Why not? It's as good at decision making as anything."

He laughed. "I'm not sure you really believe that, but if you're comfortable continuing as we are, then I shan't complain."

She plucked up the eight she'd laid down in front of him

and deposited it on the pile of eights. "Tell me more about the meeting with your parents. They were unhappy, and then what happened?"

"My mother stalked out, but she was…calmer when we left for the ball. She informed me that the betrothal ball will be next Saturday."

Her lashes fluttered. "So soon?"

"I was surprised too. It's probably for the best since it seems the news is spreading quickly." He picked up his tankard and took a sip of ale. "You will need a new ball gown before then. Will that be a problem?"

"Min is setting an appointment with Madame Demarest on Monday afternoon and will come along. I suppose it will depend on if the modiste can make one that quickly."

"She definitely can, and Min will make sure of it. Is my mother accompanying you?" Sheff hoped not, but wasn't sure it was avoidable. The duchess might be upset about his choice, but she'd want to be involved in things—why else would she plan a betrothal ball so quickly? She'd also want to ensure Jo was appropriately attired.

"Min wasn't sure. She assumed your mother would be disappointed in your choice of bride and couldn't determine how she might react."

"I'm sorry, Jo." Sheff held her gaze. "I won't allow her to be rude to you."

"I appreciate that." She finished sorting the cards in her hand, then picked up the stack of twos and began to sort them by suit. "I think it's best if we just minimize our inter- actions. I should like to keep my attendance at Society events to no more than two per week."

"Including walks in the park? We should endeavor to be seen there perhaps once a week. In fact, we should go one day this week before the ball." Sheff couldn't stop staring at Jo's hands as she moved the cards. She had elegant fingers, long and slender. He imagined them touching him in a variety of ways and began to grow hard. Clearing his throat —and his mind of salacious thoughts—he went back to the thread of their conversation. "Perhaps Wednesday?"

"I would prefer for those two events to include walks in the park," she said. "Would that be acceptable?"

"It may not be, but after the first couple of weeks, I'm sure we can do less."

"I suppose that makes sense," Jo replied as she continued her sorting. She was currently separating the fours by suit. "Wednesday should be fine, though I don't know if I'll have a fancy new walking dress by then."

"You'll be surprised at the wonders Madame Demarest can work." He fell silent as he watched her sort the cards, easily enchanted by the flick of her fingers and the arc of her narrow wrists. He imagined clasping her there and pressing his lips to the inner part, where her pulse beat strong. Would it speed for him?

"We could have an actual marriage of convenience."

Had he said that out loud?

Jo's hands stopped moving, and he realized he had indeed spoken. Raising his focus to her face, he saw her arrested expression.

"You aren't serious," she said, her tone low and incredibly arousing. What the devil was wrong with him? He was barely even flirting with her, and he was overcome with desire.

"Both our parents seem to have that," he managed to reply. "Marriages of convenience."

Her lips pressed together into a faint frown. "I would argue their marriages are highly inconvenient for all involved. Why would you want that?" A shudder moved over her shoulders. "I don't. I'd much rather remain unwed, thank you."

Right. How could Sheff have forgotten why he'd avoided

marriage for so long? He didn't want what his parents had, and he'd no reason to expect he was capable of anything different. He enjoyed women and freedom too much and would not expect his wife to endure what his mother did.

Sheff had become carried away by his surprisingly persistent attraction to his partner in this scheme. While also contemplating if this entire plan was worth the effort. "You are right, of course. I was only thinking of what you told my sister, and wondered if you might want a true marriage of convenience."

"I do not." Jo paused her sorting and cocked her head. "Min was surprised to learn that I would agree to that. I explained that I was planning for my future, which—thanks to your generous fee—I am actually doing."

"I'm sorry you can't be completely honest with your friends. I imagine that is difficult."

"I worry they'll be angry with me," she said quietly.

Sheff moved around the table to stand next to her. She pivoted to face him. "I won't let them. Blame me entirely."

"Except I am a party to this. I agreed to your scheme, and I'm even accepting money to play my role." She shook her head. "I don't think I can blame you."

"Tell me what I can do to ease your concern." He searched her face, hating that he was causing lines between her brows.

"Nothing at the moment. Keeping our social engagements to a minimum will be most welcome."

"You have my word that I'll only drag you to what is absolutely necessary. The park and the betrothal ball this week, and the park again and probably two events next week. I think Sir Alfred Hightooth is hosting a rout, and he always displays the most fascinating objects."

Her features lit with excitement. "The botanist? I should actually love to attend that. My father took me to one of his routs perhaps five years ago. He's been to South America since then, I believe."

"He has. Just last year. This is the first time he is displaying what he brought back."

"I am incredibly interested in seeing his specimens."

Sheff chuckled. "I'm glad to know what sort of Society event thrills you. I'll find more of the same."

She blushed, and he found it surprising. He'd never met a more confident or forthright woman, except perhaps his sister. "I do like scholarly lectures and literary salons."

"Noted."

The door opened then, and Becky stuck her head into the cupboard. "Oh, I didn't realize his lordship was in here."

Resisting the urge to laugh since Jo had already determined that Becky had told him where to find her, Sheff moved back toward his tankard and picked it up.

"Do you need something, Becky?" Jo asked.

"Things have picked up, and we could use a hand," Becky replied. "If you're free." She glanced at Sheff.

"I will come out directly." Jo set the cards down on the table as Becky retreated. "I'm afraid I must return to the common room."

"Pity, for I was enjoying our conversation," he said, meaning every word. He could have stayed in the cupboard with her all night. But would he have kept his hands to himself?

He would have had to, for that was their agreement, and he would not breach it again.

"I was too," she murmured before preceding him from the cupboard.

Once they were in the common room, he could see how much busier the club had become. He realized he'd never paid much attention before. He watched Jo move into action, greeting gentlemen with her characteristic smile and charm.

And wit—though he couldn't hear her, he knew that to be true.

Sheff found himself trailing her like a lovelorn puppy, attempting to overhear snippets of whatever she was saying as he nursed his ale.

"Can't believe you're betrothed," one man said to her.

Another looked at Sheff. "And to a blackguard like him." The man winked at Sheff and roared with laughter.

"Well, now he's *my* blackguard," Jo replied, directing a saucy smile toward Sheff that made his knees weak.

This went on for several minutes as she half flirted with the men ribbing her about being engaged to a reprobate like Sheff. He began to grow uncomfortable. No, Sheff was becoming angry. Not because of what they said about him, but because Jo was batting her lashes at them and laughing and being altogether too enticing.

That wasn't anger. That was jealousy.

Sheff tossed back a good portion of his ale, then set his tankard on the nearest table, uncaring that it was occupied. He'd been about to stalk out of the club when he realized that if he left without saying something to his betrothed, his behavior might be noted. And likely disdained. He wouldn't do anything to draw unpleasant gossip toward Jo.

He made his way to her and had a powerful urge to slide his arm around her waist as he moved close to her side. He wanted to kiss her cheek and whisper in her ear that he would miss her and to have a good evening.

Clenching his hands, he took a breath, then straightened them before moving toward her. He did not touch her, but he leaned close and whispered, "I want them all to believe we are a true match, so I'm making this look as though we are one."

She turned her head, and the green in the depths of her hazel eyes was more vibrant than he'd ever seen. "I see."

"Have a good evening, my love," he said more loudly so those closest to them could hear.

"You too," she said, her gaze darting ever so briefly to his mouth.

With Herculean effort, Sheff turned from her despite wanting nothing more than to kiss her until they were both senseless.

Instead, he would make his way to the Rogue's Den and try to forget about his hazel-eyed, silver-tongued, fake bride. He couldn't help doubting that would be possible.

~

Min had sent a note to Jo on Sunday indicating that the duchess would, in fact, be joining them at the modiste on Monday. Jo had responded that she would meet them there at the appointed time. She did not want the duchess coming here, even if she would not leave her coach.

When Jo's mother had heard of the meeting and that the duchess would be there, she'd announced her intent to go too. Jo wasn't entirely sure how she felt about that.

On the one hand, she was glad to have her mother's support, especially since Sheff's mother would be present. On the other hand, she worried that the duchess and her mother would not get on well. Or that, perhaps, her mother would even provoke the duchess. There were occasions when Jewel Harker did not hide her disdain for the upper crust of Society, whereas Jo's father always sought to curry their favor.

Perhaps he should be accompanying her.

Jo and her mother rode in a hack to Madame Demarest's shop on Bond Street. As they arrived, her mother gave her an even stare. "We will not permit the duchess to control what you select."

"I want to make a good impression, Mama. If that means I allow my future mother-in-law to choose some of the designs, I am happy to do so."

Her mother's gaze softened on Jo. "That is smart of you. But do remember that she is your fake future mother-in-law, thank goodness."

Jo had thought a great deal about Sheff asking if they should, perchance, actually wed for convenience. Not that she was considering it, but she had wondered why he'd asked. Did he truly want that? She didn't think he would, which she'd communicated to him. "Would it be terrible if I married him? Not that I am, but I am curious why you would be against it."

"I am against marriage in general, unless you want to have a child. Since I don't believe you do, at least not at this point in your life, I would not want to see you wed. All that aside, marriage to someone like Shefford would be awful, and not just because of his terrible reputation. As a countess —and someday duchess—you'd have all manner of duties and responsibilities in Society." Her mother made a face. "Can you think of anything more tedious than hosting balls and striving to always be above reproach? And that means whatever people judge that to be on any given day. I much prefer mingling with people in a less formal environment at the Siren's Call. There, we see people as they are, for the most part, and I find that far more engaging, don't you?"

Jo didn't think it would be tedious to host Society events. Balls might be too much, but soirees or salons could be entertaining. Not everyone she'd met at the events her father had taken her to or the literary salons she'd attended had been insufferable. In fact, many were very pleasant, and she'd enjoyed their conversations about travel and books and other topics. To Jo, the interactions at the Siren's Call could, in fact, be tedious. However, she didn't say that. Now was not the time to broach the idea of not taking over the club.

The hack stopped in front of the modiste's shop, preventing Jo from answering her mother's query. They stepped out and went inside. There were other patrons, but not Min or the duchess, as far as Jo could see.

A moment later, the door opened, and in walked an exceptionally slender woman dressed impeccably, her brown-and-gray hair styled artfully beneath a fetching bonnet. Though Jo hadn't yet seen Min, she felt certain this was the Duchess of Henlow.

And then Min stepped from behind her. She smiled upon seeing Jo and came toward her. Her gaze flicked to Jo's mother.

"Min, this is my mother, Jewel Harker," Jo said.

Min's face flickered with concern. "Allow me to present my mother, Her Grace, the Duchess of Henlow."

Jo realized she'd likely done that incorrectly. She should not have introduced her mother first. Dipping into a curtsey, she addressed the duchess. "It's a pleasure to make your acquaintance, Your Grace."

"I'm sure." The duchess looked to Jo's mother, who did not curtsey.

"Good afternoon, Your Grace," Jo's mother said with a vague smile. There was a slight edge to her tone that seemed to carry some sort of context. Had they met before? Perhaps years ago?

The duchess inclined her head as the edge of her lips appeared to curl in displeasure. "Mrs. Harker."

Jo's mother gave a proper smile to Min. "I'm pleased to meet you, Lady Minerva. Jo has told me about what a wonderful friend you've become. I'm always so glad when women form strong bonds."

"Come, let us inform Madame Demarest of our arrival," the duchess said stiffly, moving past them into the shop, where she addressed a young woman wearing an apron with a D stitched on the front.

"I'm sorry for ruining that introduction," Jo whispered to Min.

"Do not concern yourself. My mother will take time to accept you, but she *will*. She will see how lovely and capable you are."

"I hope so," Jo's mother said before turning and going to join the duchess.

"Let us pray this does not become awkward," Jo said, eyeing the two older women, who stood next to one another but did not speak.

Min chuckled. "I think it's too late for that. We shall simply have to keep it from becoming unpleasant."

Jo looked at her in horror. "You don't think it would?"

"I think we must steer things to ensure everything remains amenable. Shall we join them?"

They linked arms and stepped toward their mothers as Madame Demarest also approached. Tall, with dark auburn hair and bright blue eyes, the modiste was perhaps thirty years of age. She greeted them warmly, but her attention was primarily reserved for the duchess.

"Your Grace, let us adjourn to the private chamber to discuss your needs." Madame Demarest didn't sound French, which Jo had assumed, given her name. In fact, her voice almost carried a lilt of…Irish?

The duchess led their party through an arched doorway into a corridor. Turning left, she moved into a spacious sitting room with a tall, wide mirror as well as a dressing screen. A book sat on a table near the door. The duchess picked it up as she walked in and situated herself in a chair.

Jo's mother took another chair, opposite the duchess,

while Jo and Min sat on a settee situated between the two mothers. Madame Demarest stood near another chair. "Would you care for tea?"

"Not today, thank you," the duchess replied without looking up from the book she was perusing.

"I would, thank you," Jo's mother said with a smile. She glanced toward Jo and Min.

Jo nodded. "Yes, please."

"Er, that would be lovely." Min sent a worried glance at her mother, who did not look up from the book.

"Is that a book of fashion plates?" Jo's mother asked. "We're here to outfit my daughter, Miss Harker, as she has just become engaged to the Earl of Shefford. I'm sure she would like to look at what you have to offer."

"Certainly," Madame Demarest said. "May I offer my congratulations, Miss Harker," she said to Jo with a warm smile. "I'll return directly with a book, and the tea will arrive shortly." She departed with a brisk stride.

The duchess made a slight sound in her throat, again not lifting her attention from the book. "I declined tea, because it will be best if we choose quickly so Madame Demarest will be able to begin as soon possible. There is a ball Thursday night and, of course, the betrothal ball on Saturday."

Jo wasn't aware of a ball besides the betrothal one at Henlow House. "I have not received an invitation to a ball on Thursday." Nor did she wish to attend.

"That is because I have just procured one for you this morning," Min's mother replied crisply as she glanced toward Jo. "It is likely being delivered as we speak."

"I'm afraid Jo isn't able to attend a ball on Thursday," Jo's mother said. "She is otherwise engaged. We did not think she would have social requirements until after the betrothal ball."

Jo hadn't been certain of how to respond and was grateful for her mother stepping in.

The duchess frowned, and judging from the lines on her face, Jo surmised she did that often. But that was perhaps due to her unhappy marriage. Jo couldn't help feeling sorry for the woman. Seeing her was a good reminder of why Jo eschewed marriage—and would continue to do so.

Lips pursed, the duchess looked at Jo's mother with disdain. "It would be best if she accepted the invitation. She will need to participate in such events when she is wed to my son."

"Perhaps, but she is not yet married to him," Jo's mother said evenly. "It would be best if you ascertained someone's availability before seeking to commit them to something. Perhaps you are accustomed to doing things without concern for others, but that is not our way."

The duchess's chest moved as she sucked a breath through her nose. Jo braced herself for further conflict, but Min's mother tipped her attention back to the book on her lap.

Jo exchanged a look of relief with Min. "Your Grace, Sheff and I do plan to promenade in the park this week." Perhaps that would soothe the duchess.

"While that is nice, it is not an invitation," Min's mother replied without looking up from the book. "Anyone can promenade in the park. Declining the invitation from one of Almack's patronesses is just not a good way to begin." She snapped the book closed. "I do hope your other engagement is something that is worthy of missing the ball." She looked at Jo expectantly.

There was no engagement, however. Jo was simply… working at the club. That would not be seen as worthy at all, even if there wasn't a ball. She was saved from having to respond by the return of Madame Demarest carrying a slender book.

"Here is my latest collection of designs." She handed it to

Jo. "The tea will arrive in a moment. For now, let me make a list of what items you require and when." The modiste whipped a small notebook from the pocket of her apron along with a pencil and took one of the two remaining empty chairs—the one closest to the duchess.

Jo opened her mouth to respond, but the duchess began listing what was needed, starting with the betrothal ball grown. She went so far as to detail how it would look and what color it should be.

Frustration boiled inside Jo, and she opened the book the modiste had given her to distract herself from the duchess's cavalier behavior. The very first plate was a gorgeous blue ball gown. It was simple and elegant, precisely the sort of style that appealed to Jo. She held it up toward Madame Demarest.

"I'd like this for the betrothal ball." Jo didn't care that she was interrupting the duchess. In fact, she took pleasure in doing so. She glanced toward her mother, who was watching her with rampant approval.

Madame Demarest smiled with glee. "I just sketched that yesterday, and you are the first to see it."

"Then you shall retire the design," the duchess said. "She must have a unique and original gown."

"Of course," Madame Demarest said, making notes.

"The other item I need right away is a walking costume," Jo said. "I'll be promenading in the park on Wednesday. I do realize that is very soon, so if that's not possible, I understand."

The duchess sent Jo a perturbed look. "She will have it ready by Wednesday morning."

"Of course," Madame Demarest said with a nod. "What else can I provide?"

Jo flipped through the rest of the book with Min at her

side. Together, they selected several items. Jo was grateful for her friend's presence.

Min pivoted toward her mother. "Mama, I think you'll find our choices meet with your satisfaction." She handed the book to her mother and pointed out which ones they'd chosen while Madame Demarest made notes.

The duchess looked over at Jo's mother. "Don't you want to share your opinion?"

"Not at all. It does not signify. Only Jo's matters."

Walnut-colored brows climbing, the duchess appeared unimpressed with that declaration. "Then it is very good that I have come. Will you also be joining us at the cobbler and milliner?"

Jo watched the shadow that passed briefly over her mother's features. Min and her mother likely hadn't caught it.

"I know you are busy, Mama," Jo said. "I can meet you at home later."

Madame Demarest stood. "I just need to take your measurements, Miss Harker."

Jo rose, as did her mother, who moved toward Jo. "I can see that you are able to handle yourself with the duchess. Are you sure you don't want me to continue on to the cobbler with you?"

"No, I'll be fine. I can manage things. Perhaps later, you can tell me how you know the duchess," she added with an arched brow.

Her mother lifted a shoulder. "It is not an interesting tale. I'll see you later, my darling." She kissed Jo's cheek before bidding good day to the modiste, the duchess, and Min—in that order. Jo was not at all surprised that her mother would give precedence to the working woman, regardless of what was socially correct.

After Madame Demarest measured every part of Jo, they departed. When they were settled in the coach, the duchess settled her gaze on Jo. "You chose a lovely gown for the betrothal ball. And your other selections were indeed satisfactory. It seems Min has had a good influence on you."

"Actually, Mama, Jo had excellent taste before she knew me," Min said. "It just so happens our preferences are aligned. I'm sure that's one of the many reasons we are such good friends."

Jo had never had a female ally outside of her household. Min's support was both surprising and incredibly welcome.

"It is good that you are friends," the duchess said, her gloved hands clasped tightly in her lap. "Minerva, your guidance will be critical to Josephine's success."

Jo bristled at the duchess's use of her full name. She did not wish to correct her, however. More accurately, she did not want to provoke the woman, not when there were still shoes and accessories to grapple over.

The duchess pinned Jo with an unnerving stare. "I do hope you know that after Saturday, invitations will arrive at your door in large quantities. While you do not have to accept every single one, you must accept a great many. I shall send word to you daily of what you need to accept."

Must.

Need.

There was absolutely nothing she *must* accept or anywhere she *needed* to go. But Jo would not quarrel with her about the matter. She would leave that to Sheff.

After spending even a short time with the duchess, Jo could understand why Sheff was so desperate to deflect her attention away from him. Desperate enough to fabricate a betrothal and suffer the disappointment when it disintegrated.

She hoped he knew what he was inviting.

CHAPTER 8

Sheff was quite looking forward to meeting Jo as he strolled into Hyde Park and headed straight for the Ring. He'd stopped in at the Siren's Call last night to make sure she was still able to meet today. She'd appreciated him checking and said she would have a new walking dress to wear. That had been the extent of their conversation, for she'd been rather busy. It was too bad because Sheff had been keen to hear how the appointment with the modiste had gone the day before.

He could have asked his mother or Min, but he hadn't seen them, nor had he wanted to ask. At least, not his mother. He found avoiding her to be the best course of action currently, since she was unhappy with his choice of bride.

Scanning the Ring and the surrounding area, he spotted his mother, along with Min and Ellis. But where was Jo? She'd said she would be coming in the company of Lady Droxford, who, as a married lady, could act as chaperone.

But really, did a woman who worked in a gaming club

need a chaperone? Particularly a woman who was already of a spinsterly age?

She did if she was betrothed to an earl. Sheff exhaled. Was it any wonder he hadn't ever been enthusiastic about playing by Society's rules?

As he approached the Ring, he decided he might as well visit with his mother, sister, and Ellis. His mother would be put out if he did not.

"Good afternoon," he greeted them as he drew near.

"Shefford, I'd begun to think you weren't coming," his mother said, sounding perturbed. "Not that your betrothed has shown up either."

"There she is now," Min said, with a somewhat triumphant smile.

Sheff turned his head and saw a pair of ladies coming toward them. He recognized Droxford's wife, of course, but the beauty beside her was unknown to him. She wore a wide-brimmed bonnet decorated with flowers and feathers that were smart without being fussy. Her walking dress was a pale green with a unique ivory trim that was cut to show the green beneath. She wore a darker green spencer, expertly cut to accentuate her feminine form, and she carried an elegant muff of ivory silk. A smart accessory since the weather was still cool, though it wasn't trimmed with fur. Indeed, it appeared to be finished with swan feathers.

But he did know the woman. As she drew closer, he saw her features quite clearly. He should have known at once that the baroness's companion was none other than his faux betrothed. He'd just never seen Jo look so elegantly garbed. Indeed, many heads were turning, their attention riveted on her progress.

"Everyone will be clamoring for a muff like that since the weather has been so unseasonably cool," the duchess said with an approving nod.

Sheff relaxed as relief spread through him. His mother seemed to be satisfied with Jo, and that was all he could want. The point of this scheme was to prevent his mother's harassment and displeasure.

"Jo, you look stunning," Min said with a wide smile.

"Doesn't she?" Lady Droxford agreed. "And you may count me as one of those desperate to have a muff like that," she added with a laugh. "I shall be ordering mine tomorrow."

Jo curtsied to the duchess. "Good afternoon, Your Grace." She looked to Min and then Ellis, inclining her head. "Ellis, your spencer is so attractive. I adore that trim."

"Thank you," Ellis murmured.

"She stitched it herself," Min said.

Jo smiled. "How clever of you. I'm afraid my needle skills are abhorrent."

"You may not want to advertise that fact," the duchess said with a slight frown. She sent an irritated glance at Ellis, probably because she didn't like it when Ellis attracted attention. Sheff wondered why Ellis had been included today and assumed it was because the duchess might leave sooner than Min. And while Ellis was not exactly a chaperone, more and more, the duchess was treating her like one since Ellis was not just of spinster age but an actual spinster who did not plan to wed.

Sheff realized that Jo was also an actual spinster since she didn't plan to marry either. He generally thought of spinsters as lonely women who missed out on a great many of life's pleasures, particularly those involving the flesh. He hated thinking of Jo, whom he saw as a passionate woman, not experiencing such things.

Min looked at their mother. "Why, Mama? It's not as if Jo needs to lure a husband."

Sheff stifled a laugh. "No, she does not, for that task has

been accomplished. Shall we promenade, my dear?" He offered Jo his arm and gave her his most disarming smile.

She fluttered her lashes prettily, a demure smile teasing her full lips, whose impression he could still feel upon his. "Indeed, we shall." She curled her hand around his arm, and they started along the circular path.

"I didn't recognize you at first," Sheff said, looking over at the breathtaking woman on his arm.

"Because of a new dress?" She made a face. "You've been in Society too long."

He laughed. "My entire life. But if you're implying that I put too much weight on appearances, you may be right. You are a beautiful woman no matter what you are wearing. Or if you're wearing nothing at all, I would imagine."

Her brows rose. "Is that how you flirt with other young ladies?"

Damn, she had him there. "I am horrible. My apologies. I wasn't even trying to flirt. I'm afraid my mouth ran away from my brain."

"I imagine that happens with many parts of your body," she murmured, the edge of her mouth curling up.

Sheff grinned. "You are so bloody delightful. But let us begin again. You look lovely today, Miss Harker."

"I am your betrothed. Surely you can call me Jo." She sent him a sly glance. "And thank you. I do apologize for the expense for this new wardrobe. I fear it will be considerable. Your mother has expensive taste."

Sheff grimaced. "She didn't force her will upon you, did she?"

"She tried, but Min was most helpful in supporting me in my own choices. My mother was also a great help, though she left us at the modiste and did not continue to the cobbler or milliner."

"I didn't realize your mother went along. How was that?"

"There were tense moments, and apparently, my mother and yours are acquainted, though I don't know the details. My mother said it wasn't an interesting story."

Sheff stared at her. "Why do I not believe that? You must share it with me if you find out."

"I will." She clasped him more tightly and pressed herself against his side as they walked.

His body instantly reacted, desire pooling in his core. "What are you doing?"

"Pretending we are in love. Isn't that what we're supposed to be doing?"

Yes, but he was not supposed to respond in this way. As if nothing about this was fake. The stirring of his body certainly wasn't.

Sheff coughed. "Er, yes." He bent his head toward her and inhaled her spice and floral scent. A deep yearning burned inside him. She was utterly intoxicating in every way.

"Why does your mother not pay attention to Ellis?" Jo asked. "I wondered why Ellis didn't join us on Monday for the wardrobe shopping."

"My mother doesn't particularly care for Ellis."

Jo gaped at him. "How can that be? Ellis is lovely."

"I agree, but my father insisted my mother accept her into the household when she was orphaned, and my mother never warmed up to her." Sheff contemplated whether he ought to reveal the truth and decided he could. He trusted Jo. "For, what seems to me, obvious reasons." He gave her a meaningful look, but she only blinked at him.

She lifted a shoulder. "It is not obvious to me."

"Why would my father want to take in an orphan? She is the daughter of an old family friend, but no one I was acquainted with while I was growing up."

"You think your father lied?"

"I think my father has probably sired a number of illegitimate children, and it's likely that Ellis is one of them. He felt badly when she was orphaned and brought her into the household, where she has been a daily reminder to my mother of her husband's infidelity."

Jo shook her head. "I had no idea." She looked over at Sheff, her eyes dark with concern. "Does Ellis know?"

He shrugged. "I don't know. It's never discussed. I can't see how she doesn't at least suspect it."

"*Nobody* ever talks about it? Not even Min and Ellis?" Jo asked. "They seem so close, like sisters."

"Perhaps they do discuss it. I wouldn't be privy to their private conversations."

"How awful for Ellis—to live with someone who detests your presence."

Sheff thought it went deeper than that. His mother didn't just despise Ellis's presence. She seemed to loathe her as a person, which Sheff usually did a good job of ignoring. However, this conversation was making him uncomfortable with his own complicity in how his mother treated Ellis. On the other hand, it wasn't as if she asked for her husband to be unfaithful. All the time. And with any number of offspring as a result.

Still, none of that was Ellis's fault.

A shriek rent the air, followed by several shouts. Sheff turned his head to see a horse thundering toward them. The beast was clearly out of the rider's control. People ran, but no one was in the direct path of the animal— except them.

Sheff turned toward Jo and gathered her in his arms. He did so awkwardly, but he reacted with urgency and fear. Launching himself forward, he did his best to propel them out of the way. That meant he was not entirely in control of his movements, and while the velocity of his action took them away, it also sent them crashing to the grass off the path. He was able to twist and position himself mostly underneath her. He was certain his shoulder and back would be quite sore tomorrow.

He still held her tightly against him as he felt the hard ground beneath him. His gaze found hers. "Are you all right?"

"I'm not the one who slammed into the ground." She brushed her hand along his temple and cheek. "Are *you* all right?"

"Ask me tomorrow." He smiled at her, glad he'd managed to move them both out of the way.

"I shall," she said softly, her gaze burning into his.

Sheff was all too aware of her body pressed to his, of how her back and…backside felt in his grasp. He hadn't meant to grab her posterior. He hadn't thought about body parts at all when he'd sprung into action. But he really ought to move his hand now. He should help her up.

He did neither of those things. At least not immediately. For one lingering moment, he enjoyed having Jo in his arms.

"All right there, Shefford?" someone asked, jolting him back to reality and the impropriety of their position. Though, surely it was forgivable since he was merely trying to save them from disaster.

Moving his hand from her backside, Sheff nodded. "Fine, thank you."

Jo shifted as she pushed herself up. Her pelvis pressed against his for the barest moment, and Sheff wondered if he would hurt in more ways than one. He reacted instantly to her, his cock lengthening.

Dammit.

The person who'd inquired after him helped Jo to stand, then pulled Sheff to his feet. "Quick thinking there," the man said, clapping Sheff's shoulder.

"What happened?" Jo asked.

"Silly chit lost control of her mount over on Rotten Row. Evan Price has saved the day, however. He actually grabbed the horse's bridle and managed to pull himself onto the animal behind the young woman. It was astonishing to behold!"

Sheff had seen Price ride and credited him as a fine horseman, but this was another level of skill. "I'm sorry I missed seeing that."

"Glad you're all right," the man said before taking himself off in the direction of a crowd of people.

In the distance, Sheff saw the horse who'd nearly mowed them down, as well as two figures, one of whom—Price, evidently—was walking the horse. "Remarkable," he murmured.

"I'm also sorry we missed that," Jo said. "Gwen will be shocked to hear of her brother's actions."

"He does enjoy daring pursuits, but what the man described him doing sounded dangerous. I'm glad he isn't injured."

"Unlike you," she said with a smile, but there was concern in her eyes. "I hope you aren't suffering later. Turn. I think you have grass stuck to your coat."

Sheff pivoted, displaying his back to her. She brushed her gloved hand over his shoulders and back, moving down to the tails. He was surprised she didn't stop, then was titillated once more as she stroked his backside in her efforts to dispel the grass.

Arousal struck once more, and Sheff turned again, not caring if she was finished. "Thank you."

While he would have liked nothing more than for her to fully caress his backside, preferably without clothing, he didn't want to draw more attention than they likely already had. He could only hope that people had been paying attention to the runaway horse instead of him and Jo tangled together.

Rather than complete their circuit of the ring, Sheff

located Lady Droxford—she was still with Min and Ellis—and started toward them. His mother was nowhere to be seen.

The three ladies were looking toward the horse, which Evan had led to a small group of people, a few of whom had dismounted from their own horses. Presumably, they were from the young woman's party.

"Did you see that?" the baroness asked, her eyes round.

"We were nearly trampled," Jo replied wryly. "Sheff had to tackle me to the ground to avoid being run down, though he was kind enough to take the brunt of the fall."

"Good heavens!" the baroness declared. "Are you both all right?"

"I suspect I may be sore tomorrow." Sheff smiled despite the fact that he was actually in pain now. His shoulder had taken much of the impact.

"I do hope you're all right," Jo said, her brow creasing. She touched his arm. "Seek a physician if you are in too much pain."

"I will." He rather enjoyed her concern. What's more, he didn't think she was pretending.

"Go home and take a warm bath," Min said. "Let Spears dote on you." She referred to his valet.

"That would give him great satisfaction." What would give Sheff satisfaction, however, would be to take Jo home with him into the bath. He'd soap her body, then explore every contour of her flesh.

Dammit, he was growing hard again. Before he rushed off, which he was highly inclined to do, he made himself take Jo's hand. They needed to play their parts, and she'd done such a fine job of appearing to be enamored. He ought to do the same.

Lifting her hand, he pressed a kiss to the inside of her wrist, managing to find her bare flesh above the edge of her glove. He ought not to have done that, for it probably violated their contract. But he could not bring himself to regret doing so. Not when he had felt the pulse of her heart against his lips. It beat strong and sure, if perhaps a trifle fast.

He met her gaze. "Until Saturday, my love."

"Please send word tomorrow with how you are feeling."

Nodding, he released her hand, then bade good day to the others before striding away from them, grateful for the cool breeze dampening his ardor. He needed to bring that under control. He could not spend the next several weeks pining after his faux betrothed.

"Did you see how they were so indecently entwined on the ground?"

The question came from a pair of women standing off the path, their backs to where Sheff was walking by. He froze, knowing they were talking about him and Jo.

"It's not surprising, though, is it? Shefford is a horrible rogue, and that Harker chit is no better than a common strumpet."

"That is why he's marrying her," the first voice replied. "She is lowborn enough to suffer his rakish behavior. Honestly, it's kind of him not to expect someone of his own class to deal with his appetites. A woman such as Miss Harker is the right match."

"I suppose you're right. If he married someone appropriate, she'd be as miserable as his poor mother."

"Well, at least she'd be a duchess. One can endure a great deal for such a lofty position. I'm sure that is what enticed Miss Harker to lure Shefford into her bed. Not that it took much," the woman added with a deep chuckle. The other woman joined her in laughing.

Shefford began walking again, his stomach roiling. He couldn't listen to another word. In truth, he'd wanted to rage at them for speaking about Jo that way, but what good would it have done? People saw her—and him—as they wanted to, not as they truly were.

Except, wasn't he a rogue? His behavior was the very definition of rakish. And then to hear them mention his mother and her suffering… Sheff was reminded of his legacy, of who he was and would always be. They were right. He wasn't worthy of an "appropriate" young lady, and that included Jo. She was perhaps the most appropriate woman he'd ever met.

Though, appropriate didn't begin to encompass everything that Jo was: fiercely intelligent, incredibly capable, passionately independent. Those were the traits that came to mind when he thought of her. Which was far more often than he should, considering their entanglement was entirely fake.

Sheff didn't think it was entirely fake anymore. At least, not for him.

And that was a problem.

CHAPTER 9

As Jo sat in the coach with her parents on the way to Henlow House for the betrothal ball, she couldn't help thinking how strange this had all become. She'd never thought she would be betrothed, and certainly not to an earl with all the Society trappings that accompanied that. And she'd never, ever imagined her parents together for a social event as they were this evening.

She had no idea what to expect next, except the unexpected.

"I know I've already complimented your gown, but it really is stunning," Jo's father said from the rear-facing seat. "The fabric is so unique, and the design is beautifully original. I love the simple elegance of the style. Fussy flounces don't suit you. Everyone will be watching you tonight, as if they weren't going to be already," he added with a low chuckle.

Jo hated that she would be the center of attention, but it was just for one night. "Thank you, Papa."

The coach stopped in front of Henlow House, one of the

largest homes in Grosvenor Square. The door opened, and a footman in the Henlow livery helped Jo down and then her mother. When her father stood on the pavement, they made their way to the front door, which was held open by another footman.

They'd arrived early in order to position themselves in the receiving line so attendees could be sure to greet the betrothed couple. Jo anticipated an ache in her cheeks from smiling too much and hoped refreshment would be accessible as her mouth was likely to become dry from talking.

The butler welcomed them and showed them to the drawing room on the first floor. The duchess was the only person present.

Dressed in a lavender gown trimmed in mulberry, Sheff's mother appeared cool and serene, her narrow lips pressed together, and her hands clasped before her. "Good evening," she said. "I expect Shefford any moment." Her gaze moved over them, starting with Jo's mother on Jo's left, then sliding to Jo, then fixing on her father. The duchess's eyes narrowed for the barest moment, and color rose in her cheeks.

Did she know Jo's father?

Jo glanced at him to see his reaction, but there was none. He smiled benignly as he looked about the room.

"Your décor is so very tasteful and elegant, Your Grace."

"Thank you," she replied, her voice tight. Jo couldn't tell if that was still a reaction to her father or simply the way the duchess sounded. Her tone had been much the same the other day when they'd been on Bond Street.

The duchess returned her focus to Jo. "The gown is spectacular. It was a very good choice. And I'm pleased to see your hair looks fashionable. I'm glad you are wearing the combs I loaned you."

Jo hadn't really wanted to use the duchess's diamond-encrusted combs, but she wanted to quibble over it even less. Besides, wearing them would send a message that she was endorsed by Sheff's mother, and since Jo hadn't been certain that was the case, she'd taken it as a positive sign.

"Thank you, Your Grace," Jo replied. "I appreciate you lending them to me. I'll return them tomorrow."

"That would be acceptable," the duchess said. Her brow creased, and her brows pitched low over her eyes, making her appear rather distressed. "What is not acceptable is the reason for your missing the ball the other night. You said you were otherwise engaged."

"Actually, *I* said that," Jo's mother interjected.

The duchess sent Jo's mother a withering stare before looking back to Jo. "I have come to learn that you were *working* at that gaming club. You must cease doing so immediately."

Jo heard her mother's sharp intake of breath just as her own belly somersaulted. But it was her father who spoke. He took a step toward the duchess and summoned his most charming smile. "My dear duchess, let us not speak of such matters tonight when we are celebrating such a glorious occasion—the joining of our two families."

The duchess's eyes nearly popped out of her face. It was almost comical, in fact, despite there being nothing amusing about this conversation. Jo appreciated her father's efforts, but felt certain the duchess hadn't considered a union between her son and Jo to be a joining of their families. No, she would hope to never encounter the Harkers ever again, especially the woman who owned a gaming club.

Sheff strolled in then, his features set in a pleasant smile that seemed to crack as soon as he looked at them. "Good evening," he said robustly. "I'm sorry I'm running late. One of my coaching horses picked up a pebble. I had to take a hack."

"I'm just glad you are finally here," the duchess murmured, her expression settling into one of mild irritation instead of raging anger. "You must ensure your betrothed understands that she can no longer work in that gaming club." She turned her attention back to Jo and her parents. "We will stand in the receiving line for at least an hour, at which time I will assess whether we need to continue. I would estimate it may be closer to two hours. If you would like a drink before we move to our places, Percy, our butler, will make sure you have it."

The duchess swept from the room, leaving the four of them to stare after her. Jo's father went to shake Sheff's hand.

Jo's mother leaned toward her and whispered, "I'm so relieved this betrothal is fake. I fear the duchess will make any woman who is foolish enough to wed her son quite miserable."

"Do you think she knows Papa?" Jo whispered back. "I had the sense she recognized him. But then, you've also met her before."

"Mmm, yes."

Jo was beginning to grow frustrated with her mother's vague responses on this issue. "You said it wasn't an interesting story, but I should like to know how you all know one another."

"Why?" Jo's mother shrugged. "We met years ago, and as you can see, we did not become friendly. Indeed, we've had no reason to cross paths since. And this confluence will, thankfully, be temporary."

Before Jo could query her further, her mother went on to say, "Don't let Shefford talk you into not working at the club."

Jo bristled. "I wouldn't let him talk me into anything."

"You went along with this ridiculous faux betrothal," her mother noted, making Jo bristle even more. "You should also inform him that no one is going to believe this is a love match if he continues to visit the Rogue's Den. He's been there multiple times since your 'betrothal.'"

"I don't care if he goes there." Except Jo felt a peculiar twist in her gut upon learning this information.

"Of course not, but if you were actually betrothed and in love with him, you sure as hell would."

"What are you two whispering about over there?" Jo's father asked pleasantly.

"Boring things that ladies discuss," Jo's mother replied.

Jo's father smiled wickedly. "Now, you know I don't find any of that boring. And I daresay my future son-in-law doesn't either." He clapped Sheff on the shoulder.

Sheff looked at Jo. "Shall we adjourn to the antechamber to the ballroom?" He moved to Jo and offered her his arm.

Placing her hand on his sleeve, Jo ignored the jolt of heat that shot through her, disrupting the knot that had formed with her mother's mention of the Rogue's Den. She glanced back at her mother just as her father offered her his arm, but she did not take it. Rather, she glowered at him and started after Jo and Sheff.

Jo did not mind if they didn't appear to be happily together just so long as they were both here. Sheff's parents wouldn't appear to be happily together either. "Will your father be joining us in the receiving line?" Jo asked.

"I think so?" Sheff lifted a shoulder. "One can never know what my father will do. To be honest, I'm not even sure he's here."

But there he was, handsome and striking in his dark blue ensemble accented with an embroidered gold waistcoat. He didn't look like a man whose son had to constantly rescue him from potentially embarrassing situations.

He stood next to the duchess, who rather looked as if she preferred to catch on fire than be in his proximity. Indeed, she directed everyone where to stand, and she put him at the start while positioning herself at the end of the line. Jo wanted to point out that *her* parents didn't have to be separated, that they were mature enough to stand next to each other for a whole two hours.

The duchess had put Jo's father next to the duke, then Jo's mother, then Jo, and then Sheff who had the great pleasure of his mother's direct company for the duration. Jo felt a little sorry for him. She would rather have stood next to his father than his mother. In that moment, she realized that both of Sheff's parents were difficult, that he'd grown up with a very different sense of family than Jo had.

Though her parents had lived apart, they both loved her, and she never doubted that they wanted her happiness above all. Indeed, they'd come together to support her in this endeavor, and that alone showed how much they cared.

Guests began to arrive, and time passed quickly, for which Jo was most grateful. The best parts of the reception were when her friends showed up. She'd been thrilled to greet Gwen and her husband, Somerton, as well as Tamsin and her austere husband, Droxford. Jo went out of her way to coax a smile from him. Gwen's brother, Evan, arrived with their parents, and Jo enjoyed speaking with them.

The awkward moments, however, far exceeded the pleasant, as there were many gentlemen whom Jo knew from the Siren's Call. She'd seen a number of them roaringly drunk and even a few in tears as they'd lost great sums. A few others couldn't meet her gaze as they'd once attempted a flirtation with her that she'd batted away with the efficiency of swatting a fly.

It wasn't that she didn't flirt—innocently—with gentlemen. Except, when she really thought about it, she didn't behave with anyone the way she did with Sheff. It was clear she was battling an attraction to him. But had she always felt drawn to him, or was this a new sensation brought on by their fake betrothal? She hadn't ever thought about it, and now she was consumed with trying to determine the origin.

Then she needed to squash it as she would a fly.

The receiving line dispersed, and the duchess directed Jo and Sheff to the dance floor, where they would lead the ball with a waltz. Jo knew her mother planned to leave as soon as the receiving line was finished. Their eyes met, and Jo gave her a nod. Her mother blew her a kiss and then departed.

Jo's father planned to stay until the bitter end of the festivities. Or so he'd said with a gleeful cackle.

Taking Sheff's arm, Jo walked with him into the ballroom, where the majordomo announced them. There was applause, and Jo felt the attention of every person in the massive space, which looked more like an oblong gallery than a ballroom, but what did she know?

The candles in the chandeliers had to number nearly a thousand, their light flickering in the mirrors that lined one wall. Windows cloaked with ivory damask lined the opposite wall, and there were two sets of doors that led out onto a balcony. Though the evening was cool, the doors were open to let in the air. Soon, the ballroom would be sweltering.

Sheff guided her to the center of the dance floor and took her into his arms for the waltz. "Are you ready?" he asked softly, a hint of mischief in his gaze.

Jo arched a brow at him. "Are *you* ready for your feet to be mangled?"

He laughed. "You learned the dance quite well by the time we finished last week. I have no concerns for the state of my feet this evening."

"I hope you don't overestimate my abilities. Give me a moment or two to settle into the rhythm." The music started before she finished speaking, and he swept her into the dance.

Jo focused on counting and moving her feet and was surprised at how much easier it was this time. "This isn't so bad."

"Not at all. You are a natural." His hand pressed into her back, sending a pleasant, dizzying sensation up her spine.

Other couples moved onto the dance floor, and they were no longer alone. This helped Jo relax even more. She was soon waltzing without counting.

That allowed her mind to turn to what her mother had said about Sheff visiting the Rogue's Den. Jo considered bringing it up; however, she wasn't going to demand things of him, even if her mother had made a good point about appearances. What Sheff did was none of her business, not even in a fake betrothal. He only had to follow her rules, and, so far, he'd done a reasonably good job, the proposal kiss notwithstanding.

There had also been the kiss he'd pressed to her wrist at the park—after tackling her and holding her in a rather intimate position. Both of those activities had technically violated her rule, but she hadn't complained. Because she hadn't minded either one of them.

And now his hands were currently on her, his body so close to hers that she could smell his scent of pine and sandalwood. Not only did she not mind, she was enjoying the dance.

He spoke, and she was grateful for the interruption to her troubling thoughts. "I want you to know that I have no intention of convincing you to stop working at the Siren's Call. That was not part of our arrangement, and I would not change the rules now."

Jo was glad to hear that neither one of them wished to dictate to the other. "Does that mean if you could go back and make a rule that I don't work there, you would?" she teased.

He grinned. "I am fairly certain you would have declined my offer."

"You are correct. I can't stop working, particularly now because my mother is preparing to be away from London for a time, and I am taking on more responsibility."

His brow furrowed. "This can't be a good time for you to be away from the club several nights a week."

"Which is a primary reason I asked that I only have to attend two social events per week. Your mother did tell me that invitations would come pouring in after tonight, and that I would need to accept most of them." Jo shook her head. "There is no way I'm doing that. Your mother won't be pleased—about that or my continuing to work at the Siren's Call."

He shrugged as if it weren't a problem at all. "We'll manage it."

"'We'll'?" Jo asked, slightly annoyed by his cavalier attitude. "*You* will manage her. I do not want to put up with her snide comments or judgmental glowers."

"She can't have been that bad," he said as they moved across the floor.

"Why would you say that?" Jo blinked at him, somewhat incredulous at his obtuseness. "When you have initiated an elaborate scheme—at no small expense—to avoid her *cheerful encouragement* of your participation in the Marriage Mart," she remarked with considerable sarcasm.

Sheff stepped wrong, and his foot came down on her toe.

"Ow!" She winced as pain shot up her foot.

"Sorry!" He clenched his jaw. "For the foot and my mother. I didn't realize she was being that awful."

"I can only hope that I won't have to endure her company after tonight."

"You won't," he said quickly. And firmly. "I promise."

The music ended, and Sheff escorted her from the floor.

Jo couldn't shake the bead of irritation that had worked its way into her mind after his reaction to his mother's meddling and obnoxious attitude. She could only hope that he would keep his promise. She wasn't sure he could in the face of his mother's demanding nature.

Jo caught sight of the duchess standing nearby and immediately extricated herself from Sheff, saying she needed to speak with her friends. Then she stalked off with no idea of where to even find them.

Thankfully, Min located her. "Jo, I'm sorry I didn't see you before the ball." She looped her arm through Jo's. "My mother insisted I oversee the final placement of some flowers." She rolled her eyes. "Come and have a respite with us. You must want some lemonade."

What Jo really wanted was a large tankard of ale. Alas, that was not available. She settled for the lemonade, which they plucked from a table on their way to the relatively quiet corner where Tamsin, Gwen, and Ellis stood together.

Jo hadn't had time to see Gwen this week to tell her about the "marriage of convenience." She'd informed Tamsin when they'd gone to the park together.

"Here is the bride!" Tamsin said with a smile as Jo approached.

Jo removed her arm from Min's and took a long drink of lemonade.

"During the waltz, we told Gwen about it being a marriage of convenience," Min said softly.

Gwen gave her a supportive smile. "I understand you've been busy. And I have not been entirely available due to my recent marriage and the wound in my arm. I'm feeling much better now, especially since I don't have to wear the silly sling any longer. I'm clumsy enough without making one arm unusable!" She laughed, and they joined with her.

A few days before she wed, Gwen had been shot by an

angry mother who'd wanted Somerton to marry her daughter instead of Gwen. It was an incredible tale, but the truth had been kept quiet to keep the mother from being arrested. Everyone thought a book had fallen on Gwen, which, given her deep love of reading and persistent clumsiness, was completely believable.

"Is the marriage truly in name only?" Gwen asked. "Is there any hope it might turn out like Tamsin's?"

Though Jo hadn't known them when Tamsin and the baron had become betrothed, she'd heard the story. A compromising situation had prompted Droxford to propose. Tamsin had accepted, despite them not having any feelings for one another or even discussing their expectations for the marriage. They were fortunate in that they fell deeply in love. Their marriage was most enviable—if a love match was the objective.

Jo shook her head in response to Gwen's question. "Sheff and I will not be falling in love. We have specific rules for navigating this union." How she longed to tell them the truth!

"Perhaps you'll change your mind," Tamsin said with a shrug. "You never know what may happen."

Jo knew enough to not only avoid an actual marriage—even in name only—to Sheff but to avoid any attachments whatsoever. And not just to him. This ruse had shown her how lucky she was to have avoided marriage and how she must continue to do so. The idea of a mother-in-law even half as demanding as the duchess was enough to make a young lady of marriageable age run screaming for the remote Highlands of Scotland.

"Just be sure not to kiss him then," Gwen said with a laugh. "I'm teasing. Of course you won't."

But she *had* kissed him. And it had been shockingly delightful. So much so that Jo thought of it often and imagined what a longer, deeper kiss with Sheff might be like. Or if he caressed her. It had been hard not to imagine his hands exploring intimate parts of her body when he'd held her in the waltz.

"Honestly, I am starting to reconsider this marriage," Jo said, tiptoeing as close to revealing the truth as she dared.

"Did Sheff do something?" Min asked.

"Actually, no. It's your mother. I'm afraid she is...domineering."

Min exhaled, her eyes closing briefly. "I assume she said something awful before the ball when you assembled in the drawing room?"

"She insisted I stop working at the Siren's Call." Jo made a sound of disgust in her throat. "Sheff is going to manage her. He's promised I won't have to engage with her very much after tonight."

"Well, except for the part where you're married to her son for eternity," Tamsin said with a grimace.

Thank goodness that wasn't actually happening.

Min looked at Jo with sympathy. "I hope that's the case. She will not be happy that you continue to work at the club. And really, how can you continue to work there and be married?"

Jo wanted to answer that it was her livelihood, that her mother would have to replace her, that she was beholden to the Siren's Call and her mother's plans for the future. But she couldn't say any of that. "Since we aren't marrying immediately, I have time to decide what I will do. In the near term, however, I must continue with my work. My mother is traveling to Weston in July and will be gone at least a couple of months. There is no time to train anyone new."

There probably was, but Jo wasn't going to leave the Siren's Call to marry Sheff. If she did leave, it would be to follow her own dreams.

"Your mother will be in Weston in August?" Tamsin asked excitedly. "That's when we'll be there. You must come too!"

"That won't be possible," Jo said, ignoring the disappointment sweeping through her like an icy wind. "I'll need to be here overseeing the Siren's Call."

Not just in August, but forever. Her mother would be relinquishing more and more of her responsibility, which meant Jo would take on more and more. There would be no trips to the seaside with friends.

The reality of being tied to the club settled into Jo's brain and crept down her spine. It sent tendrils of anxiety and even dread through her belly and into her extremities until she felt as though she needed to sit down. She really wished she had that ale.

"Are you all right, Jo?" Ellis asked. "You look pale."

"I think I just need to visit the retiring room."

Ellis moved toward her. "Come with me."

Jo followed Ellis to the nearest doorway and into another room. "Thank you for showing me. I'm not sure I would be able to find the retiring room."

"I'm not taking you there," Ellis said. "Wouldn't you prefer to be alone?"

"Yes, thank you." Relief rushed through Jo, and she considered hugging Ellis. She recalled what Sheff had told her about Ellis's parentage and wished she didn't know. Not that she planned to say anything. She only hoped that Ellis wasn't unhappy about her place in this household. Perhaps she would be interested in coming to work at the Siren's Call.

Jo finished her lemonade and deposited the glass on a footman's tray as she left the ballroom with Ellis.

"There's a quiet sitting room downstairs," Ellis said. "I like to read there in the mornings. The light is lovely." She led Jo down to the ground floor.

"How did you know I wanted to be alone?" Jo asked as they descended the stairs.

"You just seemed to fade, like a flower closing at sunset," Ellis said, taking her into a small chamber at the back of the house. There was a bay window with a cozy seat.

"That does look like the perfect place to read," Jo said. "Thank you for bringing me here."

"Take all the time you need." Ellis gave her a warm look but didn't smile.

"I shouldn't be gone long. People will be looking for me." Jo would have liked to just leave. She'd done the receiving line, and she'd waltzed with her fake betrothed. What more could be expected of her?

One of Ellis's shoulders rose. "Probably. Take your time anyway. It's not as if you have to put up with this for very long. I do hope Sheff is paying you enough for your effort."

Jo narrowed her eyes. "What do you mean?"

"I may be wrong, but I don't believe for a moment that you plan to marry Sheff—for the sake of convenience or any other reason. Unless you *need* to marry him, which I don't think you do. Sheff *needs* to wed. It's his duty. You can enjoy your independence for as long as you like. Forever." There was a wistful quality to her voice.

"Is that what you want?" Jo asked softly.

"Yes, but I don't have reliable employment like you do. I've no idea how much revenue the Siren's Call earns, but your mother seems to do well. Your future appears secure. Is that not the case?" She blinked at Jo. "Do you need to marry Sheff?"

"No, I do not. And you're right—I am not going to." Goodness, but it felt wonderful to be completely honest. "I'm so glad you guessed the truth. I've hated lying to all of you, but Sheff said it was necessary to keep his mother from learning the truth."

Ellis gave her a knowing nod. "I completely understand. I am curious why you agreed to that when, as I pointed out, your future is secure."

"Because I'm not sure I want that future." Jo whispered the answer, her limbs quivering as she finally gave voice to her thoughts and hesitation.

Ellis touched her forearm, and a gentle smile lifted her mouth. "What is it you want?"

"I'm not entirely sure. I just don't enjoy running the club the way my mother does. She works so much and so hard. She's only recently begun to take time for herself. I was quite shocked when she told me she was going to Weston." Jo cocked her head, curious about Ellis since she seemed to be so aware of Jo's disquiet. "What do *you* want?"

"Security," Ellis said almost before Jo finished asking the question.

"I don't suppose you're interested in running the Siren's Call?" Jo asked with a laugh.

Ellis studied her a moment, and Jo thought she was perhaps actually considering it. "I don't know that my talents lie in running a business of that nature, but I could probably do the accounting and management. I'd like to be a secretary. However, there are precious few positions of that nature available to women."

"I know you sometimes dress as a man to walk about town on your own," Jo said. "Have you considered doing that to work as a secretary?" Although, it might be difficult to convince an employer that she was a man, for Ellis was rather pretty.

"I have, actually." Ellis chuckled. "But I daresay it wouldn't work for long. The prospect of binding my breasts *every* day is fairly distasteful. Still, I may not have a choice. When Min marries, and, like her brother, she must, I must find my own way. The duchess will not allow me to stay in her household without Min as my excuse for being here."

"How is Min your excuse? Because you're her companion?"

Ellis nodded. "That is how the duke convinced the duchess to let me join the household. Once Min is gone, I will be too. I can't expect Min to take me with her." Her lips curled into a wry smile.

"That's so unfair. Surely the duke won't allow you to be on your own without support, not after he took you in. Sheff told me how he welcomed you after your parents died." Jo hoped she hadn't said too much in case Ellis didn't know the truth of her parentage. Though they were exchanging confidences, Jo wouldn't be the one to reveal a secret that wasn't known—not one of that magnitude.

"Henlow might try to help me, but I'm not sure he'd set me up in a household or anything. That would generate gossip that would upset his wife, and he won't do that. Furthermore, I don't want that. Because of his reputation, people would assume I am his illegitimate daughter, and I am *not.*"

She wasn't? Or she didn't believe herself to be? Jo didn't ask because she didn't want to reveal what Sheff had told her. But now she was perplexed. Not that any of it was her business. "Well, I am here to support and help you if I can. Do think about working at the Siren's Call. I will be taking over its management at some point, and I appreciate competent, intelligent employees."

"I will keep that in mind," Ellis said warmly. "I confess I wouldn't want to join Min's household after she wed. I'd much prefer to find my own way."

Jo felt a strong affinity for Ellis in that moment. "I deeply understand that."

Ellis gave Jo a quick survey. "You look as though you're

feeling better. Do you want to come back to the ball with me?"

"I think I'll take just a few minutes alone," Jo replied. "Thank you again."

"Take your time," she repeated before turning and leaving the sitting room, closing the door behind her so that Jo was truly alone.

How long could she linger before she would be missed?

CHAPTER 10

*A*fter dancing with Jo, Sheff had been stopped by a number of people wishing him well and asking him, now that he was betrothed, when he would assume his duty and take a seat in the House of Commons until he inherited the dukedom and moved into the House of Lords. It wasn't as if that *was* his duty, just something that some people expected of him.

Sheff began to think Jo's suggestion that he run away and hide wasn't a bad idea. He could remove to the Grove near Weston for the entire summer. Or to his father's remote hunting lodge in Scotland. Either would do nicely.

Since he couldn't dash off immediately, he would have to settle for a few moments alone. The press of people and the lie of his betrothal were weighing on him.

He hated that Jo was uncomfortable, that his mother was causing her undue stress. And what was he to do? His future wife *shouldn't* be working at a gaming club. But Jo wasn't really his future wife.

Disgruntled and in need of a glass of something stronger than ratafia, he went downstairs to his father's study. The instant he opened the door, he knew something was amiss.

The air reeked of perfume—roses and neroli, a cloying scent. He didn't see anyone, but that didn't mean they weren't hiding. Had he stumbled into an assignation? How embarrassing. For everyone involved.

Still, he wasn't going to yield the room. He needed that bloody drink and a respite.

Closing the door, Sheff walked toward the liquor cabinet. His gaze swept the space, and he froze when he saw a familiar body lying across the settee, one leg dangling on the floor, his fall open so that far too much of his flesh was exposed.

"Dammit," Sheff breathed, his irritation blooming into full-blown anger. "You can't even behave yourself at your son's *bloody betrothal ball?*" He didn't yell, but he wasn't quiet either. His emphasis on the last words provoked his father to both open his eyes and slide from the settee onto the floor.

"What's that?" the duke slurred.

How was he this intoxicated already? "Did your paramour leave?" Sheff asked in disgust.

"I think so. You know me, I am so relaxed after a good shag that I can barely keep my eyes open." He smiled drunkenly.

"It helps that you are three sheets to the wind."

"Suppose it does." He glanced down. "Blimey, didn't even fasten myself up." He fumbled at trying to button his fall, but Sheff wasn't going to help him. The duke wasn't that far gone tonight. Still, he would need help up to his chamber.

Sheff stepped out and found a footman, whom he tasked with fetching his father's valet. Returning to the study, Sheff saw the duke was attempting to pour himself a glass of port. However, the dark wine missed the glass entirely and pooled on the tray.

"You don't need more wine." Sheff took the decanter from him and set it down before steering his father away from the liquor.

"Always room for more wine," the duke said, pouting slightly.

"Jackson will be here shortly and will take you upstairs."

The duke wrinkled his nose as he attempted to focus on Sheff. "Back to the ball?"

Sheff's shoulder twitched. "God, no. He'll put you to bed. You aren't fit for my betrothal ball."

"Hardly spent time there anyway. Your mother prefers it that way." He swayed a bit, then straightened. "Rather go to my club. Have the coach brought around."

"Definitely not." Sheff shook his head. Sometimes, he wasn't sure which version of his father was worse—the incapacitated one he had to wrestle home and into bed or this one, who would argue and be difficult.

"You can't order me about, my boy." The duke started toward the door but stumbled. Sheff raced forward just as the door opened. The valet, Jackson, caught Sheff's father before he fell. The footman entered behind him and moved quickly to the duke's other side.

"Careful there, Your Grace," Jackson, a man of nearly forty who surely needed greater compensation for what he endured in taking care of the duke, said. "Let's get you up to bed."

Sheff wondered if he should have let his father have the additional glass of wine. He might be unconscious by now, and then they could just carry him up.

But no, Sheff would never give him more drink. "Jackson, I think you and the footman will need to watch over the duke to make sure he stays abed. I doubt he will try to join the ball, but he just asked for the coach."

"Of course, my lord," Jackson replied. "We'll make certain he rests."

"He's already had enough excitement for one evening." Sheff scrubbed his hand down the side of his face.

Jackson nodded, and he and the footman guided the duke from the study. They left the door ajar, but Sheff didn't care. He ought to return to the ball, except he'd come here seeking a moment's peace—and perhaps a glass of brandy—which he now needed more than ever.

Turning toward the liquor cabinet, he frowned at the mess his father had made. He reached for the brandy, then startled when he heard his name.

"Sheff?"

He knew that sultry, feminine voice. Setting the decanter down, he pivoted to face Jo. Though he'd seen her already tonight, she still took his breath away in her stunning new gown. The blue was ravishing on her. Had she chosen it to match the betrothal ring? His gaze moved to where it flashed on her finger.

"How did you know I was here?" he asked.

"I was next door having a respite—Ellis took me there. I was going to return to the ball when I saw two men helping your father toward what I assume were the back stairs." Her expression was full of sympathy, her gaze warm and just what he needed at this moment.

"Yes, I found him in here in a…state. Suffice it to say, he is not fit to return to the ball."

Jo came toward him, her skirts making a faint rustling sound as they moved about her ankles. "Were you going to have a drink?"

"Brandy. Like you, I was seeking some quiet."

"Only you found the opposite. I'm sorry this is a recurring problem for you."

He turned and picked up the decanter once more. "Do you want a glass?"

"Why not?"

Sheff poured brandy into two glasses and handed her one. Their hands touched, but since they wore gloves, it lacked the intimacy that he wanted from her.

Yes, he wanted that.

From her.

His body had begun to stir the moment he saw her. Now that she was close and they were alone, it was all he could do to keep from becoming fully aroused. He could not let that happen.

Jo went to sit on the settee. She sipped the brandy, and Sheff tried not to stare at her lips pressing against the glass.

Sheff joined her, careful not to sit too close. He probably ought to have taken a chair so as to avoid temptation, but apparently, he enjoyed the sweet torture of her proximity.

"I want to apologize for my mother," he said. "I didn't think she would be this disagreeable." He should have, though. He'd chosen a faux bride who would upset his parents and, in doing so, had subjected Jo to their chaotic natures. It had somehow taken this situation for Sheff to realize just how aggravating his parents were.

Jo surprised him by laughing. "I think your mother is very set in her expectations, and I do not meet them in any way. She is not going to be pleased when I don't stop working at the Siren's Call. And she'll know. Do you know how many gentlemen coming through the receiving line were familiar to me from the club?"

"A great many from what I could hear." He sipped his brandy and set his glass on a table behind the settee as he angled himself toward her, resting his arm on the back of the settee. "I don't want you to stop working at the club. That was not part of our agreement. My mother will have to learn to accept your employment."

"Except I couldn't continue to work there after we are wed—not that we are actually doing that. I just think you should have a story for your mother since one of your goals is to make her happy."

He blinked at her. "You think that's what I want? My goal was for her to leave me alone."

"It's become apparent to me that your mother is not happy, and I don't think it has much to do with your lack of marriage." She took a drink of brandy. "But I could be wrong. I don't know her very well—or you, really—and I am merely making observations."

Sheff considered what she said. "You aren't wrong at all. Do you know why she's not happy?"

"I would guess it's to do with your father. I can imagine it's difficult living with someone who is unfaithful and constantly does things that are both humiliating and devastating. She's also had to live with his illegitimate offspring, although I had a very interesting conversation with Ellis, and she insists she is not his child."

"You *asked* her?" Sheff hadn't wanted to upset Ellis. On the contrary, he cared for her like a sister.

"I did not. We were talking, and she offered the information. Perhaps I should not have shared it with you."

"It's likely that she doesn't want to think of herself as his daughter—illegitimate or otherwise—and I can't blame her. Often, I wish he were not my sire." Sheff gripped the back of the settee as a wave of anger passed through him. If he'd had a different father, perhaps he would not be the way he was.

Jo touched his thigh. It was just a light brush of her gloved fingertips, but the rush of desire that assaulted him was devastatingly thorough. "You seem upset. I hope you aren't with me."

He met her gaze. "Absolutely not. You are a very bright spot. It's just…my father. I look at him, and I see what I could become." His voice nearly broke, and he looked away from her.

She scooted closer to him, her body turning toward his. "Why would you think you would be like him? I don't see that."

"Not now, but what's to say I wouldn't, particularly after I'm shackled to a wife?"

"Is that what you think will happen? That you're destined to be like him?"

"I am already enough like him." He couldn't change who he was.

"I've never seen you drink to excess, even when you're with other gentlemen at the Siren's Call to whom we refuse to keep serving liquor." Her gaze was fierce. "So, it's not that. Tell me how you think you're like him. Is it the women? I know you've continued to visit the Rogue's Den since pretending to ask me to be your wife."

She knew? "I've tried to be discreet."

"The owner of the Rogue's Den is a friend of my mother's."

Sheff hadn't known that, but neither did he find it surprising. Both women were highly intelligent, accomplished business owners. "You're not upset with me, are you?"

What an asinine question. Of course she wasn't. Just because he felt a strong attraction to her didn't mean she felt the same. And even if she did, they'd made no agreement about satisfying their physical needs—other than it wouldn't be with each other.

"No," she said firmly. "But perhaps you should take my mother's advice and try celibacy for the duration of this scheme. Then you can prove to yourself that you aren't your father. It will also lend credibility to this betrothal."

"The truth is that I *have* been celibate," he said quietly. He held her gaze. "I have visited the Rogue's Den this past week. Several times, in fact. But all I did was have a drink and chat with one of the ladies. Then I went home."

Her brow creased. "Why?"

"I don't really know. I just wasn't…in the mood." Because when he thought of giving and receiving pleasure in the past week, only one woman had entered his mind: Jo.

"See, you aren't like your father," she said, completely unaware of the lurid thoughts that were currently running through his brain.

"I *am*." His hand curled around the edge of the settee again, his fingertips digging into the ornamental wood trim. "If you only knew the inappropriate things I think about."

Her gaze flicked to his groin. "You seem to be in the mood at the moment."

He'd suspected she wasn't an innocent, and perhaps he found that particularly enticing. But to have her notice his arousal was unexpected. It escalated his desire. "That's because the inappropriate things I think about are all to do with you."

The high mounds of her breasts pressed against the edge of her bodice and moved swiftly as her breathing grew more rapid. "We have an agreement."

"To not touch one another. You didn't say I had to lie about *wanting* to touch you."

"*Is* that what you want?" she whispered.

He watched her chest rise and fall and her throat move as her pulse fluttered. She was also aroused. He knew what that looked like in a woman.

Sheff moved his hand down the back of the settee until his

fingertips, encased in horrid gloves, nearly grazed her shoulder. "Yes. I want to kiss you again, but for longer and far more deeply. I want to feel your tongue against mine. I want to stroke your cheek, your neck, your breast. I want to put my mouth on you in forbidden places and make you moan until you cry out with your release. And then I want to do it all again."

Saying all that wasn't doing anything to diminish his desire. On the contrary, it was making him desperate with need. And he would not be satisfied. Not this night, and not ever with her.

"I'm afraid I must add a new rule to our agreement." Her voice was higher than normal, her tone breathless. "You can't say such things to me."

"What things are those? I need you to be specific."

"You can't speak to me of your desires. You can't explicitly say what you want to do. To me."

He leaned toward her and inhaled her intoxicating scent. "Why not?" When she did not immediately answer, he slid his gaze down over her heaving chest and to where her hand clutched her skirt, dimpling the fabric. "Because it arouses you?"

She stood abruptly, and Sheff clutched at the settee lest he follow her. "This conversation has veered from its course," she said, keeping her back to him as she poured the rest of her brandy down her throat.

Sheff didn't dare stand, not with his cock straining against his fall. He forced himself to think of what they'd been discussing, to abandon his hopelessly prurient thoughts. "I will continue my celibacy for the duration of the scheme."

She spun around to face him. "You will?"

"You made a good argument." He blew out a breath. "Perhaps I can prove I am not like my father. It's just...you also mentioned that I want to make my mother happy—and I do. However, the only way I can truly do that is to marry."

"To marry for someone else's happiness other than your own—and your bride's—wouldn't be right."

"No. Only look at my parents. I don't believe they were ever in love, though my father claims he was. Whether that is true or not, he wasn't able to remain faithful to my mother, to uphold the covenant of marriage."

Her expression was sympathetic. "Many men—and women—don't."

"While that is true, I have seen firsthand what it has done to both of them. I won't put my wife through that, nor do I want to endure it myself. I think some people aren't meant to marry."

"That you would be so thoughtful about it says to me that you may, in fact, be the opposite of your father." Her features softened. Her breathing had returned to normal. "Try celibacy. Try not thinking you are like your father. Try finding what will make *you* happy."

Sheff's body had begun to settle—enough that he stood. "You are incredibly wise. How is that?"

She shrugged. "It's easier to give advice than to follow it."

He laughed. "What advice aren't you following?"

"I don't know. Probably what I just said to you."

"Are you going to look for happiness too?"

"I have to think about some things," she said slowly. "My mother wants me to take over the club, which I've always known. But she seems to be accelerating that plan, and I'm not ready. I'm not sure I will ever be."

He saw apprehension in her gaze and noted that she fidgeted with her fingers. "You don't want to run the club?"

"I'm not sure. But now, thanks to you and your payment for my services as your fake betrothed, I have the freedom to do what I want. I just need to determine what that is."

"It sounds as though we both have work to do." He picked up his brandy and finished it, then moved to take her empty glass. After depositing them on the tray, he faced her.

She was watching him intently. "Are you certain you still want this agreement? We could call a halt at any time."

"I know. But I think I may take another piece of your advice and just leave London." Not just to avoid his parents, but to remove himself from temptation. It was becoming difficult to be with Jo and not pursue a deeper connection.

"Will you go to Scotland?" she asked.

"I'm not sure. I need to be in Weston in August, so I may just go there. Or perhaps I'll travel to Wales first. It's not as far as Scotland, and the Prices have a beautiful estate there."

"That sounds like an excellent plan. When will you leave?"

"Not immediately. That will look strange. My departure would raise questions. I think we must endure everyone's focus for a bit." He knew they should return to the ball, but he was enjoying this time alone with her. "Will you permit me a personal question?"

Her brows climbed. "That depends. How personal?"

"You noted my arousal earlier, so I am curious about your experience. Are you a virgin?"

Her lips quirked. "No. Though I could be and still be knowledgeable about a man's arousal. In fact, my mother taught me at a young age what I could expect from men. I am grateful for her tutelage, for it has saved me from a great many awkward situations—and worse."

"I can imagine. And I'm glad." Sheff didn't like to think of her having to defend herself from unwanted attention, but he knew she could. He'd seen it firsthand when she'd elbowed his father at the Siren's Call.

"I'm glad to hear you aren't a virgin. I confess I worried that as a spinster, you would miss out."

She stepped toward him, her hips swaying in a most

distracting way. But then she could just stand there and say and do nothing, and he would be distracted by her. "You think I'm a spinster?"

"I meant no offense. You are twenty-five and unwed, are you not?"

"Twenty-six, actually, as my birthday was at the end of April. I am unmarried by choice. Surely you must realize that spinsters have a certain freedom. Without everyone watching us, we can do things nonspinsters cannot. Indeed, I could recline on that settee and invite you to do all the things you mentioned earlier."

Sheff groaned. "You're breaking your own rule."

"I am not being explicit. But perhaps you're right. I was merely trying to make a point: that spinsters are to be celebrated, not disparaged."

At that moment, Sheff wanted nothing more than to celebrate her in every way imaginable.

"My lord?"

They both turned to see a footman—the same one who'd helped Jackson guide the duke upstairs—in the doorway.

"Yes?" Sheff croaked.

"His Grace is sleeping. Jackson is with him and will remain so for the duration of the ball."

"Thank you." Sheff watched the footman leave.

"We should return to the ballroom," Jo said. "We've been gone an awfully long time. And we should not enter together, else tongues will be wagging."

Sheff wanted to wag his tongue, but it had nothing to do with gossip and everything to do with bringing Jo to orgasm. Alas, that was not to be. "You go on ahead." He needed a moment to let his body cool, for he'd become overheated again.

Her gaze flicked to his cock once more, indicating she'd noticed it too. "You seem to need a few minutes to recover.

My apologies. I should not have provoked you. Now that I know of your…desire, I shall not contribute to it."

He was afraid she did that by merely breathing. "I should not have provoked you either. Don't pretend you are not immune."

She held his gaze a moment, then left the study in a flurry of blue silk.

Sheff exhaled. How he longed for a cooling bath. But he needed to return to the ball. Where he would need to spend more time with Jo.

He would resist temptation, but it would be torturous, especially now that he knew she was attracted to him too. Was there any way their betrothal could not be fake? Could he be different from his father? Different from how he'd always imagined himself to be?

Even if he was, Jo would never consider him. Nor should she. She'd perfectly laid out the benefits of spinsterhood. He had a duty, and she had freedom.

Perhaps that was what he wanted: the freedom to be who he wanted to be, to live the life *he* chose. He only needed to determine what those things were.

CHAPTER 11

After Saturday's ball and a busy night at the Siren's Call on Sunday, Jo was glad to be doing what she wanted to do on Monday evening. Smiling as she departed the hack, she stepped through the wrought iron gate to the front door of the Davenports' house. It opened before she could knock.

"Good evening, Melrose," Jo said.

"Good evening, Miss Harker." The rather short butler closed the door behind her and took her cloak and hat.

Jo made her way upstairs to the drawing room, more eager than usual for tonight's literary salon.

"If it isn't the future Duchess of Henlow!" Mrs. Davenport exclaimed loudly so that everyone who had already arrived, perhaps ten people, quieted and turned to look at Jo.

In any other situation, Jo would have been horrified to have brought everything to a standstill, but she had known these people a few years now. She considered some of them friends, though not in the way of her new friends who were near to her own age.

Jo smiled. "Good evening, Mrs. Davenport."

Mrs. Davenport, a petite woman in her late sixties who wore ornate white wigs that were firmly out of fashion, grinned at Jo. "Shall we have a toast to your good fortune?"

"That isn't necessary," Jo said. "Truly, though, I do appreciate your kindness."

"It isn't kindness so much as envy," she said with a laugh. "Oh, to marry an earl!" She glanced toward her husband, who, as usual, was dozing in the corner. "You must tell me everything. When is the wedding?"

"I want to hear!" Mrs. Fletcher-Peabody hastened toward them. A widow in her early sixties, she possessed a round figure and surprisingly dark hair. Mrs. Fletcher-Peabody hosted the literary salons on the first and third Mondays of the month, while Mrs. Davenport hosted the second and fourth. If there was a fifth Monday, they took a respite, and the next salon was invariably at least an hour longer than normal.

"I would also like to hear," said a third woman, Lady Standish. Her cane tapped on the floor as she approached. In her seventies, Lady Standish was a poetess and occasionally shared her work. Tonight was one such evening, and Jo was particularly looking forward to it. Lady Standish wrote of the intersection of love and nature, and her work moved Jo to seek out beauty and peace. With everything happening, she felt rather in need of the latter.

"What did I miss?" Lady Standish asked, looking at the two older ladies before settling her gaze on Jo. "Here's our beautiful bride."

"You haven't missed a thing," Jo said. "Mrs. Davenport asked when the wedding will be. Not until autumn or winter. We haven't set the date yet."

Mrs. Fletcher-Peabody pouted. "Why so long?"

"Please make it November or later," Lady Standish said. "I won't have returned from the country until then."

Jo kept herself from laughing. As if she would plan a wedding based on Lady Standish's plans. Even so, the woman's desire to be present was incredibly sweet. Jo realized she would have liked all of them at the wedding breakfast. If she were actually getting married.

"I have noted your preference," Jo said before transferring her attention to Mrs. Fletcher-Peabody. "To answer your question, we are waiting because I have always wanted to marry in the autumn or winter. That way I can wear a fur-trimmed cloak." She grinned at them, glad that Sheff had provided her with a reason.

"How splendid. And when will you host your first salon?" Mrs. Davenport asked.

"I'm not sure," Jo replied. "Perhaps in the new year?" How she wished that were true. But perhaps it could be if she used Sheff's payment to set up her own household and establish herself as a literary hostess. More and more, she was truly beginning to see that future. It was both exciting and a trifle daunting. Or perhaps it was the idea of telling her mother that was the daunting part.

"Where will you live?" Lady Standish asked. "I believe the earl resides at the Albany. I can't imagine you want to move in with his parents at Henlow House."

Definitely not. Jo hadn't thought about where they would live because they weren't going to live anywhere. "We haven't decided yet."

"Perhaps Henlow owns another property here in town," Mrs. Fletcher-Peabody said. "How lucky you are to have snared Shefford! He's very handsome. And roguish, but that can be exciting. My husband was somewhat of a rake in his day." She arched her dark brows in a mischievous expression.

"You did not regret marrying a man like that?" Jo asked.

"Absolutely not. Once we were wed, Erasmus only had time for me. The key is to keep them very busy—and satisfied." She smirked at the other ladies. Mrs. Davenport appeared nonplussed while Lady Standish swallowed a giggle.

"Thank you for that advice," Jo said, hoping there wouldn't be any more.

Mrs. Davenport sent Jo an expectant look. "Shall I invite Lord Shefford to my salon next Monday?"

Hadn't he said he should attend one? "Certainly. I'm sure he'll come if he is able."

Jo tried to imagine him at a literary salon. She didn't even know if he liked to read, or, if so, what.

The idea of hosting her own salons as the Countess of Shefford held a surprising appeal. As a countess, she could invite anyone she wanted, and chances were, they'd want to attend. She could invite writers from all over the world.

Her heart beat a little faster until she realized that none of that was actually going to happen.

Another party arrived, and Jo saw that it was Tamsin and Ellis. But where was Min? Excusing herself from her hostess and the two other ladies, Jo made her way to her friends.

"There you are, Jo," Tamsin said with a smile.

"Where is Min?" Jo asked.

Ellis exhaled. "She had to attend a dinner with her mother, who hopes to match her with a gentleman who is attending. Min was so hoping that Sheff's betrothal would keep the duchess occupied, but with the betrothal ball past and the wedding not happening for months, she has plenty of time to try to match Min."

Poor Min. Jo would talk to Sheff and see if there was anything he could do. Perhaps he could take Min with him when he left London.

Jo would miss Min if she left. Shockingly, she realized she was going to miss Sheff too.

But she understood why he needed to go. His revelations at the ball the other night had clung to her mind. She hoped he could find some truth for himself and see that he was more than his father's son. When she thought of how much energy he'd likely expended throughout his life caring for his parents and dealing with their difficulties, she felt rather badly for him. Was it any wonder his view of himself was distorted?

She wanted to support him. To show him that *he* was cared for.

She even wanted to kiss him again. The things he'd said to her in the study at the ball… Just recalling them brought heat to her core. She had to be careful it didn't show in her face.

"Jo?"

Blinking, Jo realized she'd been woolgathering. "My apologies. I was thinking about the duchess and how she needs something to do that interests her besides managing her children's lives," she fibbed.

"Such as attend literary salons?" Ellis quipped.

Jo stared at her in horror before laughing. "I suppose she could, but not these. I daresay they wouldn't be lofty enough for her. Surely one of her duchess friends hosts one."

"I don't know that I've ever seen her read a book," Ellis mused. "Newspapers and magazines, but not books."

"Some magazines contain literature," Tamsin said.

Ellis arched a brow. "I think the duchess is more interested in fashion and gossip."

"Either of you want something to drink?" Tamsin asked. "I'm going to fetch a glass of wine."

"Nothing for me just yet," Jo replied.

"Me neither," Ellis said with a shake of her head.

As Tamsin moved across the room to the refreshment table, Jo angled herself toward Ellis. "Thank you again for your help the other night."

"You were gone awhile," Ellis noted, her gaze curious. "I couldn't help noticing that Sheff was also absent, and that he returned to the ball not long after you did."

"We ran into each other while we were both seeking a respite." Jo didn't want to say anything about Sheff helping his father in case Ellis didn't know. Though, Jo began to suspect Ellis knew a great deal about what happened in that household. And why wouldn't she?

"I hope that didn't disturb your peace," Ellis said with a smile.

"Not at all. Sheff and I are friends. He apologized for his mother. I was just grateful that I barely interacted with her the rest of the evening."

Ellis chuckled. "How fortunate for you. It was a nice ball. I met your father and found him rather engaging."

"Be careful," Jo warned with a smile. "He's a charmer."

"Is it true that your parents don't live together?" Ellis asked.

"Yes. I've never shared the same household as my father."

"But you are close? I saw you with him at the ball later on, and you seemed to be."

"We are," Jo said. "He's the reason I come to literary salons. He likes to take me to different events."

Ellis smiled, an almost wistful look in her eyes. "That sounds lovely." Her features sobered. "Do your parents know the truth of your betrothal?"

"My mother does. My father would not be able to keep the secret."

"That must be difficult. To have to lie to him, I mean."

"I don't enjoy it, but it's necessary. Sometimes, I think I

was foolish to agree to help Sheff, but talking to you at the ball actually helped me feel good about my decision. I will have a chance at the life I want, and I'm incredibly grateful." Jo laughed softly. "And don't ask me if I decided what that will be. I'm still mulling things."

"Fortunately, I don't think you have to rush." Ellis winked at her.

Tamsin returned with her wine, and Gwen arrived. Her husband had dropped her off on his way to the Phoenix Club.

"I'm surprised he didn't want to come in," Jo said with a mischievous smile. "Isn't this where you had your first kiss?"

"Yes. The whole evening was so daring." Gwen giggled. "I don't know where I summoned the courage to dress and act as Lazarus's 'great-aunt.'"

Jo laughed. "You certainly didn't behave as his 'great-aunt' when I caught the two of you in the retiring room."

"That's because he's a rogue," Tamsin said, her eyes dancing with mirth. "Or *was*, anyway."

"He still is," Gwen said primly, though her gaze held a devilish glint. "He's just *my* rogue."

That had to be a heady feeling—to know a man who'd enjoyed female company, perhaps to excess, had chosen *her* above all others. And he was so clearly and desperately in love with her... It was enough to almost make Jo want that for herself.

Almost.

A few minutes later, they all took their seats to hear Lady Standish speak. Jo lost herself in the poetess's words, and by the end of the first poem, she had come to one decision.

Jo would host her own literary salon one day. It might not be for quite some time, but she would work toward that goal.

How easy it would be if she were actually the Countess of

Shefford. Lady Standish started another poem. It was about the sea. And sexual gratification, apparently.

> The waves crash upon the shore. My body rises
> and falls. The rhythm is intrinsic and intox-
> icating.
> Over and over, the sea advances and retreats.
> Until a rush of water overtakes the sand. I
> cry out in ecstasy.

Or so it seemed to Jo that Lady Standish was comparing the ocean to an orgasm. Perhaps it was merely that Jo had been thinking too much of sex and having an orgasm. With Sheff.

So long as she only thought about it. They did not need to be entangled any more than they already were.

When their ruse was finished, Jo could consider taking a lover. She hadn't done so in more than a year.

Those were the kind of entanglements she preferred. Nothing deep or permanent. Nothing that would make her feel trapped. Because nothing was more important to her than freedom.

Thanks to Sheff, she would have it.

~

Sheff strolled into the library at the Phoenix Club and was shocked to see so many of his friends present. They occupied the largest seating area, and it appeared as though Somerton had recently arrived, for he had just sat down. With dark blond hair and an easy smile, he was too handsome for his own good and women fell at his feet. Or they used to anyway. Now that he was married, the viscount only had eyes for his wife.

"Sheff, join us!" Evan Price called. He and Somerton were now related by marriage since Evan's sister was the new viscountess. At one point, Price had been upset that Somerton was paying his sister attention. No one could blame him since Somerton's reputation had been only slightly better than Sheff's.

A footman asked Sheff what he wanted to drink as Sheff made his way to the table. He'd barely sat down before the footman had returned with a glass of claret.

"We're all here," Somerton remarked. "Except Bane."

"Even Wellesbourne," Sheff noted, looking toward the duke. His dark eyes looked a bit tired, but he had a very young son at home. Indeed, this was the first time he'd been to the club since the birth of his heir. "Shall we drink a toast to your return?"

"If you must," Wellesbourne said with a grimace. "I won't be here terribly long. I confess I am exhausted. We try to let the nurse manage the babe, but we usually allow him to fall asleep in our chamber. We are hopelessly smitten." He shook his head.

"Enjoy it," Keele said softly as he raised his glass. "To happiness and fatherhood."

Everyone lifted their glasses and drank.

"And to Bane," Wellesbourne said, keeping his glass aloft. "He was robbed of both those things, and I can only hope he will find them again one day."

"Hear, hear," Sheff said, and everyone drank again.

They were all quiet a moment. Sheff had written to his friend but had to think his words wouldn't do much to ease Bane's grief.

"Even *I* am finding this to be too maudlin," Droxford said drily, lightening the mood that had fallen over them. A few of them chuckled, and Droxford continued, "Seems like we should all be giving Sheff a hard time about finally being caught in the parson's trap."

"And with Jo Harker!" Wellesbourne said, his eyes rounding. "I would never have guessed. Can't imagine your mother is happy about that," he added with a laugh.

Sheff frowned. "She's even angrier than I anticipated. I thought she would at least like Jo and see why I would choose her. She's clever and capable, and she isn't going to try to overtake my mother as a hostess." He looked at his glass. "Actually, perhaps my mother doesn't realize the latter. I shall underscore that point to her."

"I still don't understand why you're betrothed," Price said, studying Sheff over the rim of his glass. "You don't seem the type to fall in love. But then neither did Somerton." He sent his brother-in-law a wry look.

"It just takes the right woman," Sheff said. He thought of what he'd told his mother recently about Min finding a husband, that she only had to find one who was right for her. Did Sheff think his sister could fall in love? Why her and not him?

Because she was not like their father.

Still, she'd grown up with the same parents as Sheff had. Perhaps his mother was right, that neither one of them would have any romantic inclination. He didn't think he did, but he realized he didn't really know how Min felt. He couldn't blame her if she didn't ever want to wed either. Their parents' marriage had all but ruined the notion of a happily ever after.

Somerton inclined his head. "And Jo is a very fine woman. Truly, you could not have chosen better, Sheff. She is quite perfect for you, really."

"I agree," Price put in before taking a drink of whisky.

"What makes you say that?" Sheff was most keen to hear.

Lifting a shoulder, Somerton said, "She's too smart to let

you misbehave, which makes me think you must truly have forsaken your rakish ways."

"That would mean you've all fallen," Price said. "Except me." He sounded smug.

"It's not a bad thing to fall in love," Keele said quietly as he contemplated the port in his glass. "And it can certainly happen when one least expects it." His lips rose in a faint, humorless smile before he sipped his wine.

"I didn't realize your marriage was a love match," Somerton said.

"It wasn't. At first." Keele spoke in a clipped tone that did not invite further curiosity.

Sheff had no hope to be fortunate enough to find love even once. He looked around at his friends, some of whom were newly married, newly in love. He couldn't imagine the emotion would last.

"When are we losing you to matrimony?" Price asked, his dark eyes narrowing slightly.

"Not until the autumn or winter," Sheff replied.

"I confess that makes me question whether you are actually in love," Wellesbourne said skeptically. "When I realized I loved Persephone, I couldn't wait to be wed. It was actual torture to be apart from her."

Somerton nodded vigorously. "Obviously, I felt the same since I married Gwen with the utmost haste."

Price stuck a finger in his ear. "I don't want to hear about how you couldn't live without my sister."

This provoked laughter, but Sheff was thinking of Jo. He definitely understood the torture aspect. Being near her was both delicious and agonizing. The torment was being in her presence, not away from her. Away from her, he felt... as though he wanted to see her again. Indeed, right now, he was thinking when that would be. Not for two more days. How disappointing.

But it wasn't torture! He was *not* in love. He was, however, in lust, but that was to be expected. He was, after all, a rogue cut in the image of his father.

Sheff considered telling them that he planned to leave town, but he didn't know how to explain why, not without revealing that he was having some sort of introspective crisis. How could he talk about it when he barely allowed himself to think about it?

"What I would like to know," Sheff said, moving to change the topic, "is how Price leapt on a moving horse behind its rider without injuring himself, the rider, or the horse." He pinned Price with an expectant stare, his mouth lifting in a teasing smile.

Price shrugged, and everyone turned toward him.

"That is a very good question," Somerton said. "Do tell."

Wellesbourne held up a hand. "I think I need to hear what happened first."

Droxford explained that his wife had seen it and went on to describe the escapade.

"The rider nearly ran me and Jo down," Sheff added. "What you did, Price, was nothing short of terrifying."

"Something needed to be done. Miss Pilkington was not going to be able to control her mount. And she was in danger of trampling people." Price looked to Sheff. "You and Jo included."

"But how on earth did you learn to do that?" Sheff asked.

Again, Price shrugged. "I like horses, and sometimes I practice…things."

"If working for the treasury doesn't meet your satisfaction, you could seek employment at Astley's," Somerton suggested.

This was met with more laughter as Price smiled. His expression carried an almost mischievous cast as he sipped his whisky.

It felt good to be with friends again, Sheff realized. Even if most of them were now married. He actually found himself feeling slightly envious. They just seemed so bloody happy, especially Wellesbourne with his newborn son, and in spite of the exhaustion hiding in his gaze.

Sheff reminded himself that their joy wouldn't last. Nothing did.

CHAPTER 12

Jo settled into the hack with her father, who was accompanying her to Sir Alfred Hightooth's rout. As they began moving along Coventry Street, he gave Jo an approving look.

"That ensemble is fabulous. The vibrant orange-red is perfect for you." He patted her hand.

"I was concerned it was too garish, but Min convinced me it would be striking." The style was simple, and the ivory trim helped to mellow the main color. Looking back, Jo probably chose the flame color because the Duchess of Henlow had wrinkled her nose at it.

His gaze flicked to her neck. "I see you are wearing the pearl-and-coral necklace I gave you for your eighteenth birthday. It's a lovely adornment."

Jo touched the necklace lying at the base of her throat. "I am glad to have occasion to wear it."

Her father rubbed his gloved hands together. "I'm so pleased to be escorting you tonight! I was hoping for an invitation to Sir Alfred's rout, but he can be somewhat discerning. It is my good fortune that you are now engaged to Shefford. You've likely received invitations to nearly everything." He looked at her expectantly, and she realized he was probing for information—and perhaps inclusion.

"I've received a great many, yes. However, I have declined most of them. I do not wish to attend more than two or three events each week." Three was excessive to her, particularly when she usually attended a salon on Mondays. "I am busy with the club."

"Oh, that gaming club is such a distraction," he said somewhat testily. "I was never enthused that your mother raised you in such a place."

Jo knew her father didn't particularly care for the Siren's Call. Her mother said it was because he envied its success, the rewards of which she did not share with him. "She didn't raise me *in* it."

"I would argue she did. You've lived above it as long as you can remember. You have never been able to escape the shadow of the club. But now you will. When you become the Countess of Shefford." He pierced her with a curious stare. "Why aren't you leaving your role there now? I should think you must."

"I can't, not with Mama leaving London this summer. I need to be at the club."

He cut his hand through the air before him. "Balderdash. Your mother needs to hire someone to manage the club if she isn't going to be here. That cannot be your role. Not any longer. I will speak to her."

"Please don't, Papa." She touched his arm. "I *will* transition to not working at the club, just not yet."

"I would ask that you do so in the near future. It does not help your status in Society to be perceived as unworthy of your soon-to-be husband. *I* don't think that, of course."

Was that what people were saying? Jo didn't care. She

couldn't. But she also didn't want Sheff to be adversely affected by her behavior.

They arrived at Sir Alfred's house near Bloomsbury Square. Jo alighted from the hackney coach and made her way to the door, which was held open by a liveried footman.

Inside the entrance hall, she gave her cloak to another footman who directed her upstairs. Jo waited for her father then took his arm as they ascended the staircase.

Jo glanced over at him. "I know you will likely want to stay until the very end of the gathering, but I do not wish to stay that late."

"As you wish, my dear." His gaze fixed ahead of them as they reached the first floor and turned toward the drawing room. "There is your betrothed."

Sheff walked toward them, his brown hair artfully styled so a lock caressed his forehead. He wore black with a scarlet waistcoat, and a ruby pin sparkled in the pristine white folds of his cravat. "Good evening, my dearest," he said to Jo, a flash of heat in his gaze as he took her hand and bowed to brush a kiss against her glove. Straightening, he addressed her father, "Evening, Harker."

"And to you, Shefford. I shall leave my daughter in your capable hands for now. Behave yourselves," he added with a chuckle before taking himself off toward the drawing room.

"You look stunning," Sheff said as he slowly perused her from head to toe.

"I am not a selection of sweets you are contemplating," she murmured.

"No, you are far more enticing than that," he replied softly. He offered her his arm. "Do you wish to see what Sir Alfred brought back from South America?"

"Desperately." She smiled as she took his arm and ignored the rush of desire that claimed her for a moment. For several moments, really.

Inside the drawing room, she forced herself to focus on the curiosities placed about the room. Each had a card describing it, including where Sir Alfred had found it. There were dried flowers, leaves, insects, and wool from an alpaca.

"Come along and feel it," Sir Alfred said as they approached the white fluffy wool. "It's one of the few things here I'm encouraging people to touch. There is some wood on the other side of the room, I would suggest you feel as well."

Average in height and build, Sir Alfred wore thick spectacles that made his eyes seem larger than they were. He was in his middle fifties, probably, with thinning gray hair and an engaging smile.

"You'll have to remove your glove," Sir Alfred added with a chuckle.

Jo did so, as did Sheff, and she reached for a small ball of fluff. It was soft and springy. "I imagine this makes a beautiful blanket."

"Indeed. I brought several home with me. One is hanging over there." He gestured toward the wall, where a vibrantly dyed blanket hung. "But I do ask that you not touch that. This here is what an alpaca looks like." He lightly touched the edge of a framed drawing that stood on the table with the wool.

"Did you sketch that, Sir Alfred?" Sheff asked.

"Indeed, I did. I'm compiling a book of my drawings and descriptions. It should be available later this year."

"How splendid," Jo said with enthusiasm. "I look forward to purchasing a copy. Will you be giving any lectures about your experiences there?"

"I will indeed. I shall ensure you receive an invitation," Sir Alfred said jovially before turning his attention to someone else who'd arrived at the table.

"Did you feel it?" Jo asked Sheff.

He touched the wool she still held, his fingers grazing hers. "Very soft. And so is the wool." He gave her a crooked smile, and Jo smirked as she rolled her eyes.

"You are a terrible flirt."

"I can't help myself with you," he said with a light laugh, his head tilting toward hers.

She set the wool back on the table but did not draw on her glove just yet. "Shall we go find the wood he mentioned?"

"We'll make our way in that direction."

Tucking her hand around his arm once more, Jo realized the folly in not putting her glove back on. It was far more intimate to touch him with her bare hand. And tantalizing.

As they moved to the next table, they encountered Mr. and Mrs. Davenport, who'd hosted the literary salon on Monday. "How pleasant to see you here," Mrs. Davenport said.

Jo looked toward Sheff. "Do you know Mrs. Davenport?"

"I think we have met at some point," Sheff said with a smile. "You host the literary salons Jo is so fond of."

"Yes. We look forward to when she joins us as a hostess in her own right," Mrs. Davenport said with considerable glee. "I do hope you enjoy literature, my lord."

"I do, indeed. I look forward to my wife's salons and hope you will come. Perhaps you'd even see fit to invite me to one of yours," he added with a flirtatious wink.

Jo squeezed his arm provoking him to glance at her. She gave him an exasperated look. His lips twitched in response.

"I most certainly will," Mrs. Davenport said.

They chatted a bit longer before continuing on their separate ways.

"I wanted to ask if you liked to read," Jo said to Sheff. "What type of literature is your favorite?"

"I enjoy reading historical accounts. I haven't ever been terribly fond of novels."

"What about poetry?" she asked.

"The more risqué the better," he said with a laugh.

"You would have appreciated Lady Standish's offerings the other night. She had one poem in particular that was rather…stirring."

He arched a brow. "As in, it aroused you?"

"It spoke of arousal. She compared the ocean to having an orgasm." Too late, Jo realized this was not a good topic for them to converse about. "Shall we go feel the wood?"

And that was somehow better?

Sheff choked out a laugh. "If you are trying to arouse *me*, you are doing a fine job. But then, all you need do, really, is exist."

How had that happened? She didn't think she'd aroused him before they'd launched this scheme. If so, he'd never shown it. "What has changed to make you feel that way?" She should not be asking him such things in a place like this. Or anywhere. "Never mind."

He pulled her to the side of the room. They'd been speaking softly, but now he lowered his voice even more. "I don't really know what has changed, but something has. And I know you feel it too."

Jo said nothing, but she absolutely felt it—deep in her core. Standing here with him, her bare hand on his sleeve, their bodies close, she wanted nothing more than to give in to that something.

His eyes locked with hers. "But we aren't going to do anything about it."

She managed to exhale despite the stranglehold that desire had placed on her ability to breathe. They took a step away from the wall, and two ladies crossed their path.

"Pardon," Sheff said.

They both looked at him, then flicked glances toward Jo.

Without a word, they turned and strode in the other direction.

Jo had never received the cut direct, but she believed that might have been it.

"Bloody prigs," Sheff breathed. His eyes had darkened with anger, and his features were pulled into a furious glower as he stared after the two women.

"Who cares what they think?" Jo said.

"I do."

"Do you?" Jo thought of what her father had said to her just before they'd arrived. "I don't want to cause problems for you," she said softly.

"You aren't. At all. I care what they think about *you*."

"You shouldn't. I'm a temporary accessory." Regardless, she couldn't deny she felt a prick of agitation at the ladies' reactions. She would not share that with Sheff, however.

He turned his gaze toward her, and she saw the fury there. "You are not an accessory. And I will ensure those women are excluded from every Society event for the rest of the Season."

Jo moved to stand in front of him, blocking his view of the women who'd scorned her. "No, you will not." How would he even do that anyway?

"Their behavior cannot go unpunished," he said fiercely.

"What an arrogant thing to say. As if you are the arbiter of their actions."

His expression gentled—slightly. "I won't allow them to be rude to you."

"Even if it doesn't bother me?"

"It bothers *me*," he grumbled. "I won't permit people to denigrate my future wife. Even if you aren't actually going to be my future wife. They don't know that." He sounded possessive and…hurt. Jo couldn't find fault in either of those things. Indeed, she couldn't help feeling flattered.

She took her hand from his arm and drew on her glove. "I'm going to the retiring room. If you want to have words with those women while I am gone, I can't stop you. But I don't want any part of it."

She turned on her heel and strode from the drawing room, passing the women who'd cut her without sparing them a glance. In the corridor, she stopped to ask a footman where the retiring room was located.

"I can show you," a woman said. She was petite and curvaceous, her blonde hair streaked with white. "I am Sir Alfred's sister, Miss Hightooth."

"I'm pleased to meet you," Jo said. "I'm Miss Josephine Harker."

"Ah, the Earl of Shefford's betrothed," Miss Hightooth said with a knowing smile. "You are a courageous woman. I don't know you at all, but I admire your spirit." She led Jo along the corridor to the back of the house.

"Why, because I am marrying an earl?" Jo asked with a chuckle.

"Yes, of course! That is not for the faint of heart. I declined to wed a viscount in my youth. My mother was horrified, but I realized I was not meant for that sort of marriage. Or any marriage, as it turned out. I am a happy spinster."

Based on her smile and enthusiasm, Jo could see that. "What is it about spinsterhood that you love?"

"Freedom, mostly. I am fortunate to have a brother who cares for me financially. In return, I manage his household and take care of things while he's traveling." She opened the door to a small sitting room that had been made into the ladies' retiring room. "Alf wasn't meant for marriage either, but that is because he is wed to his studies and exploration."

"It's nice that you have one another." Sometimes Jo wished she had a sibling. Especially now that she had friends her age and saw the relationships Gwen and Min had with their brothers.

"It is, but sometimes I wonder if it might be nice to have a romantic partner," Miss Hightooth said. "But then I scoff and remind myself that I never wanted that, nor do I need it." She turned toward the door. "I'll leave you to it."

"Thank you." Jo looked about the empty space wondering how long she should linger. The only reason she'd left was to give Sheff time to do whatever he planned with those two women.

Was that the only reason?

She was also perhaps seeking a respite from being in his presence. Particularly from the desire growing between them. The end to their ruse—or his departure from town— could not come soon enough.

Satisfied she'd been gone long enough, she started for the door. A woman in her forties stepped inside, her gaze falling on Jo. She pursed her lips and jerked her focus away, moving past Jo with alacrity.

Another cut direct. Or almost.

Jo caught the door before it closed, but before she could leave the room, she heard the woman say, "A title will not make you welcome. There are people in Society who will never accept you. Think about that before you saddle a highly respected family with your presence."

Shock mingled with anger as Jo gripped the edge of the door. She ought to keep going and find her father to tell him that she was ready to leave. But she hadn't yet finished looking at Sir Alfred's objects.

Turning, she released the door and let it swing shut.

"Unrepentant strumpet," the woman muttered as she gazed at her reflection in a mirror in the corner.

"I'm still here," Jo said.

The woman turned around sharply, her jaw dropping.

Jo curled her lips into a malevolent smile. "A title doesn't make anyone anything. Their character does. You and your ilk willingly accept rogues and rakes—men who are 'highly respected' but should not be. How dare you judge me when you don't even know me?"

The woman sniffed. Her cheeks flooded dark pink. "You are not from our class. You should know better than to mingle with us."

"So far, I have been most fortunate. Perhaps the best thing about being a countess—and a duchess someday—is that I will choose with whom I mingle. You may rest assured it will not be with you." Jo returned to the door and opened it. "Enjoy the rest of your evening," she called before slipping from the room.

Her hands were shaking as she made her way back to the drawing room. She heard her father laugh and saw him standing to one side with a small group of people, a glass of wine dangling from his fingertips. Did anyone ever give him the cut direct? She'd never witnessed it. But then, he wasn't welcomed everywhere. He hadn't even received his own invitation to this rout.

What was Jo doing here?

It was a stupid, rhetorical question. She had a lucrative reason for being here, and she could suffer the ignorant and judgmental harpies of the ton. They'd be relieved when she cried off and didn't marry one of their precious members. Part of Jo wanted to wed him out of spite.

Sheff joined her. "You'll be happy to know I didn't say anything to those horrible women. But I still plan to cut them at every opportunity. It's the least I can do."

"That seems fair," she said, deciding she wouldn't tell him about the woman in the retiring room. What would be the point? "Let's finish our perusal of Sir Alfred's items."

"We still need to stroke the wood," he said with a comical leer.

Jo giggled, glad for his humor. She shook off the lingering irritation from her encounter with the obnoxious woman in the retiring room and hoped she wouldn't come face to face with her again.

"Lead the way," Jo said.

"I thought we might promenade in the park tomorrow," Sheff suggested. "I spoke with Somerton about it the other night, and he said that he and his wife would chaperone."

Jo was always amused that a woman younger than her could serve as a chaperone—married or not. "All right. I'll send Gwen a note in the morning. Then we have a ball to attend on Saturday." She resisted the urge to make a face. How many more cuts would she have to endure?

"Yes, but we needn't stay long. In fact, you can be back at the Siren's Call to work just after midnight, I should think."

His support of her obligations warmed her. Would he do the same if they were actually betrothed? Of course not. There was no way he could endorse such behavior from his future wife. He was able to do it now because it didn't really matter.

Soon enough, she wouldn't have to endure any of this. And it would all be worth the freedom she would earn.

~

The following evening, Sheff found himself at the Siren's Call. He hadn't had to escort his mother and sister anywhere, and there wasn't anywhere else he wanted to be. He found himself increasingly seeking Jo's company and missing her when he didn't see her.

When he thought about what that could mean, he decided it was due to their unresolved mutual attraction. If they could put that behind them somehow, perhaps he would not feel as though something was absent. Something almost viscerally important.

Jo was not in the common room when he arrived. Becky said she was dealing vingt-et-un in the cardroom. Sheff made his way there, a tankard of ale in hand, and stood near the doorway to watch her work.

In the past, he would have joined the game, but now it would be odd, for she was his betrothed. Or perceived to be anyway.

So, he observed instead. He noted her mischievous smile as she turned over the dealer's card, her laugh when one of the players lost melodramatically, her genuine glee for the player who won.

She reset the table, her gaze moving about until she met his. Her brows arched briefly in surprise. He lifted his tankard in a silent toast.

Then she dealt the cards, and Sheff watched another hand. Then another. Her fingers were long and slender, her nails neatly trimmed. She was not wearing her betrothal ring.

That made him frown slightly. He liked seeing it on her hand. Because it was the only physical claim he could make on her.

That afternoon, they'd enjoyed a wonderful promenade in Hyde Park. The weather had finally been slightly warm, with the sun making a prolonged appearance. But then the wind had picked up and rain clouds had moved in, prompting them to hasten their departure.

But for a time, he'd enjoyed laughter and ease with Jo and their friends. He began to see how a man like Somerton had traded his bachelorhood for marriage. Not just any marriage, but a lifetime with a woman he clearly adored. Sheff had never seen Somerton so happy. Giddy, even. And it was obvious his wife felt the same. What would happen when one of them inevitably stopped feeling that way?

What would happen when neither of them did?

The voice came from the depths of Sheff's mind, and he wanted to shove it right back where it had come from. Love like that was rare. What were the odds that three of his friends—Somerton, Droxford, and Wellesbourne—were fortunate enough to have found that?

And what about Bane? Sheff didn't even know if his friend had loved his wife. Bane had been caught in a compromising position with Pandora Barclay, and his reaction had been to say he was already betrothed to the woman he'd ended up marrying. The woman who had recently died in childbirth. Had Bane loved her? Was he, like Keele, grieving the loss of something that was already nearly impossible? How cruel to have that only for it to be ripped away.

That alone was enough to warn one away from love and marriage. Better to just avoid those entirely. Then there would be no hurt. Not like the humiliation his mother endured. Or the emptiness Keele sometimes spoke of.

Sheff took a long drink of ale. He needed to stop thinking of love. Especially in relation to Jo. He wanted her. Desperately. And that was not the same thing.

"How delightful to see a man unabashedly enamored of his betrothed."

Startled, Sheff turned to address the man who'd walked up beside him. In his midforties, Allard was a regular patron of the Siren's Call. Sheff knew him fairly well. He was an MP for some constituency on the outskirts of London.

"Evening, Allard." Sheff couldn't think of a single thing to say in response to the man's initial observation. He couldn't very well tell him he was dead wrong about what he thought he was seeing.

"Do you plan to move the wedding up? I hear you haven't even set a date."

"We have no plans to do so. Marry soon, I mean," Sheff clarified, though the latter part was also not happening.

Allard cocked his head. "Why not? Judging by the way you look at her, I must wonder why you'd want to wait." He chuckled, then sobered. "Forgive me, I didn't mean to be indelicate."

"But you are being intrusive." Sheff realized he sounded like an ass, but he didn't like what Allard was saying.

And why not?

Because it was true. Sheff looked at Jo the way a child looked at a sweet or a toy they'd been denied. No, it was more than that. He yearned for her in a way that went beyond simple want or even desire. He *ached* for her.

"I didn't mean to offend," Allard said, turning slightly as if he would leave.

"My apologies, Allard. As you can imagine, many people ask me about when we will wed, particularly my mother."

Allard smiled. "I *can* imagine. You must do what you wish, though. Even if that means escaping to Gretna Green," he added with a laugh. "That's what my wife and I did."

Sheff turned his head toward the other man. "Really, why?"

"My mother-in-law was perhaps like your mother. She wanted to manage every aspect of the wedding, and a week before it was scheduled, my wife asked me to whisk her away to Scotland instead." He shrugged. "So I did."

"You've been married how long?" Sheff asked.

"Twenty-one years. I love her more today than I did yesterday, and I shall love her even more tomorrow." Allard's green gaze turned wistful. "That kind of love is the reason I asked why you wanted to wait to marry. I can see you have that for Miss Harker, and in my experience, once you've fallen in love and know you want to spend forever with someone, you can't wait to begin."

"You are not the first gentleman to tell me that," Sheff said wryly. "However, I don't know that I truly feel the kind of love you are referencing."

"Indeed?" Allard sounded surprised. "You appear, to me, to be a man far gone, but perhaps I am wrong." He blew out a breath. "I have had too much ale tonight. You must ignore me. I'm waxing romantic and offering unsolicited advice. Have a good evening." He nodded at Sheff, then departed the cardroom.

Sheff frowned after him, then returned his attention to Jo. But she was gone. Another employee had taken her place.

Scanning the cardroom, Sheff didn't see Jo anywhere else either. He returned to the common room, his heart beating faster than he would like—it wasn't as if Jo had gone missing, for heaven's sake.

There she was, standing at the bar, talking to the woman behind it who was dispensing ale. Sheff exhaled, relieved to have found her. Warmth spread in his chest. He wanted to go to her, to spend the rest of the evening in her company.

He turned away and brought the tankard to his lips, his hand shaking. What was wrong with him?

Allard's observations flooded Sheff's mind. He realized there might be truth in them. He could very well be in love with his make-believe betrothed. But why would that even matter? It wouldn't last, and—anyway—she would never marry him.

A touch on his arm sent heat racing through his body. He didn't have to turn or hear her voice to know it was Jo.

"Sheff?"

Taking a deep breath to steady his raging pulse, he turned to face her. "Evening, Jo."

She wore one of her "regular" working gowns, something

between a day dress and an evening gown. "I saw you in the cardroom, but then you were speaking with Allard, and I had things to check on."

"You're a busy woman. It's surprisingly attractive."

She arched a brow at him. "Can we have just one conversation without your blatant flirting?"

"I wasn't flirting. I was being honest." He sighed. "Perhaps I shouldn't be that either, though."

"Just keep your feelings of attraction to yourself. It would be…best. Is now a bad time to ask how your vow of celibacy is going?"

Sheff couldn't help his shout of laughter. "Now you're just being cruel." He laughed some more. "It's progressing without incident. And I wouldn't call it a vow. It's a requirement of our arrangement."

She put her hand to her chest. "*I* didn't make it one."

"I did."

"Who said you could make rules?" she asked saucily, her eyes glinting with humor.

"I'm only making them when they apply to me. I would never presume to make a rule for you."

"I appreciate that," she said softly. "Just as I appreciate your…protective nature. I was thinking about what happened last night at the rout, and I should not have prevented you from doing what you wanted with those busybodies."

"That is too kind a term for them. You were only trying to save me from my baser, vengeful nature. I must thank you for that. I'm afraid I became rather primally defensive of you."

Her gaze met his, and Sheff felt a connection that stole his breath. "You should not be, but I thank you," she murmured. "It's disconcerting to think of someone wanting to protect you in that way. But also exhilarating."

God, this dance they kept doing was going to kill him. They flirted. They admonished each other for flirting. They acknowledged their mutual attraction. They dismissed that attraction.

He wasn't sure how much more he could take. It seemed he was going to have to leave London as a matter of self-preservation.

Sheff took a long drink of ale, finishing the tankard. "I should go."

She took the empty vessel from him. Their fingers did not touch, and he was incredibly disappointed.

"I'll see you at the ball Saturday. Ten o'clock?"

He nodded. "Thank you."

She gave him a quizzical look. "For what?"

"For agreeing to this silly scheme. For putting up with what other people say and do. For suffering my ceaseless roguery."

"You're making it very worth my while," she said, her eyes gleaming with things he couldn't discern and decided he was better off not knowing.

CHAPTER 13

*A*fter arriving at the Billingsworth ball on Saturday night with Gwen and Somerton, Jo danced with Sheff and visited with her friends. She recalled what Sheff had told her about being back at the Siren's Call by midnight —or thereabouts—and decided she could leave soon.

The question was how?

She didn't think Gwen and Somerton would want to leave yet. And she couldn't simply hail a hack. Could she? Perhaps Min or Ellis would have an idea.

Going to the last place she'd seen them, Jo found Ellis seated against the wall. She didn't look bored, exactly, but she also didn't seem to be enjoying herself. But why would she?

Jo slid onto the empty chair beside her. "Do you think I could leave the ball without causing a stir?" she asked quietly.

Ellis looked at her sideways. "That depends on what you mean by a stir. The duchess will not be pleased."

Exhaling, Jo slumped against the back of the chair. "I suppose not."

"There's a ladies' entertainment room," Ellis said with a sly smile.

"What is that?"

"Gaming, liquor, probably ribald jests. Lady Billingsworth is known for offering a ladies' version of the men's gaming room."

"What a marvelous idea. Could we hide there for the rest of the ball?" Jo asked.

Ellis shrugged. "We could try. Though I daren't stay long. The duchess will notice, and I'm supposed to be available to Min."

"Min can join us," Jo said.

"Oh no," Ellis said firmly, shaking her head. "The duchess would lose her temper, and then the fact that she'd lost her temper would make matters worse."

"I can see how that would happen," Jo murmured. "But could we at least go for a short while?"

"We can say we were in one of the retiring rooms." Ellis rose.

Jo leapt up, eager to depart the cloying heat of the ballroom. She followed Ellis into the antechamber and then along a corridor.

"Where are you going?"

The duchess's shrill voice sounded from behind them. Jo and Ellis exchanged looks of disappointment before turning to face her.

"To the retiring room," Jo said brightly.

"That isn't the way." The duchess moved toward them. "I might think you were trying to find Lady Billingsworth's ladies' gaming room, but you must know that is only for those of us who are married."

"Is that where you are going?" Jo asked. She glanced at Ellis who pressed her lips together in an apparent attempt not to smile.

The duchess's eyes narrowed. "You need to return to the ball," she said, as if that was a response to Jo's question. "You don't attend enough events as it is, and you must be seen. You must *engage*. You need to show people that you are up to the challenge of becoming a countess."

Jo wanted to ask why it was any of their business, but she feared she knew the answer. Instead, she summoned a smile. "I will do that. Excuse me." But before she could return to the ballroom, the duchess held up her hand.

"Just a moment. I need to speak with you first." She looked—briefly—at Ellis. "Do excuse us."

Ellis blinked, then gave Jo an apologetic look before hastening back to the ballroom.

Jo braced herself for a possible lecture.

The duchess moved into an alcove and motioned for Jo to join her. She spoke quietly. "This isn't going to work."

"What is that?" Jo asked, thinking she could mean any number of things.

"Your behavior. Your working at a gaming hell." The duchess's eyes blazed. "You *must* stop working there. You *cannot* be a duchess and work at a club!" She kept her voice low, but her tone managed to remain shrill.

Jo hesitated to respond because she didn't know what to say. But the duchess wasn't finished.

"Furthermore, when you do attend events, apparently you haven't the slightest inkling how to behave properly. You insulted Lady Balliol at that rout the other night. And you actually drew your soon-to-be father-in-law into the matter! I can't believe even you would be so crude."

Even her. *So* crude. As if *some* crudeness were to be expected from her.

Jo didn't recall mentioning the duke at all. "I'm afraid I don't know what you mean about His Grace. He was not discussed."

"Not by name, apparently, but you indicated that one's position was not representative of good behavior." She narrowed her eyes at Jo, and her anger was palpable. "What else would you have meant besides my husband, who behaves as if he has no decorum whatsoever?"

It was difficult for Jo not to become upset in the face of this woman's ire. "That is not what I was trying to say. Lady Balliol—I didn't even know who she was—gave me the cut direct and was very rude." Jo felt herself growing more agitated. "Should I not stand up for myself? When I am the Countess of Shefford, I don't think I should tolerate such discourtesy, do you?"

"You should never be the Countess of Shefford!" the duchess ground out, her lip curling. "You are no one from nothing. Worse than that, your parents are the worst sort of people. Your mother is in trade, and a ghastly one at that, and your father's pathetic attempts to gain a foothold in Society are pitiable."

Jo gaped at the duchess. Fury surged through her. It was one thing to insult her, but to denigrate her parents? She opened her mouth to speak, but Sheff stepped between them.

"Mother, you cannot speak to my betrothed like that," he bit out. Though his back was to her, Jo could imagine the storm in his eyes as he practically growled at the duchess.

"Come, Mama, let's find you a glass of wine." Min was there too.

Jo then saw Ellis standing off to the side. She'd fetched Sheff and Min to help. Jo wanted to hug her. But she couldn't. She was still shaking with anger from what the duchess had said.

"Go, Mother," Sheff demanded. "Before I say something I will regret as you have already done. I will expect a complete and detailed apology—*in writing*—to Jo tomorrow. You will show it to me first so I can determine if it is acceptable."

He was blocking Jo's view of the duchess, which was disappointing. Jo imagined her jaw dropping and her eyes goggling. She also never expected to receive an apology of any kind. What she most wanted was to understand why the duchess hated her so much. It seemed to go beyond simply not approving of her. But perhaps that was all it was.

"You must rethink this betrothal," the duchess said. "You can't marry a woman who works at a gaming hell. You just *can't*."

"She won't work there forever, Mother. Not when we are wed. You're going to have to become accustomed to having Jo in our family."

The duchess made a strangled sound in her throat. Then she marched away.

Min sent Jo an apologetic look and turned to follow her mother. Ellis joined her, leaving Jo to stare at Sheff's back.

But then he turned, and she saw the concern in his dark blue eyes.

"Jo," he whispered, lifting his hand to cup her cheek. His glove was soft against her flesh. He muttered a curse, then whipped the offending accessory off and pressed his bare palm to her face. "I'm so sorry for the things my mother said."

"You can't be sorry for that," Jo said quietly. "And I don't think *she* will be. She doesn't need to write me an apology. I don't want it."

"Dammit." He breathed the word, his eyes shuttering briefly. When he opened them, they fixed on her with a ferocity that made her breath catch. "I will make sure you are never alone with her again. No, I should halt this entire ill-plotted scheme." He nodded. "Tomorrow, I'll tell her we aren't marrying."

Jo clutched his arm—the one that was still at his side. "*No.* After what she said, I'm tempted to make you marry me. You can't let her win, and she'll see that as a victory, especially after what she said tonight and the fact that you witnessed it."

"You make a good argument—for actual marriage," he said wryly, his hand moving from her face to her collarbone. "But how can I ask you to continue with this ruse after the way she treated you? I can't expect you to put up with that."

"I won't. I held my own with her." Right up to the part when she'd denigrated Jo's parents. Jo had still been formulating her response when Sheff had arrived. "How much did you hear?"

"I heard you saying you didn't have to tolerate discourtesy." His lips spread in a heart-stopping grin. "That was brilliant. Then I heard what she said about your parents," he added soberly. "What did I miss?"

"Just her telling me I had to stop working at the Siren's Call. And she took me to task for insulting Lady Balliol the other night at the rout. Apparently, it's fine for Lady Balliol to cut me, but when I take offense and address her rudeness, I am in the wrong." Jo rolled her eyes.

"When did that happen?" he asked, his brows dipping.

"When I went to the retiring room."

He searched her face. "Why didn't you tell me?"

She lifted a shoulder—the one he wasn't touching. "You were already upset about those other women."

He took his hand from her, and she nearly asked him to put it back. Raking it through his hair, he ruined the style somewhat. "This is unsustainable. We must put an end to this farce."

Jo saw the anger and worry in the lines in his brow. She lifted her hand from his arm and brushed his hair back into place. "I can manage. Perhaps we can just keep our engagements to the park." Except she could just as easily face a Lady Balliol and her superiority there.

Too late, she realized the nature of his expression had changed. The anger and worry were gone—mostly—and had been replaced by hunger. Heat blazed through her, and she knew she had no time to lose if she wanted to escape before she broke her own rule.

The rogue rules flashed in her mind. She was alone with him. She would gladly flirt with him. And if she wasn't careful, she was going to give him a chance...

To kiss her, at least.

"You should go," he rasped.

She gentled her hand against his head and slid it down the back, tucking it into the top of his collar until her palm met his nape. Unfortunately, she had not removed her glove as he had.

"I should, but I won't. Not just yet." She stood on her toes and angled her head slightly before pressing her lips to his.

His arms came around her, pulling her body against his. The contact with him intensified her longing. She pressed her fingers into him and slid her other arm around his waist.

Eyes closed, Jo reveled in his embrace. His lips moved over hers with devastating precision, stirring her desire. She opened her mouth to deepen the kiss, and it was all he needed to claim her mouth completely.

She was suddenly swept into a realm of dark need and brilliant ecstasy. Her body ached for his, to be possessed in the same way he'd taken over the kiss she'd started.

His hands clutched at her back and backside, pressing her into him so she could feel the hard length of his arousal. Jo kissed him ravenously, as if it were the most important thing in the world—absolutely vital to her survival. In that moment, nothing else mattered except the two of them together, demanding, giving, sharing, relishing.

Voices sounded from somewhere along the corridor. They broke apart, their breathing rapid. Sheff stepped back, his hand moving across his mouth as he worked to catch his breath.

Jo brushed her fingertips along the sides of her mouth and inhaled deeply. "Sorry," she murmured. "That was my fault."

"Don't ever apologize for kissing me. As you could tell, I didn't mind."

She chanced a look at him—she didn't want to, for fear she'd leap on him again, but they could *not* continue. His expression was sardonic, his eyes still glowing with heat.

"I am going to leave the ball now, if that's all right with you."

"You don't ever need to ask me permission for anything either," he said. "How will you get home?"

"I'll walk if need be," she said drily despite being quite serious.

He pulled on his glove and offered her his arm. "I'd take you, but that would be potentially ruinous since this betrothal is fake. I'll find someone to convey you."

She put her hand on his sleeve. "Thank you."

"I'll fix things with my mother," he said as they walked back toward the ballroom.

Though Jo couldn't imagine how, she knew he would try. She felt quite badly for him, because while Jo's time enduring the duchess was temporary, poor Sheff had to deal with her forever.

~

Somerton and his wife had taken Jo home from the ball last night, leaving Sheff to decide if he ought to confront his mother or wait until the following day. But here it was Sunday, and Sheff hadn't been able to bring himself to go to Henlow House. The disgust and anger he felt toward his mother was too great. Greater than he'd ever experienced. Indeed, he wondered where the woman he'd grown up with had gone. She'd never been this vitriolic or awful, even when Sheff's father was at his worst.

Why did she loathe Jo so very much?

It wasn't just that Sheff was upset by the duchess's attitude. He was hurt. Because Jo was an extraordinary woman. She was helping him, and she'd been a good friend. Sheff had grown to care for her.

Deeply.

So, he'd spent today focused on her instead of his mother, and he didn't regret a moment. What he did regret was bringing Jo into the mess of his life. But he would end that tonight.

She'd asked him not to end the scheme, and he would not. At least not immediately. He *would* leave London, however. Then his mother would leave Jo—and him—alone.

Tomorrow, he would travel to Weston for the remainder of the summer. For the first time in his life, he would seek solitude and quiet contemplation. Away from his parents. Away from Society. Away from his own reputation.

Sheff accepted his hat from his valet and made his way out of the Albany, where he lived, and caught a hack to the Siren's Call. He hoped Jo would have time to speak with him.

He entered the common room and immediately saw her standing at a table chatting with the occupants—three gentlemen Sheff knew somewhat. As he watched her laugh and smile, his chest pulled. He was going to miss her.

Becky approached him with a smile. "Evening, Sheff. I'll grab your ale."

"Thank you," he said absentmindedly, his focus still on Jo. When what Becky had said actually permeated his brain, he touched her arm before she could walk away. "No. Could you tell Jo to go to the supply cupboard or whatever you call it?"

She gave him a puzzled look. "Why?"

"Because I want to speak with her privately." He flashed a brief, closed-lipped smile.

"I will," Becky said, taking herself off as Sheff made his way to the cupboard.

Only one of the lanterns was burning when he stepped inside. He moved away from the door and surveyed the shelves as he waited for Jo.

A moment later, the door swung open, and she came inside. "Becky said you were here."

He turned to face her, and the truth smacked him in the face more surely than any pugilist. He was falling in love with her. He'd no idea what that meant until now. And he still had no idea if it would last. But in this moment, he felt incredibly strong emotion for her.

"I needed to see you," he said, his voice sounding rough. He coughed. "I'm going to leave London tomorrow."

She'd closed the door and now stood in front of it. Her brow pleated as she tucked a loose curl behind her ear. "Is that wise?"

"It seems the best option, particularly given your argument on why we shouldn't just dissolve the betrothal right now." It occurred to Sheff that he could force her hand. He had only to do something scandalous to provoke her to cry off.

"I won't give your mother the satisfaction," she said with a defiance that only made him fall harder for her. "Are you leaving town now in order to accelerate the end of this scheme? Do you plan to cause a scandal wherever it is that you're going?"

"Not immediately. I am following our original plan."

"The plan does not involve you leaving town mid-Season.

People will question the betrothal if you leave. They may presume you have regrets."

"I certainly regret proposing this ridiculous scheme." He went to brush his hand through his hair only to meet his hat. Taking it off, he set it on the table. "I'm going to tell my mother that I'm visiting Bane—Banemore—to support him in his grief."

"I know who Bane is," Jo said softly. "Will you really do that? I know you two are close friends. He would likely appreciate your company. At least, I think he would, but I don't know him as well as I have come to know you."

He hoped not. When he thought of how close they'd grown, of their shared attraction, their kisses, he didn't want to imagine her with any other man.

"Actually, I hadn't thought to actually visit him. He hasn't replied to my letters. I'm not sure he wants a visitor."

"Want and need aren't the same thing."

They felt that way when he considered Jo. He wanted and needed her most desperately. "Perhaps I will travel north to see him." He had plenty of time to do that and make it to Weston before August when he would meet with his friends for their annual frolic.

Why did that not hold the same allure as in years past? Hell, he'd fallen squarely into the trap he'd feared. He was in love, and he wanted to spend time with the woman who'd stolen his heart instead of his closest friends.

Wasn't she his close friend?

Perhaps that was the emotion he was feeling—the love and camaraderie one felt for a dear friend. Except he didn't want to shag his other friends. Just Jo.

He could try to find excuses for the way he felt, or attempt to explain it away, but there was no denying the truth of things. There was also no point in accepting it or pursuing it. He was alone in his feelings, and he would remain that way.

"You're leaving tomorrow, then?" she asked, her gaze meeting his almost tentatively.

He nodded. "I plan to speak with my mother first. I will give her strict instructions to leave you alone. Any communication she wants to have with you must be with Min present. I will demand she not expect anything from you. No Society engagements. No leaving your job."

Frowning, Jo put her hand on her hip. "I have clothes that you've paid for that I haven't even worn."

"Consider them payment for the extra harassment you've endured." He blew out a breath. "I can't believe I was foolish enough to think this would work. Instead of relief, I've invited a whole new campaign of disappointment from my mother."

"It goes beyond that," Jo said with a great deal of irony. "I do think this plan may have worked if you'd chosen someone other than me."

"I didn't want anyone else." He'd chosen her because she wouldn't suffer when this was finished. But that claim—that he didn't want anyone else—meant so much more now.

"You shouldn't want me," she whispered.

"I know." He picked up his hat and started toward the door, but he would have to pass her.

He tried. He really did.

But her gaze locked with his, and when he reached her, he simply...stopped. She took his hat and set it back on the table. "Kiss me before you go, then."

He wanted to be gentle. He clasped her face and lowered his head. But the moment his lips met hers, he lost control. His mouth slanted over hers. When she clasped his lapels and pulled him against her, he groaned.

Her movement caused him to push her back against the

door. Her hands moved up his front and curled around his neck as he plunged his tongue into her mouth. She met his kiss eagerly, grasping at his nape and hair.

Sheff caressed her face, her neck, her collarbones. Their kisses were long and deep, relentless in their passion as they explored one another. They made inarticulate sounds, their bodies moving with each other to feel as much as possible.

She dug her fingers into his neck as he kissed down her neck. He licked the hollow at the base of her throat, and she moaned her approval.

Desperate to touch her bare flesh, he lifted her skirt and skimmed his hand along her thigh. She widened her stance, then lifted her leg to curl it about his waist in open invitation. He moved his hands to her backside and guided her other leg around him, lifting her so that he held her pinned against the door.

She raised her skirts, bunching them between their bodies. His rigid cock, constrained by his clothing, pressed against her wet heat. All he had to do was unbutton his fall and sink into her.

God, how he wanted that. But not here, not in a storage cupboard.

She ground against him and pulled his head up, her mouth claiming his as she squeezed her legs around him. Sheff pumped his hips, his body raging with need. He swung her around to the table, setting her on the edge.

He slipped his hand between her legs while he ravaged her mouth. She opened for him, her foot moving around his leg.

Stroking her flesh, he brought his fingers to her sex. He paused—his hand and their kiss—and looked into her eyes. "You must stop me if that's what you want."

"I do not want you to stop. I want you to make me come."

"Like this?" He found her clitoris and moved his fingertips over the sensitive bud, slowly at first, then with more pressure and speed.

"Yes," she hissed. Her eyes closed, and her head tipped back.

Sheff watched her face, desire and need etched into every contour. Her lips were parted as she whimpered with each stroke of his fingers. He pushed a finger into her wet sheath, gliding easily inside. He pumped once, twice. She cried out, and he kissed her, stealing the sound and devouring it for himself.

With two fingers, he thrust into her, curling them to find that elusive inner place that would drive her toward the brink. He could feel her muscles clenching as she sought release. Nothing had ever felt so good. So right.

But it wasn't enough. He wanted to do what she asked—to make her come. But in the most spectacular way possible.

"Lie back," he rasped, guiding her backward atop the table. Then he pushed her skirts up to her waist with his free hand, exposing her sex to him. He watched for a moment as he fucked her with his fingers. He'd never seen anything so arousing in his life.

Her hips moved with him, her body seeking whatever he would give her. Needing to taste her as well as give her even more, he bent his head and licked her clitoris.

She cried out his name and clutched at his head. He pushed at her thigh, making her open to him even more. She slid back on the table and braced her feet on the edge. Moving one hand to her backside, he held her as he drove his tongue deep into her sex.

Shuddering, her hips bucked up. He brought his hand around to her front and held her down, gently, as he slid his fingers into her once more, his lips and tongue teasing her clitoris until her body began to quiver.

Her muscles clenched, and she stiffened as her orgasm

exploded. A high-pitched keening sound filled the room, but she muffled it with her hand; at least, he assumed that was what she was doing. He didn't look, for he had a job to finish.

He moved his fingers inside her, licking and suckling her clitoris, until she began to calm. Then he kissed her mound, her thigh, her hip.

"I hope that kiss was satisfactory." He stared down at her sprawled atop the table, her eyes closed and her chest rising and falling.

"Quite," she murmured, her voice drunk with sexual satisfaction.

Sheff's cock was begging for release, but this was already so much more than he'd anticipated. "I should go."

She opened her eyes and bolted up. Her gaze dipped to his groin. "If you think I'm letting you leave like that, you would be wrong."

He arched a brow. "What do you suggest? I pleasure myself while you watch?"

Her eyes rounded, then narrowed to seductive slits. "That is a marvelous idea, actually. But I've my own plan." She pushed her skirts down and slid from the table. Moving to the door, she gave him a saucy smile. "Grab your hat and follow me."

Sheff bent to pluck his hat from where it had fallen to the floor. "What do you have planned?"

"Nothing you didn't already do to me." Her sultry expression made him groan as he imagined her mouth around his cock.

"If you insist."

Then he followed her from the cupboard and up the back stairs. She opened a door, and they arrived on a landing that looked familiar. He realized the other end was where he'd come up the stairs from the front door to her lodgings.

But she didn't lead him that way. She took him through

an archway to a corridor and opened the first door on the right. "My chamber. I doubt my mother is here as she is likely at Marcel's, so you may be as loud as you like."

Sheff closed the door behind him as he followed her inside. "Marcel?"

"Her lover." She began to loosen her hair, setting the pins on a dressing table on the opposite side of the room.

As her dark locks began to fall around her shoulders, Sheff stood stock-still. He'd had more sexual experiences than he could count, but this was somehow the most intimate act he'd seen. When her hair was down, she removed her earrings and put them on the dresser with the pins. Then she turned and ran her fingers through her wavy hair.

Sheff crossed the room in just a few strides and swept her into his arms, grunting just before he kissed her. She kissed him back—ravenously—as she pushed at his coat.

Tearing his mouth from hers, he stepped back to toss his coat away. Then he collapsed into a chair near the hearth and pulled his boots off. His stockings followed them to the floor, and when he looked up, he saw that Jo had undone the front of her gown. The bodice fell, exposing her stays. Her breasts pressed up against the top, but not in the revealing way they did in her ball gowns. Her costume for the Siren's Call was more modest, and her undergarments covered more of the flesh he so desperately wanted to see.

After pulling the gown over her head, she set the garment over the back of the small chair at the dressing table. Then she removed the petticoat and draped it atop the gown.

Lifting her hands behind her back, she began to pull at the ties of the corset. Sheff had undressed enough women to know what she was doing. He moved toward her. "Turn."

Without comment, she presented her back, and he made quick work of divesting her of the garment. She took it from him and casually dropped it to the floor. "It's almost as though you've done that before," she murmured, a playful smile teasing her lips.

"I've never enjoyed it as much as just then." And he meant that. His gaze dipped to her breasts, her nipples visible through the thin lawn of her chemise.

She took his hand and pulled him toward the end of the bed. "You are exceptionally handsome," she remarked as she plucked at his cravat, expertly loosening the knot before pulling the silk away from his neck and letting it fall to the floor.

"It's almost as though you've done that before," he said, clasping her waist, then massaging her hip.

She smirked at him. "Can we not discuss our past experiences? I can't think of anything more tedious. Especially at this moment. I'm only interested in right here. Right now."

"Agreed."

She unbuttoned his waistcoat, and he shrugged out of it. She pushed it from him, and neither of them made an effort to catch the garment before it hit the floor.

Tugging the hem of his shirt from his breeches, she put her hands beneath the garment and ran her palms over his abdomen. Sheff whisked the shirt over his head and threw it across the room. She explored his chest, her fingers moving over his flesh, pausing here and there. Leaning forward, she licked one of his nipples. He groaned and cupped her backside.

She dropped onto the bed and unbuttoned his fall. His cock jerked as she pushed the breeches down over his hips. She tugged them farther down until he was able to kick them off, leaving him nude.

"Lovely," she breathed as she caressed his hips and thighs, her hands coming close to his groin but not close enough.

Sheff could barely contain himself. He wanted nothing

more than to slide himself into her mouth and thrust back against her throat.

She curled her hand around his shaft finally, and he groaned low and long. He closed his eyes and let his head fall back as she stroked him. He had no idea how long she worked him, her hand moving faster, then slowing once more. It was the most delicious torture.

He felt her mouth close around the tip of his cock. He sucked in a breath and lightly clasped her head. She cupped his balls, and he thought he might come right then.

Opening his eyes, he tipped his head down to watch her take him more deeply into her mouth, her tongue gliding along the underside of his shaft. He twined his fingers in her hair, utterly enchanted as he watched her pleasure him. His balls tightened. He really was going to come in an embarrassingly short amount of time.

He pulled away from her. "Jo, I can't."

She blinked up at him, her lips parted. "Are you going to leave?"

"God, no. I'm just not going to come in your mouth. Not when I want so desperately to feel your sex around my cock. Unless you want me to go?"

"I have a new rule," she said, pulling her legs up and scooting backward up the bed. "You have to spend the night with me before you leave town." She crooked her finger at him as she pushed back the covers of the bed.

Sheff grinned as he fell onto the bed and crawled up to join her. "You do make the rules. And I am honor bound to follow them."

CHAPTER 14

A small part of Jo questioned the choice she'd made downstairs, but the vast majority of her wanted this. She wanted Sheff—in a way she'd never wanted anyone before.

He was going to leave, and when he returned, their fake betrothal would be over. Now was the time to give in to their mutual attraction and put it behind them. One night to satisfy their hunger and move on.

As he prowled up the bed toward her, she quivered with desire, her breasts tingling and her sex pulsing. She'd pulled the covers back, but hadn't slid between them.

His blue eyes were dark, riddled with storms. She saw passion and need, even stark lust as he unabashedly raked her with his gaze.

He clasped her ankle and skimmed his hand up her leg, his thumb sliding along her inner calf, her knee, and then moving beneath her chemise to stroke her thigh. He gripped her, squeezing her flesh, as he came over her, his body looming above hers.

Sheff braced his other hand beside her head. "I will pull out before I come."

She nodded, grateful someone was thinking clearly. She usually inserted a sponge, but things had progressed quickly. This hadn't been at all planned—at least not for her.

"Were you hoping this would happen tonight when you came to the club?" As soon as she uttered the question, she wished she hadn't. She didn't want to know if this was a premeditated seduction, probably one of dozens in his experience.

He shook his head, surprising her but also pleasing her more than she cared to acknowledge. "No, I came to tell you I was leaving. Everything else is…unexpected. But desperately wanted." He bent his head and kissed her, gently at first. She clasped his head and held him to her, allowing the joy of the moment to wrap around her.

His tongue dipped into her mouth, and she met him with her own. When his hand moved farther up her thigh, she parted her legs and arched her hips slightly, seeking his touch. He stroked her folds, stoking her desire.

Lifting his head, he looked down at her with such vulnerability that she couldn't draw a breath for a moment. "May I remove this?" He lifted his hand from the bed and touched the sleeve of her chemise.

"Please."

His hand left her sex as he pushed the garment up over her hips. She lifted from the bed and wriggled as he drew the chemise up her body and over her head. Her arms were up, her hands against the headboard, and he clasped her wrists in his hand, holding her there.

"Let me look at you," he breathed, his gaze moving down to her breasts. With his free hand, he caressed each one, settling on the left. He cupped her, massaged her, rolled her nipple between his fingers.

Jo arched up with a whimper as he toyed with her. If her hands were free, she would have put his head to her breast and urged him to suckle her. But she could not. "Sheff, please. I want your mouth."

"Here?" he asked, pinching her nipple hard enough to send a shaft of pleasure straight to her core, but not so much that it hurt.

"Yes."

He pulled on her nipple, teasing her relentlessly. "You're so beautiful. And so aroused. I could stare at you all night. Perhaps I will."

"Please, Sheff." She writhed beneath him and pulled against his grip on her wrists.

"I am enjoying your torment," he said rather wickedly. "I think you are too." But then he lowered his head and drew her nipple into his mouth, sucking on her flesh so she cried out. Pleasure built in her core, making her desperate for his touch.

He released her wrists and brought his hands to her breasts, cupping and caressing her as he feasted on her nipples. Eyes closed, Jo arched her neck and clasped his head, holding him tightly and tangling her fingers in his thick hair.

One of his hands trailed down to her sex, where he teased her clitoris before sliding his fingers into her sheath. Jo bucked up, moaning with ecstasy.

"Give me your cock," she demanded.

"In due time," he murmured at her breast as he used his teeth to gently score her nipple.

"*Now.*" She bent her legs and tugged at his shoulder. Then she reached down between them and searched for his cock. She would bloody well do this herself if she had to.

Sheff laughed as he moved up her body. He caught her hand and put it around his shaft. "You want this? Where?"

"In my pussy. With due *haste*." She arched her brow at him.

"Jo, I adore you," he said with a laugh before kissing her soundly.

Their hands worked together to position him at her sheath, then he thrust into her, one long, smooth glide that filled her to perfection. Jo curled her legs around him and sighed, her eyes closing in bliss.

"Yes, this," she whispered.

"Should I move, or is this enough?"

She opened one eye. "Moving would be nice, don't you think?" She rotated her hips against his, and he groaned loudly, his eyes shuttering briefly.

"God, Jo. I couldn't hold still if you begged me." He began to move, pumping into her with deep thrusts.

Jo muttered nonsensical things as they moved together, creating a delicious friction that sent her careening toward release. She worked to hold it back, to revel in this act with him. Digging her heels into his backside, she caressed his back, then brought his head down for a long, lingering kiss, their tongues mimicking the roll of their bodies.

He brushed her hair back from her face, and she opened her eyes to see him staring down at her. He thrust hard and deep. She cried out.

"Faster now," she said softly, pressing her feet into him, urging him.

He brushed his lips against hers and braced his hand on the bed as he drove hard and fast into her. Her orgasm was imminent, the darkness curling around her, pulling her inexorably into ecstasy.

She exploded with light and joy, her body going stiff as waves of pleasure held her aloft. A few more strokes, and then he was gone. His warm seed sprinkled over her abdomen, but she was mindless, not that she would have cared. It was necessary.

Somehow, she managed to find his cock with her hand, joining his to finish him as he cried out her name. It was several minutes before their bodies calmed. He slid to the side and pulled the covers over them both before cradling her in his arms. He kissed her forehead, her cheek, then her lips.

Jo stroked his cheek as they kissed, her body thrumming with a bone-deep satisfaction. That was, without question, the best sexual experience of her life. It was both wondrous and terrifying.

Because it would never happen again.

A dark, hollow sensation formed in her chest, as if a hole were opening. She didn't want that. She didn't want what it meant either, that she felt strongly about this man in her arms. Too strongly.

Their lips broke apart, and they were slightly breathless. He caressed her shoulder, and she burrowed her face against his warm neck, inhaling his spice and sandalwood scent.

What had he said just before he'd come into her?

Jo, I adore you.

He'd laughed as he said it, proving it didn't mean love or anything close to that. He was just in love with what she was saying and doing, with this particular moment in time.

Yes, she was in love with it too. That was acceptable. That was safe. Anything else was not.

Except she feared that "anything else" was already happening, that she'd grown too attached. She would miss him horribly, she realized. And she would miss their ruse.

But she would not miss certain Society events, she reminded herself. Or the people *in* Society. Namely, his mother. Yes, she would do well to keep all that at the forefront of her mind if she grew maudlin in his absence.

"Can I stay for a while?" he asked.

"I said you could stay the night." Perhaps there would be one more chance for intimacy before he left. But she wouldn't ask for it. She'd already demanded too much.

Neither of them wanted more than this. She needed to remember that.

~

Sheff somehow woke while it was still dark despite enjoying the best sleep of his life. He never slept with his sexual partners. But nothing had ever felt as right as surrendering to slumber while he held Jo in his arms.

He listened to her even breathing as he inhaled her citrus-and-floral scent. Her hair smelled particularly wonderful. And it was soft against his cheek. He smiled to himself.

Was this heaven? It had to be. At least as close to heaven as he would likely ever be. His chest swelled with unbridled joy. He would carry this moment with him forever.

"I love you," he whispered, not quite believing he had the courage to think it to himself, let alone say it.

Not that she could hear him as she slept. Which was the point. He would not tell her how he felt, for it wouldn't matter. She could not love him, nor did he expect his love to last.

So, he would savor this time they had. That meant not leaving until he said a proper goodbye.

Sheff skimmed his hand along her thigh and down her backside, over the soft curve of one cheek. Then back up, to the small of her back, where he explored the alluring hollow at the base of her spine. He dragged his fingertip up her back, swirling it over her soft flesh as he went.

She stirred and wiggled her backside against him. He was already aroused, but her movement made him hard as stone.

He brushed her hair from her neck and pressed his lips to the sensitive spot behind her ear. She sighed softly. But was she awake yet?

Caressing her shoulder, he kissed along her collarbone. He moved his hand down to her breast and gently cupped her. She felt so good in his hand, and she'd been so responsive last night. He rolled her nipple between his fingers.

"Sheff," she murmured.

"Jo," he whispered near her ear before he licked along the outer edge. She shivered against him. "Do you want me to stop?"

She shook her head, her body arching to encourage his hand on her breast.

He tugged her nipple, then squeezed the globe. She pushed her backside more firmly against his rigid cock.

"I'm afraid I couldn't resist," he said softly, nipping her earlobe, then laving it with his tongue. "I hope you don't mind."

"More." She sounded awake now, her voice still sultry but crisper as she roused from sleep.

He played with her breast a while longer, then moved his palm down her side, stroking her hip before he slid inward to her mound. She rolled to her back, and he massaged her clitoris, driving her to lift her pelvis. He teased her folds. She was already so wet. He groaned with need.

She turned toward him and pushed him back against the mattress. Putting her leg over his hips, she climbed on top of him. Her sable hair cascaded over her shoulders and breasts, the ends grazing her nipples. She gazed down at him, her lids heavy.

"You want to ride?" he asked as she ground her pelvis against his, igniting a fierce desire. Sheff clasped her hips.

"Mmm. I want to be in control." She wrapped her hand around his cock and stroked him several times.

Sheff cast his head back and closed his eyes, his attention entirely focused on her touch. He was desperate to drive into her, but he didn't. He would give her total control.

The heat of her sex engulfed the tip of his cock as she guided him into her. He opened his eyes just enough to watch her take him completely, her body settling against his. She was warm and tight around him. He closed his eyes again, reveling in her control.

She began to move slowly, her hips rocking gently over his. Sheff followed her lead, his body flooding with pleasure.

Her hands pressed down on his chest. He opened his eyes to see that hers were now closed. She increased her speed, rising and falling over him, lifting and grinding. He watched where their bodies were joined and felt a fresh rush of need.

Lifting his gaze, he became enchanted by the sway of her breasts. He reached up to cup them. She sucked in a breath, her eyes opening to slits as she leaned over him so he could take her nipple into his mouth.

She ground down hard against him, then quickened her pace, riding him hard and fast. He felt her stiffen, her muscles tightening. She was close.

Then she cried his name and put his hand between them to stroke her clitoris. She came apart, her body moving in a frenzy over his.

Sheff's orgasm raced to claim him. He threw his head back and shouted. Then he swore as he lifted her and turned their bodies.

He'd already started to come before he was able to break free of her. But had his seed yet escaped him and found her? He gripped his cock to finish, lights dancing behind his eyes as he fell back onto the mattress.

A few moments later, he heard her breathing begin to slow. "That was nearly a disaster," she said.

"I'm so sorry," Sheff said. "I wasn't thinking."

"Nor was I. Last night, I should have inserted a sponge."

"That's what you typically do?" he asked. "I often use a French letter."

"I've used those too, but the sponge is my preference. What a lovely conversation to have with a gentleman." She sounded as though she were smiling.

"I do not wish to sire any children out of wedlock. I think I've been successful so far."

"You *think?*"

"I am not aware of any children. I'd hope that their mother would have told me."

"What would you do if that happened?" She'd turned to her side to face him, her hand bracing her head as her elbow rested on the bed.

Sheff rolled to his side and met her gaze. "Panic?"

She rolled her eyes, her mouth curving into a smile. "Really. What would you do?"

He propped himself on his elbow, mirroring her position. "Care for the child the best I could."

"Not marry the mother?"

He coughed. "In most cases, that wouldn't be appropriate."

"Because they could not be a duchess someday. I fall into that category, don't I?"

"I don't think so." He imagined marrying her. The idea made his heart speed again. He took a deep breath. "I am very careful. I am sorry I wasn't just now. I highly doubt anything will come of it. I was outside your body before my seed released." He was almost completely certain.

"I'm not concerned. Besides, it's not as if I don't know how to…manage things if necessary."

He knew what she meant. The courtesans at the Rogue's

Den used a number of preventions. "Have you had to do that before?" he asked.

"No, and I hope I never do." She tucked her hair behind her ear with her free hand. "When will you leave?"

"Here or London?"

She smiled briefly. "Both, I suppose."

Though he was loath to depart her bed, he knew he must —and soon. "I should return home shortly. I need to pack. I don't imagine I'll be on my way until afternoon. Spears will be in a dither."

"Your valet?"

He nodded. "How will you manage things while I'm gone? Will you attend any Society events? You don't need to."

"I think I will—a few here and there. I can go with Min or Gwen. Or Tamsin. That will hopefully keep your mother at bay."

He narrowed his eyes slightly. "She is not to trouble you. If she does, you must write to me at once."

"And where will you be?"

"I'm going to visit Bane north of York, but then I'll travel to Weston. I don't know how long I'll be in the north. I suppose it depends on Bane." He locked his gaze with hers. "Min will help if you need it."

"I know." Her expression softened. "It's nice that you're visiting your friend while he's grieving." Her brow creased. "It must be a terrible time for him."

"I can't really imagine what he's feeling. I didn't even know he was going to marry Lady Isabel until he already had. It was all very strange." Sheff reached over and caressed her arm from shoulder to wrist. Her hand lay flat on the bed in front of her chest. "You're sure you want to attend events while I'm gone? You really don't have to."

"Just certain invitations—things like Sir Alfred's rout. I need to assure people that all is well between us, that we are madly in love." She fluttered her lashes at him and gave him a sultry smile.

Sheff's pulse sped once more as his heart flipped over in his chest. He *was* madly in love.

But it wouldn't last.

"Will you come to Weston in August?" He held his breath, hoping she would. But why? So they could continue what they'd started tonight? It wasn't a start. It was a fleeting moment. And by August, he would likely be back to his roguish ways.

"No. I need to be here in London. You cause your scandal however you like, and make sure I hear about it. Then I'll cry off as we planned."

Though that was what he'd intended, discussing it now filled him with an icy desolation. "I won't return to London until the new year. That will allow plenty of time for everything to fade away."

"I know this hasn't gone entirely as you'd hoped. I do hope it was worth your time. And money." Little pleats formed between her brows.

"I don't want you to worry about any of that. Every moment of this scheme has been a delight—for me. I have always enjoyed your company, and it's been my pleasure to know you better." That barely communicated how he felt, but it was enough.

"I'd say you've come to know me quite well," she said with a seductive smile, her brow smoothing. "Would you like to know me one more time before you go?" She put her hand to his chest and traced her finger around his nipple.

"God, yes." He growled as he leapt on her, pressing her back into the mattress.

She giggled as he claimed her mouth. Then he lost himself in her once more.

This time, he did not forget to leave her body. And it was

the hardest thing he'd ever done—right up until he walked out of her lodging onto the street.

He didn't say goodbye, nor did she. They simply waved. Then he turned and strode into the dawn light.

CHAPTER 15

o finished updating the ledger for the club and snapped it closed. It still felt strange to sit at her mother's desk in the study, though she'd been doing it more and more the past few weeks.

A week had passed since Sheff had left London. He'd sent over the rest of Jo's fee before departing. The two-hundred-and-fifty-pound banknote sat in a drawer in her dressing table.

She wasn't entirely sure why she hadn't taken it to the bank. Perhaps it was because things felt unfinished. They were still betrothed, even if they wouldn't be together again as an engaged couple. And they would remain betrothed until he did something that would prompt her to cry off. She couldn't help wondering exactly what and when that would be.

She hoped he'd arrived in Yorkshire and that he and Banemore were benefiting from their time together. In the past week, Jo had gone to the park with Min, Ellis, and Tamsin, spent an afternoon shopping at booksellers and speaking with publishers along Paternoster Row with Gwen, and attended the Phoenix Club assembly on Friday evening, though she hadn't danced with anyone and had left somewhat early.

There had been many questions about Sheff's departure—mostly directed to Min and the duchess. Jo assumed people hadn't asked her because they didn't know her. Or, perhaps more perniciously, it was because they preferred to avoid speaking with her. Whatever the reason, she was glad to not have to answer their questions.

Jo had only seen the duchess at the Phoenix Club, and it had been a brief interlude. She'd actually said it was good that Sheff had left town, that he likely needed time for contemplation and reflection. Jo took that to mean the duchess hoped he would change his mind about marrying Jo. The duchess was going to be *so* happy when the betrothal fell apart.

While that was annoying, Jo could only hope that things would be better for Sheff in the future, that perhaps the duchess would leave him be. She hoped the same for Min but feared that would not happen. The duchess continued to press her to wed, and Min continued to resist. She hadn't met anyone that was worth taking the risk of shackling herself for a lifetime. Jo could well understand her perspective.

The trip to Paternoster Row had been, by far, the best thing that had happened since Sheff had left. Jo's mind was churning with ideas of what she could do next armed with the small fortune Sheff had paid her.

She could open her own bookshop. Or she could help people, primarily women, to see their work published. Perhaps she could even become a publisher herself.

But first, she needed to speak with her mother about not taking over the club. It was time. And Jo was dreading the conversation.

Her mother came into the study then, as if summoned by Jo's thoughts. "Finished with yesterday's entries?"

Jo nodded as she stood. "It didn't take long."

"And where are you off to now?" her mother asked.

"Just to my chamber. I've a book to read." She'd purchased several during her outing with Gwen.

Her mother frowned. "I can't help noticing you've been doing more reading than usual—and spending more time by yourself. You appear to be moping. Since Shefford left town, if I'm being honest."

Jo gave her a wry look. "When are you never not honest?"

Chuckling, her mother moved away from the door toward the desk. "Sometimes I hold my tongue, but it is difficult. I am not going to do that now, however." Her gaze gentled, making her look more like the woman who'd cared for Jo her entire life, who sometimes was lost beneath the successful club owner. "Is there a chance you fell in love with Shefford?"

Jo winced inwardly. "No. I did fall in lust, if *I'm* being honest. But that's over now. I won't even see Sheff again until next year."

Her gaze skeptical, Jo's mother didn't immediately respond. When she did, she spoke quietly. "I hope you weren't ever truly hoping to marry him. And I don't say that because I am not an advocate of marriage. I mean that being wedded to him would come with a host of problems."

"No, I wasn't ever hoping that." That was absolutely true. "I feel sorry for his eventual wife having to deal with his mother."

"Amen to that," her mother said with a laugh. "Go on and read your book. You'll have less time for that when I go to Weston."

It was the perfect opening for Jo to say what she needed to. But now that the moment was here, she wasn't sure she had the courage. She clasped her hands in front of her and probably made some sort of terrible expression where she looked as though she were trying to soothe a patron of the club who'd just lost too much money. Probably because this was nearly as discomfiting as doing that.

"Mama, I need to tell you something." She moved from behind the desk.

Her mother's brows drew together. "Is something amiss?"

Jo blew out a breath, then took a deep one. "I am so glad you want to enjoy your life away from the Siren's Call, especially after all the years you've poured your heart and even your soul into it."

Taking a step toward Jo, her mother's brow furrowed even more. "You don't feel as though I've neglected you, do you? I have always tried to put motherhood before all else. Well, until you were old enough to not need me as much."

"I don't feel neglected in the slightest," Jo hurried to say. "On the contrary, you have been a wonderful mother. Which is why it's silly that I'm nervous to tell you what I must. I don't really want to take over the Siren's Call."

There was a silence in the air that seemed to weigh a stone at least. Jo couldn't immediately read her mother's expression. Her eyes shuttered, and her lips pursed. She looked confused. And perhaps mildly upset. Then surprise flashed in her gaze.

"Why haven't you said something before now?" her mother asked, an edge of irritation in her tone.

Jo thought of her mother's advice on marriage and her expectation that Jo would follow in her footsteps with the club and realized she'd been building her life on emulating her mother. "I admire you so very much, Mama," she said with great emotion. "I've always wanted to be like you, to make you proud."

"I could not be prouder of you, my girl," her mother said

with a fierce warmth. "But you don't want to run the Siren's Call?"

Jo shook her head. "I don't feel the same pull toward it as you do. I was hoping that might change, but now that I have the financial means to do something else, I realize I don't want to be tied to the club."

"Is that how you see it?" her mother asked, sounding a bit agitated. "It has never been a burden to me. I'm sorry you see it that way since its success has provided you with anything you could need or want." She turned her head toward the window, her jaw clenched. "I didn't know you disliked it so much."

Jo rushed forward to touch her mother's arm. "I don't dislike it. In fact, I like working there. It has taught me so much, including the fact that I don't want to be responsible for it. I am not passionate about running a gaming club, Mama."

Her mother looked back to Jo, her expression gentling. "I didn't realize. And I should have."

"I should have told you before now."

"What is it you *are* passionate about? Especially now that you have this money from Shefford."

"You know I like to read," Jo replied. "And attend literary salons. I should like to have my own house where I can host such events, but I don't know if anyone will come since I will be a spinster with a minimum of social connections." Really, just what she'd made through her father and at the salons she attended.

Her mother made an inelegant sound and waved her hand. "Nonsense. Even without Shefford, you were on your way to making excellent connections. You became friends with a baroness, a viscountess, the daughter of a duke, and—I think—a duchess. You'll continue to develop your social circle, and your salons will be legendary." She had such an expression of intense pride that Jo's throat caught.

"Thank you," she managed to say. "I also thought I might like to help writers, particularly women, get their work published. I'm not sure how I'd go about that, but I'd like to try."

"You could open a library or become a publisher yourself," her mother said with considerable enthusiasm. "It wouldn't be easy as a woman, but neither was opening a gaming club." She winked at Jo, and all of Jo's anxiety melted away.

"You truly don't mind?" Jo asked, daring to hope that all would be well.

"I confess I was upset at first, which I'm sure you could see. I was just...surprised. I should have seen that you weren't excited about taking over the club. And I shouldn't have expected you to be. Just because you are good at something—and you are *excellent* at managing things at the club—doesn't mean it's what you want to do. Neither should you do something because *I* want you to." She cocked her head and smiled at Jo, then held out her arms. "Come here." Those were the two words she always said when inviting Jo for a hug.

Jo nestled against her mother and wrapped her arms around her waist. As her mother's arms came around her, she closed her eyes briefly, grateful for this woman who had always cared for her above all else. "Thank you, Mama." They hugged for a few moments before stepping apart.

"But what about the Siren's Call?" Jo asked. "You should still take time to do what you want, and I am more than happy to manage things this summer when you go to Weston."

"I do appreciate that, dear. The time has come for me to find an actual manager, but it must be a woman, of course."

She briefly tapped her finger against her lip. "Someone like Lady Evangeline at the Phoenix Club. Or Lady Warfield, who manages the finances there. Ideally, it would be a combination of the two."

"We'll find someone," Jo said, thinking of Ellis. She wouldn't be the combination Mama was looking for, but she could do anything behind the scenes.

"We will indeed," her mother said. "Now, take yourself off, as I've correspondence to complete."

"Yes, Mama." Jo stepped toward the door, then glanced back as her mother sat behind her desk. A surge of joy passed through Jo as she thought of her mother's encouragement.

She left the office thinking it was nice not to be dwelling on Sheff. Except now she was.

Her mother's question came back to her. It was possible that she'd fallen in love with Sheff. But she would just as easily fall out of it.

~

Sheff had been at the Grove, his father's estate outside Weston, for a few days now. And he was not alone.

Much to Sheff's surprise, when he'd arrived after visiting Bane, his father had been in residence. Sheff wasn't sure when the last time was that his father had visited the Grove in the summer. It had been several years, at least. He typically stayed in London until the very end of the Season, then traipsed off to a series of house parties that saw him into the autumn.

This year, however, he'd set up residence in the very place Sheff had been hoping to find peace and solitude so he could determine what to do with the rest of his life that would not see him ending up like his father.

That his father was here to witness and even participate in Sheff's ruminations was perhaps the most ironic thing ever.

They'd spent the last two days riding, playing cards, and going their own way in the evening. The duke had left every night without a word as to where he was going. Sheff was all but certain he was having a liaison.

Perhaps his father's presence wasn't *the* most ironic thing. It could also be that they were engaging in activities together, which was more than Sheff could say for his time with Bane. The man who had once been Sheff's closest friend spent most of his time closeted in his study. Sheff had only coaxed him to leave the house once. Every effort he'd made to engage Bane or to provide support and friendship had been rebuffed. Then, when Sheff had suggested that Bane come to Weston to spend time with him and their friends, to perhaps heal, Bane had told him to leave.

Needless to say, Sheff had spent a great deal of time contemplating his own situation, not that doing so had brought him any closer to determining what he wished to do next.

Well, besides ruin his betrothal. He needed to come up with that scheme, but he had time. Which was good, because the idea of being caught with another woman made him decidedly uncomfortable. He didn't want any woman but Jo.

Hopefully by August, he would be over this infatuation and feel differently.

The duke strode into the breakfast room, appearing fresh and eager. He rubbed his hands together before approaching the sideboard and heaping his plate with items from the buffet.

He sat at the table with Sheff, and the footman poured coffee. He also refilled Sheff's cup.

"Morning, Sheff. Another ride this afternoon?" the duke asked as he slathered butter and jam on his toast.

"I'm game if you are. You seem inordinately pleasant this morning. Indeed, you've been that way the entire time I've been here. What's going on?"

The duke chuckled. "Am I that unpleasant usually?"

"You are…challenging," Sheff said judiciously. "I also don't spend this much time with you in London. Sometimes, I only see you when I'm called in for rescue."

Grimacing, the duke took a bite of toast, then chewed it thoughtfully. After he swallowed, he said, "I would argue that you don't need to rescue me. I'm man enough to suffer my mistakes."

"That may be, but I am trying to protect the family's reputation, primarily so Min can make the marriage she wants."

"Bah. She doesn't want to marry. But then, neither do you." He sipped his coffee, eyeing Sheff over the rim of the cup. "Still can't imagine why you're betrothed to that chit."

"She's not a chit," Sheff said, his ire pricked.

The duke arched a still-dark brow. "I have struck a nerve. Perhaps you really do have feelings for her. Is that why you're moping around here? Why don't you go back to London?"

"Because Jo is busy with the Siren's Call, and I…wanted a respite. I was visiting with Bane."

"Yes, I know. Though, you said that was a waste of time."

That wasn't exactly what Sheff had said, but he wouldn't correct him. "Bane is struggling with his grief."

The duke's brow furrowed as he nodded. He ate his breakfast for several minutes while Sheff drank his coffee.

When the duke spoke, his words surprised Sheff. "He didn't want to marry that girl—Malton's daughter. But his father forced the issue."

Sheff had suspected as much, but Bane had never said.

"He didn't even tell me he was betrothed. And we were together in Weston just before he traveled north to be wed."

"When he was caught with that other chit," the duke said. "I'm sure Banemore has many regrets. You can let them drag you into darkness, or you can forge your way through and find peace with yourself."

Sheff had never heard his father speak in such a manner. "Is that what you've done?"

The duke swallowed a bite, then sat back in his chair, surveying Sheff for a moment. "You presume I have regrets."

"Don't you?" Sheff couldn't help gaping at him.

"Plenty, and if I were a stronger man, I would stop doing things I regret almost daily, but alas, I am not. I have made peace with who I am."

"A drunken, carousing, selfish libertine?"

The duke dabbed at his mouth with his serviette before returning it to his lap and taking another bite of toast.

"I didn't mean to offend you," Sheff said. "I was only speaking the truth."

"You are right to describe me in that way." The duke shrugged, but there was a sadness etched into his features that Sheff hadn't ever seen before. "It is what makes me happy."

"You don't seem happy," Sheff observed softly, though he had appeared happier here in Weston. Perhaps it was London—or more accurately, *who* was in London—that provoked him to misbehave. "I am often left with the impression that you are seeking something you can't have. But then I remember that you had it and tossed it aside in favor of your appetites."

"You mean your mother?" The duke laughed, but it was hollow. "If you think I had happiness with your mother, you are mistaken."

"I should have said you had the chance for it. Instead, you chose to continue your rakish ways after you wed."

The duke pushed what little food was left around his plate. "Not at first. I *was* a rake when I wed your mother, but I fell so deeply in love with her that no other woman could compare." He scowled briefly. "I was a fool, for though she'd played the coquette and charmed me during our courtship, she did not love me. It was my title she coveted."

Sheff's chest tightened. What was his father saying? His whole life, Sheff had understood the divide between his parents. His father had been a horrible rogue and had continued as one after marrying Sheff's mother. And she struggled with being married to him.

"You loved her? And she did not love you?" Sheff could scarcely wrap his mind around that. He wasn't sure he could believe his father.

"The duchess would rather you not know that. Just as she would rather you not know that she is the reason I am the way I am. Not entirely—I fully acknowledge that I have made my own choices." His jaw quivered, and he looked away for a moment. When his gaze found Sheff's again, his eyes were damp. "When I fell in love with her, she saw her opportunity to be a duchess. That was her goal. She didn't want me as a person."

There was truth in his words. Sheff had seen firsthand that social status and position were more important to his mother than anything else when forging a union. She hated that he'd chosen Jo because she wasn't appropriate. It made sense that she would choose her own husband with calculation. Cold calculation, apparently. Sheff could hear the pain in his father's voice.

"I'm sorry," Sheff murmured.

"Her rejection was devastating. I wanted to find solace—

even love—elsewhere. I'm still looking." The duke smiled sadly.

"Did you not even have that with Ellis's mother?" Sheff asked, deciding that as long as his father was sharing secrets, they could address the most obvious one.

His father's brows rose sharply then his lips flattened. "I *did* want that with Ellis's mother, which I've explained. *Your* mother is Ellis's mother."

Sheff gripped the edge of the table. "What?"

"I know you and countless other people think Ellis is my daughter, but she is not." Sheff recalled what Jo had told him, that Ellis had insisted she was not the duke's daughter.

"Does Ellis know?"

He shook his head. "Only that she isn't my daughter. She asked me a year or two after she came to live with us, and I swore to her that I was not. But I could not tell her the truth. That was a condition your mother made when I convinced her to allow Ellis to live with us."

Sheff tried to make sense of this incredible revelation and could not. "I don't understand. Who were Ellis's parents, then?"

"When your mother fell pregnant the second time—you were a few years old—I knew the child could not be mine. We did not share a bed once she was carrying you. I don't know who Ellis's father is, nor do I care. I offered to raise the child as mine, but your mother refused. She was furious to have been caught in her infidelity, and she wanted to give the child away. I arranged for friends of the family who hadn't been able to have a child of their own to adopt her."

"*You* arranged?" For his wife's illegitimate child to have a family. To say Sheff was shocked by all this was an understatement of massive proportions.

"I wanted to make sure this poor child would be loved,

and though I would have loved her—I actually do love Ellis as a parent ought, I think—your mother refused to even try."

Poor Ellis. "And then Ellis's adoptive parents died," Sheff whispered.

"Yes, and I insisted we take her in," the duke said firmly. "Your mother fought me on that as well, but I was adamant. Sometimes, I think it was the wrong decision given the way your mother treats her, but she and Min have such a close bond. Even you do too."

"I think of her as a sister," Sheff said. "Because I assumed she was."

"And so she is." His father smiled wryly. "Just not from the parent you thought."

Nearly everything Sheff had believed about his father and mother, about the dynamics of their family, blew apart. It was no wonder everything had always felt so chaotic. They'd been living in a battle zone for practically Sheff's entire life. How had it taken him so long to flee in search of peace? "But you and Mother must have reconciled...unless Min is not your child either?"

"Min is our child. After being unfaithful and birthing Ellis, your mother was most contrite. I'd long wanted a spare to go with my heir, or a daughter—I didn't particularly care which. I just wanted more children. I always envisioned a house full of joy, especially when I fell in love with your mother. She saw it as her duty to give me a second child, and so she did. We have not shared a bed since."

Sheff's heart ached for this man who'd been utterly rejected by the woman he'd loved. "Do you love her still?"

"Heavens, no. She quite killed that with her treatment of me. I finally understood there was no hope when she became pregnant with Ellis. Then, watching the way she treats Ellis..." The duke pursed his lips, and his jaw clenched with anger. "I can truly say that I loathe her now. I'm sorry to have to say that to you, but you deserve the truth."

His mind reeling, Sheff released the table and laid his hand atop it. What he wouldn't give for a glass of something strong. Gin, perhaps. "I wish you'd told me sooner."

"As much as I detest your mother, I never wanted to spoil your relationship with her."

"But it was at the expense of your relationship with *me*. Doesn't that mean something?"

The duke's eyes filled with tears once more. He blinked them away and wiped his hand over his face. "I suppose a small part of me still loves your mother—at least enough to not want her children to hate her."

A sadness settled inside Sheff. He was somehow even more petrified of marriage than ever. His father had fallen in love and wed believing a beautiful life lay in front of him. He'd been so wrong. "I think you've just confirmed that I should not wed."

"You've changed your mind about Miss Harker? I thought you were in love. You are—at your core—a romantic like me, I think." He smiled. "I was hoping you would fall in love, and it seems you have. Your betrothed can't be like your mother."

No, Sheff couldn't imagine Jo entering into a marriage because she wanted a title or money or anything but love. And she didn't even want that—marriage or love.

Sheff hadn't thought he did either. But knowing what he knew now, could he take the same risk his father had taken?

"Why did you choose to be a libertine?" Sheff asked.

"As I explained, I was looking for love, or at least comfort. I wanted to feel wanted. And I knew how much your mother hated my behavior. I'm not proud of wanting to provoke her, but there it is."

Sheff had done the same thing with his fake betrothal

scheme. He'd wanted to provoke his parents. In doing so, he'd unearthed secrets he'd never imagined.

His father shrugged. "Being a libertine is now who I am."

"You could change." Sheff realized he was addressing his own fear with that statement. He was afraid of being like his father, worried that he was already on that path. But now that he knew the truth about his father, he had to reassess that assumption. Perhaps Sheff could choose not to be that way. He'd already successfully mastered celibacy.

Of course, that was easy when you only wanted the one person you couldn't have.

The duke blinked. "Why would I change?"

"Because the drinking is going to get you into serious trouble. Or kill you. And why not just take a mistress? Someone long term. I thought perhaps that was what you'd done here since you're gone every night."

Very small swaths of pink slashed briefly up his cheekbones. "I have met someone to warm my bed while I'm here."

"Perhaps she does more than that?" Sheff could hope. With his father's revelations, Sheff wanted nothing more than for him to find—and receive—love.

"I'm always afraid to find out," the duke whispered, once again shocking Sheff with his honesty.

"Perhaps it's time to take a risk again," Sheff said, wondering if he should do the same. With Jo. He could tell her how he felt. And then what? Marry? The fear he'd felt a moment ago had not really dissipated. Even if his father was right that he was a romantic, Sheff wasn't entirely convinced.

"Perhaps," his father murmured. "But I'll still have to return to London at some point."

"Yes, but I think it's time you and Mother lived apart. Other couples do this—Wellesbourne's parents lived in different cities. Find Mother a new house somewhere fashionable."

The duke barked a laugh. "She will never consent to that. Managing Henlow House was one of the reasons she wed me. And the Duchess of Wellesbourne was—wrongly—vilified for taking their daughters and living separately. She was called a pariah for not standing by her husband. Your mother would not want to chance that happening to her."

"I'll speak to her," Sheff said with determination. "I'll find her a new house."

His father's face creased into a deep frown. "No, Sheff. This is one mess I won't let you tidy. Perhaps it *is* time I make some changes. But first, I've a party to host."

"You're having a party here?" Sheff asked.

"Yes, in a few days. This can be my last event of debauchery." He waggled his brows. "You must join in, though I can't promise there will be a great many people your own age. I'll see what I can do to rectify that since you are here."

"It's all right. I don't need to attend your party. Honestly, I'm not in the mood for debauchery."

"You do love Miss Harker, then?" his father asked.

Sheff avoided a direct response, saying only, "It won't last."

The duke frowned. "Why not?" He held up a hand. "I think I know the answer—you expect to be like me. I can assure you that you are not. My choices are the result of events that happened to me. They have not happened to you. You may have rakish tendencies, but you are conscientious and caring. You've gone out of your way to protect your sisters from my behavior while I've not thought enough about how I may affect them."

Sheff supposed that was all true. But what if his fear wasn't so much that he was like his father, it was that marriage was a battleground? That was all he'd ever observed. Now that he knew the reasons behind his parents' chaos, he could rationally see that he was not necessarily destined to suffer the same fate. Especially not if he and his wife loved one another. When he was with Jo, he felt something he never had before—a sense of rightness and belonging, harmony, even.

"I wasn't even sure that I knew what romantic love was until I met Jo," Sheff said quietly. "I assumed I was incapable of feeling that."

His father's gaze turned fierce, but there was affection too. "Do not think that you don't have the free will and ability to be a loving, devoted husband. That's all I wanted to be," he added softly.

Sheff's heart cracked. "Perhaps it isn't too late for you to find that."

His father smiled—it was the warmest expression Sheff could remember seeing on him in some time. "I had given up hope, my boy, but I am beginning to think you may have restored it."

Perhaps it wasn't too late for Sheff either. He wanted what his father had been denied—a loving partner, a joyous family. Listening to him talk about his dreams and knowing they hadn't come true was gut-wrenching, but at least his father had tried. He'd taken the risk, and while it had failed, he was still here.

"You don't regret marrying Mother?" Sheff asked, recalling what he'd said earlier about not having regret.

"Never, for then I wouldn't have you and Min. Or Ellis, even." The duke gave him a pointed look. "My only advice to you is to be as certain as you can that your love is reciprocated, that your expectations match that of your bride. Otherwise, your romantic ideals will be dashed, and I couldn't bear if that happened to you too."

That was the problem—Sheff wasn't certain at all.

CHAPTER 16

On a Thursday morning in late June, Jo was resetting tables and chairs in the common room at the Siren's Call. In a few days' time, her mother would leave for Weston, and Jo would be fully in charge of the club. She didn't mind, for it was a temporary situation, just for this summer. They'd hired a bright and enthusiastic woman a fortnight ago, and so far, she showed promise as a future manager for when Jo's mother was not present.

That very woman came from the kitchen, a pencil stuck into the knot of light brown hair atop her head. Edith Henshawe was thirty years old and had worked as a governess, a teacher at a school for girls, acting headmistress at that school, and then decided she no longer wanted to work with children. She'd responded to Jo's mother's advertisement in the newspaper, eager to try something new. Though Jo's mother had been hesitant at first, Edith's references were excellent, and what she didn't possess in knowledge, she was keen to learn. She'd already proven herself to be clever and quick.

"Sorry to disturb you, Jo," she said, glancing at a ledger in her hand. "I'm preparing the list for the pantry and don't see that there are any potatoes. But that cannot be, can it?" She looked at Jo, her brows pitched into a V over her moss-green eyes. "We just purchased some the other day."

The cook did most of the shopping for the kitchen. "I do recall that. Perhaps the cook has stored them somewhere odd. Or someone put them away who does not know where they are typically kept. I would wager that's what happened." It would not be the first time.

Edith nodded. "I'll look more thoroughly." She smiled, then hastened back to the kitchen.

"She's doing very well," Jo's mother said, coming into the common room.

"I agree." Jo set the final chair at its rightful table and faced her mother. "You may travel to Weston in a few days without a care."

Jo's mother laughed. "I will always care, but I will not worry. I would not have even without Edith since you are here." She exhaled. "Are you still going to search for a small terrace to lease? I can't believe you are going to leave our household. You don't need to."

"I do if I wish to establish myself as a woman of independent means who hosts literary salons," Jo said shrewdly but with a smile.

"I understand. I will miss you." Her mother pulled a chair from one of the tables and sat. "I did wonder if I should not go to Weston. Not because of the club, but because I will miss you. And it seems you may need me just now." She sent Jo a searching look. Without words, she was conveying her concern about how Jo was managing since Sheff had left.

"I am no longer moping," Jo scoffed. She moved to join her mother at the table, taking the chair next to hers. "I want you to go. It's only for a couple of months."

"Or less if I hate it." Jo's mother wrinkled her nose. "I

sincerely hope Sheff's mother won't be at their estate. I hadn't even realized they had one near Weston until you told me the other week. I would have told Marcel to find a different seaside village."

"I can't help thinking that is not just because of the way she's behaved during this betrothal scheme," Jo said tentatively. "It seems to me there is more to it—the uninteresting story you've never shared with me about how you know the duchess."

Her mother frowned at the table. "I don't know that I want to share it. Sometimes things are better left in the past."

"Except it isn't in the past since you both dislike each other. And the duchess's treatment of me goes beyond not liking me as her son's choice of wife. There is something… personal to it." Jo hadn't shared everything the duchess had said with her mother—especially not the woman's comments regarding Jo's parents.

"It is personal." Jo's mother's lip curled. She lifted her gaze to Jo's. "When I tell you this, please don't think poorly of your father. That is the reason I didn't want to share the history."

Jo's gut clenched. How did her father play into this? She feared she might already know. "Did he have an affair with her?"

"Yes. When I was expecting you. I was rather devastated, actually." She said that matter-of-factly, but Jo could imagine there had been plenty of emotions when it had happened.

"That was cold of him." Jo would always love her father, but learning this was upsetting, to say the least.

"He has always been a hedonist," her mother said with a shrug. "I was young and foolish. I thought he would give all that up when we wed because I believed he loved me. And he did. I think he still does. But, as he explained to me once, he was not meant to be monogamous."

Jo thought of her mother expecting a child and discovering her husband had been unfaithful. "I'm sorry that happened to you, Mama." Then she thought of the Duchess of Henlow and her stringent expectations. "I'm also shocked the duchess would do such a thing."

"She is no saint, regardless of what she'd have people believe. What's worse is I believe she might have had a child as a result of their liaison. She was gone from Society for months. It could just have been a coincidence, but she wasn't in London at all for the entire Season."

Considering what Jo knew of the duchess, she wondered why the woman would choose to miss an entire Season—unless she had to. "If true, that is worse." Jo wasn't sure she'd ever be able to speak to the woman again without wanting to throw her past mistakes in her face. How dare she say Jo's parents—particularly her mother—weren't good enough when she had betrayed her own family?

Jo counted back the years. Sheff would have been a small child when this happened, and Min would not yet have been born. Jo sucked in a breath. Was Min Jo's half sister?

"What?" her mother asked, blinking at Jo.

"I was just thinking of the timeline and wondering if Min is my half sister, but she's too young if the duchess was expecting while you were. Her child would be close to my age."

"If the child even lived," her mother said. "And she likely had it somewhere far outside London. The child could be anywhere."

Or it could be living under the woman's roof. Jo thought of Ellis's age—she was just a few months younger than Jo. What if she wasn't the duke's illegitimate child, but the duchess's? And what if she was Jo's half sister? Ellis's blonde hair *was* a bit like Jo's father's...

"I don't understand why the duchess wouldn't just have passed her child off as her husband's," Jo noted.

Her mother shrugged. "That is strange, but I don't think the duchess possesses a natural amount of reason. She seems ruled by her emotions, and appearances mean far too much to her. It may be that she couldn't even stand the thought of raising an illegitimate child, even if it came from her womb."

That certainly made sense considering how the duchess treated Ellis, as if she were anathema. Did Ellis know? "Does Papa know about this child?" Jo asked.

Her mother shook her head. "I never said anything to him, and he's never indicated awareness that the duchess was with child. Their liaison was short-lived."

Jo didn't want to voice her suspicions about Ellis. None of this was her business. Especially since she wasn't marrying Sheff.

But what if Ellis was her half sister? Wouldn't that be Jo's business? Rather, Jo's *family*?

Her mother stood. "I've much to do today. I'm just glad you are not actually marrying Shefford. And I'm pleased to see you are recovered from your tendre." She gave Jo a warm smile, then departed the common room.

Jo organized the candles on the tables, replacing them as needed, then went upstairs to their lodgings. She was going to miss living here, but it was time she embraced her independence—and spinsterhood.

She only hoped that was what she would be—a spinster—because over the past few days she'd begun to worry she might end up in another category: unwed mother. Her courses were late, but they were not always the most reliable, so she was not going to worry yet.

She arrived on the landing that led to the entrance hall where she encountered Mrs. Rand. "I was just coming to fetch you," the housekeeper said. "You've a caller. Lady Minerva Halifax."

"You can just call her Min to me, if you like," Jo said. "She's a friend."

"I will try to remember that. It's odd that you would call someone like her friend, but I suppose she must be a decent sort if you like her."

"Not all nobles are stiff and condescending." Jo thought of the contrast between Min and her mother. They could not be more different. She would also compare them to Tamsin and Gwen, but neither of them had been born noble. Or had they? Both had viscounts for grandfathers. Or barons. Or something. In fact, if Jo remembered, she herself had a great-grandfather who was the younger brother of a viscount. Or a baron. Or something. She didn't know because it had never mattered. And it still didn't.

Nobility was a construct and had nothing to do with character. That was what mattered.

"Shall I bring tea?" Mrs. Rand asked.

"It's a bit early, I think. But thank you for offering." Jo made her way to the sitting room where Min stood at the window looking down at Coventry Street below.

"You're alone?" Jo asked. "Where's Ellis?"

Min turned from the window. Her expression was tight, and Jo could see there was something wrong. "I came with my maid, but she's waiting downstairs. Ellis was engrossed in a book. Also, I didn't tell Ellis why I wanted to come. I haven't told anyone yet, but I assume the gossip will spread imminently."

Jo gestured for Min to sit, then took a chair. She clasped her hands on her lap. "What gossip is this?" She braced herself, presuming it could be Sheff. Though, she hadn't expected him to make his move this soon. The Season was not quite over. There were still enough people in London to make a meal of the gossip.

"I received a letter from the housekeeper at the Grove. She writes to me monthly to tell me what's happening." Min shrugged. "We have a fond relationship. She says my father has been in residence, which is shocking on its own, along with Sheff. Did you know he was there?"

"Yes. He's written to me a couple of times." Jo had not yet written to him. She didn't know why. Perhaps it was the short, perfunctory nature of his letters. He wrote of the weather, his travels, the latest history he read concerning the fall of Rome. He had not mentioned his father at all.

Min pressed her lips together. "I know your marriage to him is a business arrangement, but I wonder if you may want to rethink that after you hear what I say."

Sheff had initiated the next phase of their scheme then. Perhaps he simply hadn't been able to control himself. He'd made it clear to her that he saw himself as a profligate. Apparently, he was right.

"What happened?" Jo asked. "Please don't prevaricate. I'm well aware of your brother's habits."

"Does your arrangement include him continuing to behave in that way? I should think he would at least try to curb his proclivities while you are betrothed and newlywed. You can't want to live with that kind of scandal. It's torture." She looked away, her jaw working.

"Because of your parents?" Jo asked softly.

Min nodded stiffly. "I would not wish a marriage like my parents have on anyone, even someone going into it with no romantic expectations. I wanted you to hear about what happened from me so that you are not surprised. There was a party at the Grove several days ago. It seems Sheff was *with* a pair of women."

"By 'with,' I surmise you mean he was intimate with

them?" Jo asked, disturbed to feel her chest constricting in an almost painful way.

"He appeared to be. The housekeeper said he was seen in the garden with them. They were draped over him. Then she said she saw a woman outside his bedchamber late that night." Min's eyes flashed with ire. "I'm so angry with him for behaving like that. I know you don't have romantic feelings for him, but I can't imagine you want to be married to someone like that."

Jo formulated a reason as to why she would marry him, but was there any reason for her to continue to mislead Min? She could not think of a single one, not when the end of their betrothal was now imminent.

Meeting her friend's gaze, Jo took a deep breath. "I hope you won't be terribly angry, but it's time I told you the full truth. I was never going to marry Sheff. He made me a proposal several weeks ago—that I pretend to be betrothed to him for the remainder of the Season."

Min gaped at her. "The entire betrothal was fake? With my grandmother's ring and an expensive ball?"

"Yes." Jo couldn't help cringing. She and Sheff had suffered doubts all along the way, but they'd kept on with it. And for what? All it had served to do was make them fall into a torrid mutual attraction that had resulted in a night Jo would never forget. Especially if she had a baby as a reminder.

No, she would not think about that. It was far too early for her to make that assumption. Indeed, she was currently cramping in her lower abdomen. Her courses were likely about to begin.

Min stood and stalked around the room, her hands moving wildly as she talked. "What could Sheff possibly have hoped to gain from doing this? He could at least have chosen someone our mother approved of. Then she wouldn't have directed her frustration on me and increased her efforts to see me wed." She put a hand on her hip and faced Jo. "Do you know how many dances and promenades I have had to suffer the last several weeks?"

"I'm so sorry." Jo hated that Min was upset, that she was hurt. "I value our friendship more than anything. I hated lying to you."

Min frowned, then threw her hands up in the air before reclaiming her seat in a huff. She glowered at Jo. "What could you possibly have benefited from this escapade?"

"Money," Jo replied frankly. "Sheff offered me a life-changing sum that will allow me to be independent. I didn't particularly want to take over the Siren's Call from my mother, and now I don't have to."

Min blinked. "Well. That is both frustrating as the sister of the man who paid someone to pretend to be his betrothed and wonderful as the friend of the woman who now has the freedom she deserves. But mostly, I am envious," she said quietly, looking down at her lap for a moment.

"Oh, Min, don't be. Things will work out for you. They must." Even if Jo had no idea how that would be. It wouldn't be as easy for Min to choose an independent life, if that was what she truly wanted. "At least you aren't being forced to wed."

"Not yet." She looked intently at Jo. "What will happen now?"

"The plan was for Sheff to do something away from London that would prompt gossip. Something that would make it easy—and smart—for me to cry off. He chose me instead of someone from Society because he believed I would be able to survive the scandal. Someone like you would be ruined."

"*You* may be ruined," Min said.

Jo shrugged. "In what way? I won't be invited to balls?

Boo-hoo. People will give me the cut direct? They already do."

Min grimaced. "Do they?"

"Quite a few since the fake betrothal." Jo did not share how much it bothered her, not when she'd invited those reactions by daring to become engaged to marry the heir to a dukedom. And she would not moan to Min about it, not after keeping the truth from her. "I could use your help making it known that I will be crying off due to Sheff's behavior."

"I can do that." Min cast her eyes toward the ceiling. "My mother will be furious."

"Or not." Jo's social status notwithstanding, she was also the daughter of her former lover. But Jo wouldn't share that with Min, nor would she reveal her mother's inkling that the duchess may have borne an illegitimate child. "Your mother is likely relieved to be rid of me."

"True," Min replied. "When do you want me to tell her about you crying off?"

"The gossip isn't yet making the rounds here in town?" Jo asked. Min shook her head. "As soon as it does, I will begin telling people—mostly the patrons of the Siren's Call, as those are who I mainly see—that I am no longer betrothed. Then you can tell your mother." Jo brushed a hand along her cheek. "I'll find a time to tell everyone else—our friends, I mean—about the scheme."

"They will understand," Min said. "I do. Despite my initial anger, I really do." She laughed, surprising Jo. "Here, I thought I was delivering unpleasant news, but you've been expecting this."

Yes, but what Jo hadn't expected was how much it hurt. Apparently, she was not yet over her "tendre." She began to worry that it would take much longer than she thought.

Perhaps even forever. The thought of Sheff with another woman made her ache. It also made her angry—at him and at herself. She should not have expected anything different. Especially since this had been part of the plan all along.

Couldn't plans change? Jo had veered from taking over the Siren's Call. What if she also decided marriage wouldn't be terrible? Even her mother had endorsed the idea for the sake of having a child. But Jo didn't want to marry Sheff just because she was carrying—*if* she was carrying. She would marry him because she wanted to. Because she'd fallen in love with a man who made her laugh and feel special, a man who cared for others and wanted the same thing she did: the freedom to choose for himself.

Except she wasn't going to marry him. A change in the plan would have to be amenable to both of them, and he didn't want that.

"I'm glad you came," Jo said, hoping they would remain friends even after she struck out as an independent spinster, though she would understand if they could not. The hardest part would be staying friends with the sister of the man she loved.

~

*S*heff set the letter from Jo on the table in the library where he'd taken tea after riding along the beach. It was the first letter he'd received from her. And almost certainly the last.

He should have written to her about the party and the gossip that had spread, but he'd been too angry and upset. Because he hadn't been with any woman, let alone two. That hideous Mrs. Lawler—the very same woman who'd caught Bane and Miss Barclay in that compromising position nearly two years ago—had said she'd seen Sheff with two women in the garden.

It was precisely the kind of scandal that would ensure Jo

was able to cry off with little damage to her own reputation. Except it wasn't true. Mrs. Lawler, that meddling busybody, had seen two women attempt to gain Sheff's attention. Apparently, she hadn't seen him rebuff them and return to the house.

Naturally, the gossip had reached London, and now his fake betrothal was over. In her letter, Jo had confirmed that she'd heard about his activities and had already made it known that they would not be marrying after all.

The plan had reached fruition, just as he'd intended.

Why, then, did he feel as though he had nothing to look forward to, that his life had just turned…gray?

The duke came into the library, his hair damp. He wasn't wearing a coat or cravat, but since it was just the two of them in residence, they'd both neglected to fully dress some days. Why bother?

"Did you receive a letter?" Sheff's father asked as he sat at the table and helped himself to a biscuit from the tea tray.

"From my betrothed. Rather, *former* betrothed."

The duke sat up straight, his eyes rounding. "She's cried off?"

"Do you blame her?"

"She heard the gossip, then," his father said with a grimace. "You must write to her and tell her it isn't true."

"It's too late." The hollow feeling in Sheff's chest spread to his belly and to his extremities. "She's already made it known."

"She can change her mind."

"She won't, nor should she. People will pity her if she marries me, and Jo doesn't deserve that." Just as she hadn't deserved people giving her the cut direct just because she'd had the gall to become betrothed to someone above her station.

"Nonsense. She'll be a countess. No one pities a countess."

Sheff glowered at his father. The man could not be that obtuse. Sheff chose not to argue with him.

"What else was in her letter? Or was that it?"

There'd been more, but Sheff wasn't going to share it. She'd written that she'd talked to her mother about not taking over the Siren's Call, and that they'd hired someone to become a manager, perhaps in the autumn when her mother returned from Weston. Jo had said she would be free to pursue her independent life, and she'd thanked him for making it possible.

He was so damned happy for her. And utterly despondent for himself.

"Her mother is in Weston," Sheff said almost absentmindedly as he sought to say something that wasn't about Jo.

"Is she? Do you want to pay her a visit? I could go with you."

Sheff made a face and stared at his father. "Why would I want to visit her? Even if I did, you could *not* come with me. She banned you from her club a second time after you took liberties with one of the employees."

"Yes, that." The duke pressed his lips together. "That won't be happening again. I've decided to take your advice and make some changes. I'll be returning to London soon, and I won't be seeking female companionship as I have in the past. Nor will I be drinking to excess. Indeed, I haven't had anything but ale the past several days and not much of that."

"What about your new companion?" Sheff had met her at the party. Mrs. Welbeck was a few years younger than his father's fifty-eight and had the most infectious laugh. Sheff had liked her.

"She's going to stay here for the summer, but then she'll be at her primary residence in Bath for the Season starting in October. I plan to visit her there. Then, she may come to

London with me in the new year." He shrugged. "We'll see what happens. I'm trying not to look too far ahead."

"I'm glad you're at least planning for something past tonight." Sheff smiled at him, feeling genuine warmth and even pride. "I like her. She is quite jovial. I imagine you enjoy that."

"It is refreshing," the duke said with a chuckle. "Thank you for giving me the encouragement I needed. Now, it's my turn to do the same for you. Come back to London with me. Fight for Miss Harker."

Sheff shook his head firmly. "I can't do that."

His father frowned, and he narrowed his eyes at Sheff. "I've never known you to be a defeatist. You've certainly shouldered all the awful behavior I've made you a party to. I am dreadfully sorry, son."

Sheff had become used to hearing his father apologize nearly every day since he'd revealed the truth behind his horrible behavior. "I've forgiven you. You can really stop apologizing."

"Come to London with me. We'll find a way to convince Miss Harker that you love her, that the gossip was a terrible rumor started by an obnoxious busybody."

What would Jo do if Sheff showed up claiming to love her? Would she laugh in his face? Recoil in horror?

Sheff wiped a hand over his brow. "I can't do any of that because our betrothal wasn't real. The entire thing was a charade."

The duke blinked at him. "Why?"

"Because you and Mama wouldn't let me alone. I couldn't stand the constant badgering. And Mama said if I wed, you'd stop bothering her about it too." Sheff shot his father an apologetic look. "I wanted to protect her from you. But now I must wonder if you were even pestering her about me."

His father snorted. "I was not. I'm sorry she lied to

manipulate you." He shook his head. "Why would Miss Harker agree to a fake betrothal?"

"Because I paid her." Sheff rested his elbows on the arms of his chair.

"I see. Well, that changes things somewhat. It does not, however, alter the way you feel about her. Did you always love her?"

Sheff wanted to deny it, but why should he bother? Wouldn't it feel good to share his emotions with one person, even if it wasn't Jo? "No. I chose her because we were friends and because I believed she would weather the dissolution of the betrothal, unlike someone from Society."

"You think Miss Harker won't be ruined by crying off, whereas someone from your own class would." The duke stared at him. "Are you daft?"

"No. Why would you think that?"

"Because to think Miss Harker would not be affected by your behavior is incredibly shortsighted of you. There will be plenty of people who won't wish to associate with her, and I don't believe she's entirely disengaged from Society. She is friends with Min and her set, is she not?"

"Yes, but they won't drop her."

His father sent him a dubious glance. "Your mother will most certainly try to insist that Min do so."

Dammit, Sheff hadn't thought of that. "Why are we all so bloody beholden to Mother? Especially after the way she's treated you? I think we should convince her to remove to Beacon Park." That was their country seat in Bedfordshire. "No, not convince her, *demand* she go. She can't continue to make all of us miserable."

"I will deal with your mother, all right? You must focus on winning Miss Harker. Is there no chance at all she might reciprocate your feelings?"

"I would be shocked if she did. She has less desire to wed

than I did, if that is possible. She yearns for an independent life hosting literary salons."

"A countess can host literary salons," the duke said. "Indeed, a countess can do that far more easily and with greater flourish and impact than a spinster."

Sheff leveled his gaze on the duke. "You're suggesting I win her by promising a lifetime of literary salons?"

His father laughed. "If you think that will be enough, you are not the romantic I believe you to be." He stood. "I must be off to see Mrs. Welbeck." He smiled, then departed the library, leaving Sheff to frown at Jo's letter.

She didn't want to be a countess. He could hear her excitement in the words she'd written. She was looking for a small terrace house for herself—a place where she could lead the life she'd dreamed of. Without him.

He had to hope his love for her would fade. Not because he was certain it would, as he had been in the past. He needed it to fade because there was no hope for it.

He couldn't return to London with his father. It was already difficult to be around a man who was happily falling in love. And then to be in the same city as Jo? He'd have to see her probably, if only to retrieve his grandmother's ring. What about the Siren's Call? Could he never go there again?

No. At least, not until he was no longer in love with Jo. Why in the hell wasn't this emotion fleeting? It wasn't supposed to last. And it sure as hell wasn't supposed to cut through him like a knife. Or leave him feeling lost and full of despair. Wasn't love supposed to make you happy?

CHAPTER 17

Jo walked into Gwen's drawing room on a Monday afternoon in late July, precisely ten weeks since she'd last seen Sheff. With her mother gone—to the exact place where Sheff was—Jo had called an emergency meeting of her friends. But first, she'd asked Gwen to host. She'd needed to get away from the club, and that included her home since it was attached.

Gwen greeted her with a warm smile, but her brow was pleated, reflecting her concern. They embraced and sat together on a settee.

"You probably don't wish to say anything until the others arrive," Gwen said. "But if there is something you need right now, just tell me."

"Thank you." Jo felt surprisingly calm. Perhaps that was due to the various levels of distress she'd felt over the past several weeks. She'd gone from mild concern to pragmatic worry to complete panic. Now she'd simply accepted the truth—she was with child. The question was what she should do next. The future she'd planned since entering into the scheme with Sheff must be altered. As an unwed mother, she could not live a life that even bordered London Society.

She'd considered not carrying the child, but once she'd acknowledged its presence, she'd been shocked to also realize that she wanted to have it. She wanted to be a mother, to give a child the love and care her own mother had given her, which she'd done almost entirely alone.

Min and Ellis arrived then, followed by a maid who set up a tea service on a table near the windows outside the seating arrangement where Jo and Gwen were situated. The new arrivals sat with them, taking the opposite settee.

"We're just waiting for Tamsin and Persephone."

"Persey is coming?" Min asked. "How lovely."

Jo didn't know the Duchess of Wellbourne as well as she knew the others, but Gwen had said that she was keen to leave the house and visit with friends now that her son was several months old. She'd asked if Jo minded inviting her, and Jo did not. The more support and counsel she could receive, the better.

The duchess, rather, Persephone, arrived next. Everyone had just finished embracing when Tamsin walked into the drawing room.

"Oh, Persey is here!" Tamsin rushed in and hugged her with a happy smile. "It's so lovely to see you."

"It is quite lovely to be seen. And to be out of my house," Persephone added with a laugh.

"Is Wellesbourne tending to baby Jonathan?" Min asked.

"Not by himself," Persephone said wryly.

"Is he crawling yet?" Tasmin asked.

Persephone shook her head. "It's far too soon for that. Thank goodness. We are enjoying listening to him babble and making him laugh."

"I know almost nothing about children," Tamsin said with a chuckle. "Laughing and babbling sound wonderful."

The talk of babies made Jo's breath catch. She didn't know much about children either, but she was going to have to learn. How she wished her mother were here. Why was this happening the first time she'd actually left Jo?

Jo realized the others had turned their attention to her. "I, ah, suppose you're wondering why I asked you all to come today." She looked at Gwen beside her. "Thank you for hosting. And thank you for becoming my friend and introducing me to everyone else. I've never had close friends before, and I am particularly glad to have them now."

Dammit, tears were threatening. She did not want to cry! But she'd noticed her emotions had become much more intense in the last several weeks.

Jo took a deep breath. She'd thought about what she wanted to say and how she wished to say it. She would not let emotion rule. "I've something to confess. Sheff and I were never really betrothed. It was a scheme he concocted to avoid the Marriage Mart for the rest of the Season. He does not wish to marry, and his parents had been pressuring him for years to do so. The plan was for us to pretend to be betrothed then at the end of the Season, Sheff would leave town. He would then behave in such a way that would generate gossip so that I could cry off with the excuse that I couldn't possibly wed a rogue like him."

"The Rogue Rules in action," Ellis murmured with a faint smile.

"He didn't wait until the end of the Season, though," Gwen observed. "He left weeks ago."

"But he did behave badly," Tamsin said with a frown. "And can you believe that horrible Mrs. Loose-Lips was behind that gossip too?" She looked around at everyone who responded with a combination of rolled eyes, grunts, and pursed lips.

"Mrs. Loose-Lips?" Jo asked.

Min made a face. "She was the busybody in Weston who caught Pandora and Bane together, then told everyone. Then the next year, she saw Tamsin and Droxford having a private moment, followed by Droxford hitting the man Tamsin's father had arranged for her to wed. Her name is Mrs. Lawler, and she's an abomination. This is the third year running now that she's stuck her nose into someone's business. Can't she just look the other way and keep her mouth shut?"

"Apparently not," Gwen said. She looked to Jo. "So, that was all planned? You knew Sheff would resort to roguery and that would be the end of the scheme?"

Jo nodded. "It all happened according to his plan—except the part where he left town before the Season ended. He did that, in part, to save me having to attend so many Society events. His mother kept pressuring me to do more, and I did not commit to that when I accepted Sheff's proposal. I still have to manage the Siren's Call, which the duchess didn't approve of either." She glanced toward Min, who was clenching her jaw.

"I'm sorry she was so difficult," Min said. "She is pleased that you and Sheff are not going to marry. But she is also furious with Sheff for behaving like our father. I confess, I am also angry about that."

"Don't be," Jo said, lifting her chin. "That is who he is, and I certainly didn't expect any differently." Indeed, his run of celibacy had surprised her.

"You said you are glad to have friends right now," Persephone said with a concerned smile. "How can we help?"

This was the difficult part. Jo felt like such a fool. "It seems that with spending so much time together pretending to be in love, Sheff and I developed a strong mutual attraction. Before he left London, we, ah, gave in to that, and I'm afraid I am now suffering the consequences." She returned

Persephone's smile, but then her throat constricted, and she couldn't say anything more.

"He will marry you," Min said, her gaze meeting Jo's with a quiet confidence.

"He doesn't know, and I'm not sure he needs to. He doesn't want to wed, and I've no desire to force him. I don't really want to wed either." Except, she did, and not just because of the child. She loved Sheff. Her plans to follow in her mother's footsteps hadn't been what Jo really wanted. She wanted a family of her own. "Yes, we should have refrained from…roguery. We tried to be careful."

"You intend to carry it, then?" Ellis asked.

Tamsin snapped her gaze toward Ellis. "What else would she do?"

"There are ways to prevent the pregnancy," Jo said. "And I did think of that, but the truth is that I love this child, and I want to raise him or her."

"Do you love its father?" Persephone asked quietly. "You've said nothing of how you feel about Sheff, except that you were attracted to one another. Was that all it was?"

Jo took a moment to respond. It would be easier to lie, but these were her friends. "No. I fell in love for real. However, that was not the plan. I don't want to saddle Sheff with a wife he doesn't want."

Ellis's expression was sympathetic. "I see your conundrum. You love Sheff and you are carrying his child, but you don't want to be stuck in a marriage where your love is not reciprocated."

Jo thought of her father breaking her mother's heart when he was unfaithful. "No, I do not."

"But you have to tell him about the child," Tamsin said adamantly.

"I don't want him to feel obligated to marry me when neither of us wanted that," Jo said.

"Is that still the case, though?" Gwen asked, drawing Jo to turn her head. "You've fallen in love. Perhaps he has too. I think several of us—and our husbands—can say we never intended to fall in love with a rogue, and yet here we are." She laughed softly.

Min pressed her lips together. "In your cases, the rogues reformed. As much as I love my brother, I am not sure he can do that."

"You said he would marry me," Jo said to Min. "Does that mean you think I should marry a rogue knowing he won't change? What's the rule about that?"

"Never trust a rogue to change," a few of them answered nearly in unison.

"Am I to expect the kind of marriage that my parents have where they live apart and are not really married except in name only? Or worse, Min's parents, who can't even be pleasant to one another?" Jo asked, feeling despondent. She did love Sheff, but she couldn't think their marriage would be happy, not after everything he'd said to her about expecting to be like his father.

Persephone sent her an understanding nod. "Acton's parents were like that too. They didn't even live in the same city. I can understand you not wanting to subject yourself to that. But it would be better for the babe if you married Sheff."

"You don't have to live together," Ellis said. "You were already looking forward to a life of independence. You can still have that as his countess. He won't begrudge you that. In fact, I think he'd want you to have that." Her features softened with encouragement.

Ellis had described Jo's parents' arrangement. As much as Jo didn't want that, she would accept it for the sake of her child. She did not want to condemn him or her to illegitimacy.

"My father just informed me last night that he and my

mother will no longer reside together at Henlow House," Min said rather evenly. "He's told her she can spend the Season at Beacon Park and then come to Henlow House in summer and autumn, when Papa is not in town. She will never do that. Or, he said he'll purchase her a nice house wherever she would like except Grosvenor Square."

"I can't imagine she took that very well," Persephone said with a faint snort.

Min shook her head. "I confess I'm shocked my father would do such a thing, but he said he won't have her haranguing me about marriage any longer. Or being cruel to Ellis." Min glanced toward Ellis, who sat straight and unflinching, her expression serene.

Persephone blinked at her. "That is remarkable. When did your father return from Weston?"

"Just last week." Min looked back to Jo. "I did not mean to divert us from Jo's situation. She needs a plan for telling my brother he's to be a father." She suddenly smiled. "And I'm to be an aunt. I must admit I am thrilled."

Seeing Min's expression gave Jo more comfort than she'd had in weeks. She felt a surge of strength and courage. "I think I must go to Weston and tell Sheff about the babe. If he proposes, I will say yes."

"*When* he proposes," Min said with a grin, and the others nodded in agreement.

They were all so sure Sheff would marry her. Jo was still worried about forcing themselves into a marriage neither wanted. Though, if they both wanted the child, perhaps it would be all right. Especially since her friends were right— she loved him. Didn't she owe it to herself to find out if there was any chance at all they could be happy together?

Gwen took Jo's hand and gave it a squeeze. "I think you must also tell Sheff how you feel. There is every chance he may feel the same. Lazarus kept his love from me because he thought that was best for me." She rolled her eyes. "He was wrong. Please don't make that mistake. You'll never know what could happen if you don't tell him the truth."

Jo wanted so badly to have what Gwen and Lazarus did. She hadn't realized just how much until there was a child. The family she hadn't known she wanted was just within reach.

"Does anyone here think Sheff can reform himself from a rogue to a faithful husband and father?" Jo asked.

"I do," Tamsin said loudly and with a bright smile.

"That is not surprising to anyone," Min said with a laugh. "You are the most optimistic person in the room."

"In London, really," Gwen added with a grin.

"I also think Sheff can reform," Ellis said, and that *was* surprising. "Before he left London, he seemed different to me. He was more thoughtful. More reserved. As if something weighed on his mind."

"You think he loves Jo?" Min asked.

Ellis lifted a shoulder, her gaze fixing on Jo. "I think Jo should find out."

"We are all leaving for Weston day after tomorrow," Tamsin said. "You must come with us."

So that everyone could witness her humiliation when Sheff probably said he did not love her in return? "I think I might prefer privacy."

"Then leave tomorrow," Min said. "You can take one of my father's coaches."

"Does she need a chaperone?" Tamsin asked.

"No," Jo said firmly. "I've never had one before, and I'm not starting with that now." What good was a chaperone when she was already with child?

She would arrive in Weston a day ahead of everyone.

Whatever happened with Sheff, Jo would have her mother near, then she would shortly also have her friends. "All right. I'll leave in the morning. Thank you, Min. And everyone." She looked around and felt a catch in her throat. "I'm so very fortunate to have you all as my friends."

"We are just as fortunate to have you," Gwen said, releasing Jo's hand so she could put her arm around her and give her a sideways hug.

Butterflies took flight in Jo's belly. Or was it the baby? No, it was nervous anticipation, for now that Jo knew what she would do, she was anxious to do it.

She would be glad for the journey, however, as there was much to consider. What if she did marry Sheff? She would be a countess, and she'd be expected to do all the Society things, including the ones she found tedious. But she would also be able to host literary salons and be invited to all manner of scholarly discussions. She had to think there were people who would not accept her, but she didn't care. Would Sheff? Given his anger at how she'd been given the cut direct, she didn't think he would.

Perhaps everything would work out. A future Jo never imagined flitted before her.

With Sheff's love, you can do anything.

The sentiment rose in her mind, surprising her. Did she believe that? She knew that acknowledging her love for him made her feel stronger and more secure. Perhaps his love would do the same.

She had only to find out if that love existed.

Mrs. Ingram, the Grove's rather tall housekeeper, bustled into the library and stopped short upon seeing Sheff sprawled in a chair. He was reading a novel. Or trying to anyway.

"I didn't realize you were in here, my lord. I can return later." She spoke in a lilting southern Welsh accent.

"Don't let me interrupt your plans," Sheff said, snapping the book closed. He'd wanted to read a novel to feel closer to Jo, but he just couldn't focus. "I should go for a ride." He hadn't been for several days.

"That would be beneficial, I think." Mrs. Ingram, a sometimes stoic woman with assessing blue eyes, studied Sheff a moment. "You've not left the house in a few days, at least."

Five, but who was counting? Sheff's outings had dwindled after his father had returned to London.

"I can see you are moping about. Is it because your father left? Your friends will be here by the end of the week, won't they?"

Somerton, Wellesbourne, Droxford, and Price were all departing London the day after tomorrow for their annual holiday together. They would, indeed, arrive in Weston by the end of the week.

"Surely that will cheer you," she added with a nod.

Sheff grunted as he stood. He deposited the book on a table. "I know you don't approve of some of our activities, but rest assured that with most everyone married now, things will be far more sedate. Furthermore, only Price will be staying here." Sheff was fairly certain she already knew that but felt it worth repeating. Mrs. Ingram clearly preferred Min and Ellis to Sheff and his friends.

"Along with your sister and Miss Dangerfield," the housekeeper said. "We will be prepared." She hesitated, but seemed as though she wanted to say something more.

"Is there something else?" Sheff asked.

"I only wondered if perhaps you were missing the woman

you spent the evening with at the party. I would have expected you to invite her back."

"What woman?"

"I saw a woman visiting your room late that night." She shrugged. "I should not have mentioned it. You just seem sad, and I wondered if that was why."

Sheff exhaled his frustration away. It wasn't the housekeeper's fault that she assumed him to be a lothario. He had been for a very long time. "That woman came to my room, and I turned her away. I am not the same man you've known."

"But there were those women in the garden too," Mrs. Ingram said, her brow furrowing.

"Like the woman you saw outside my room, they presumed I would want to spend time with them and pushed themselves upon me without my consent. I was not interested in their attentions, nor am I now."

The housekeeper blanched. "How were they to know that?"

"They could have asked instead of assuming." He gave her a pointed look. "Just as you could have not assumed I spent the night with the woman you saw."

She pressed her lips together into a flat line. "I did make an assumption. But I did so based on years of behavior. I'm sure those women thought you wanted their attention. I'm sorry that you did not and were made to suffer it anyway."

Her words made Sheff think about his own behavior in the past. Had he ever made assumptions or taken advantage of a situation? He hoped not, but he couldn't be entirely sure. At least these women had left him alone after he'd made it clear he wasn't interested—and he'd always done the same with women.

"I must make it known that I am no longer the rake I used to be, I suppose."

"And why is that? What prompted you to change?" Mrs. Ingram asked, seeming genuinely curious.

Sheff smiled sadly. "I lost my heart." He touched his chest. "It belongs to the loveliest woman, and I truly thought it would be a temporary loan. Alas, I fear she will own it forever."

Mrs. Ingram's brow pleated again. "She rejected you?"

The housekeeper's reaction and frank question somewhat surprised him. He *hadn't* been rejected, but why did he feel as if that were the case? "She is not interested in marriage."

"Her refusal must have been upsetting. I'm sorry."

"I didn't actually ask her." Not for real. What would happen if he did? If he told her that he was desperately in love with her, and that he was nearly certain he would always be?

"Then you're daft," Mrs. Ingram said with a shake of her head. "Go and ask her and see if she really would reject you. Then you can mope about."

He could go to London—which his father had suggested several times and Sheff had declined. Now the housekeeper was going to persuade him to fight for Jo? He would have asked if the duke had put her up to this, but Mrs. Ingram had seemed unaware of Jo until now.

"Who is this young lady?" Mrs. Ingram asked, confirming Sheff's supposition.

"She's a friend of my sister's. In London."

The housekeeper's eyes rounded, then she grimaced. "I'm afraid I wrote to your sister about the woman outside your room. I thought you had spent the night together."

Sheff gaped at her. "Why would you tell Min about that?" And had Min told Jo? Did that even matter since Jo had heard the gossip about the women in the garden, thanks to Mrs. Lawler, and already cried off?

Mrs. Ingram shrugged, her expression contrite. "I have a

close relationship with Lady Minerva. I write to her once a month or so about what's happening here."

Whether Jo knew or not, Sheff needed to see her. He needed her to know that he had changed—for good. His future wasn't written. He could choose love. He *would* choose love and marriage, if Jo would have him. "I must go to London at once." As it was afternoon, he would leave at first light tomorrow.

"May I offer you advice, my lord?" the housekeeper asked.

Sheff wanted to sprint from the room and set his valet to packing, but he remained. "What would that be?"

"If you've truly changed, you may want to make that known, so you are no longer…inconvenienced by admirers." She smiled. "Perhaps you should take an advertisement in the *Times*?"

It was a ridiculous idea—a joke. But he was tempted. He yearned to shout from the rooftops that he loved Jo and wanted her to be his wife.

That he'd been mooning about the past several weeks instead of recognizing the massive change he'd undergone was infuriating. But the only thing he could do was stop it right now and step into the future he wanted.

He could only hope she might want it too.

"I'll be leaving for London as soon as the sun is up." Sheff hastened from the room then, his mind on how to woo Jo.

What if she refused him? She had plenty of reason to, not the least of which was his roguish past behavior. There was also the fact that she didn't particularly care for all of Society's aspects, nor had Society treated her very well. How could he ask her to make that her life permanently?

Finally, there was the small reality that she didn't want to wed, that it was likely she didn't even love him. She'd only written to him once since he'd left London, and that was to confirm the next stage of their plan.

Sheff faltered, his gait slowing as he entered the staircase hall. No, he wouldn't hide behind his fear any longer. If she rejected him, he would accept that.

But if he didn't try, he'd never know if happiness could be theirs.

CHAPTER 18

Jo was very glad she'd left at dawn that morning because rain had slowed the journey. Still, they'd made it to Froxfield, which was about halfway to Weston. She was now comfortably ensconced in her small room and had just finished a delightful repast.

She was sore from jostling around in the coach—something she had rarely done outside London—and eager to sleep. Not just because she was tired, but because she couldn't wait for morning so she could be on her way once more.

She tried to settle into bed, but whoever was lodging next door was pacing about. And the floor squeaked. This went on for quite some time. Jo glared at the wall behind the headboard of her bed.

Finally, it stopped.

Smiling to herself, Jo exhaled as she snuggled into the bed. Sleep began to claim her... then she jolted awake at the sound of a chair being dragged across the floor next door.

She pulled the pillow over her head and prayed for quiet.

*S*heff bolted up from the chair he'd just moved closer to the fire. He'd wanted it there because his bare feet were cold. However, he was too warm from pacing about.

Energy coursed through him, making the bedchamber feel close. He didn't want to be there. He wanted to continue toward London. However, the rain had made them stop, and they were only halfway.

He walked from the head of the bed back to the hearth on the opposite side of the room. Then back again. He removed his dressing gown and cast it on the foot of the bed. Clad in just a nightshirt, he returned to the fire.

Before he could throw himself in the chair, there was a knock on his door. Who would be disturbing him at this hour?

He strode to the door and opened it a crack since he had not thought to don his dressing gown.

"Sheff?"

"Jo!"

Was she really there? He recognized her voice, for her face was barely visible in the dim corridor. She could likely see him because he was in his much more illuminated chamber.

"What are you doing here?" he asked incredulously.

"I came to ask whoever was in this chamber to please be quiet."

He laughed at her sardonic reply and then wondered why on earth he was leaving her in the corridor. "Come in!" He opened the door wide.

She wore a garnet-colored dressing gown, and her sable hair hung in a plait against her shoulder, tied at the end with an ivory ribbon. Her expression was tentative as she stepped inside.

Somehow, Sheff resisted the urge to sweep her in his arms and swing her about the room. He was just so happy to see her. "I missed you," he said softly.

"I missed you too." She sounded almost…shy. Which was not what he would ever have expected from her.

"I'm glad to hear it. Since you only sent one letter, I thought you were pleased to be rid of me." Reality cut through his glee. She'd written about the dissolution of the betrothal. Because he'd been seen with a pair of women.

Sheff sobered completely. "Jo, I must tell you the truth of what happened in Weston."

She arched a brow. "I don't know that I need to hear it. I'd rather focus on the future."

"But it's important. I have remained celibate—in all ways. I haven't so much as touched any women."

"The gossip that you were seen with two women in your arms wasn't true?"

"In part," he said. "They had put their arms around me, and that was when we were seen. I hadn't yet had a chance to extricate myself from them. And I think you must know about another woman. Mrs. Ingram—the housekeeper—said she wrote to Min about seeing a woman outside my chamber. She stayed there—outside, I mean. She thought I would be amenable to her attention."

Her brows drew together. "But you were not?"

He shook his head. "Absolutely not. I haven't thought of another woman, let alone wanted one, since I left you in London. I've been a fair mess, if you want to know the truth." He attempted a smile, but feared it came out rather lopsided as he nervously awaited her response.

Response to what? He hadn't asked her anything yet.

"Are you angry with me?" he asked.

"Why should I be? You executed the plan we discussed. Things happened sooner than I expected, but now it seems that you didn't execute anything at all." She searched his face. "You weren't with any of those women? You didn't try to stir up a scandal?"

"No. My father had a party at the Grove. I thought I would join in, that it might cheer me up. It did the opposite. It only made me miss you more. I retired early. Then I was disturbed by that woman."

"Why did you need cheering?" she asked quietly.

"Because my heart was breaking," he whispered, his gaze holding hers. "I fell in love with you when I wasn't supposed to, and I was waiting for it to go away. Only, it did not. It has not. And I don't think it ever will."

She put her hand to her chest, her lips parting. "You love me?"

"Desperately." He couldn't keep from smiling, then, or taking her hand. But he stopped short after reaching for her. His conversation with Mrs. Ingram rose in his mind. "May I touch you?"

Jo took his hand in hers. "How can you love me? You have been adamant that you could not love anyone."

Sheff moved close to her and pulled her hand up to hold it against his chest. "I love you because you are brilliant and witty, and you have stood with me through a ridiculous time. I am so sorry that I put you through everything with my stupid fake betrothal scheme. But I don't want it to be fake."

She held up her hand, halting anything further he might have said. His breath stalled in his lungs. She didn't want him to continue.

She didn't want *him*.

"Please stop," she said, sounding almost breathless. "I need to tell you something before you can go on. I was on my way to Weston. Or did you not think it strange that I was here in

Froxfield? That we are here on the very same night is astonishing."

In truth, he *hadn't* stopped to think about why she was here. He was simply too overjoyed to see her. "You were coming to Weston? To see your mother?"

A smile lifted her lips as she gave her head a slight shake. "Can you not believe that I was coming to see *you*?"

Sheff's brain froze for a moment, and he struggled to find words. All he could manage was "You were?"

"Yes. I have something very important to tell you." Her hand moved to her abdomen. Sheff continued to feel as though he were not entirely in working order. "We were not careful enough in London. I am going to have a baby. I am not telling you to prompt a marriage proposal, but that would be best for the child. I also needed to tell you that I love you, and if you wanted to marry, I am amenable."

She didn't finish uttering the final word before Sheff had gathered her into his arms. "Yes. No. Wait." He slid down her body, setting his hands on her hips. "Yes, I want to marry. *You.* I want to marry *you.* Please marry me, Jo." He leveled his gaze at her belly. "Hello, there. I am very much looking forward to meeting you. You will have the best mama in all of England. What a lucky girl—or boy—you are."

"You think the babe is a girl?" Jo asked, her eyes shining down at him.

"I don't know. The first image that filled my mind was a dark-haired girl with hazel eyes and a fierce smile." He held his breath. "Will you marry me?"

"I can hardly believe we are standing here doing this," she said with a laugh. "Yes, I will marry you."

Sheff pressed a kiss to her abdomen. "Your papa already loves you so very much." He stood and looked into Jo's dewy eyes. "I love you too. And I always will."

"How can you be so sure when you've always believed you were incapable of doing so?"

"I was so wrong about who I am and, more importantly, who I want to be. The time I spent with my father was most enlightening. He showed me a side of himself I'd never seen before. Being with him away from my mother gave me joy—and peace. It helped me to realize that I want a place where I can always feel that way, and that place is with you. I am, apparently, quite capable of overwhelming love."

She touched his cheek. "Oh, Sheff. I was wrong about myself too. I'd been doubting my role with the club, but I should also have been skeptical about my spinsterhood. It turns out I might be happiest if I had a family of my own—with you."

He sucked in a breath, hardly believing that this was what they both wanted. "I wish I'd been smart enough to return to London sooner."

"And I wish I'd left London before now," she said with a smile. "We told each other what we thought was true, what we thought we wanted. But even the best-laid plans can change."

He laughed. "If you are referring to my betrothal scheme, it was very poorly planned. Yet, I don't regret a bit of it since it brought us together."

Her gaze turned sultry. "For that reason, it was a brilliant scheme, really." She pressed a kiss to his jaw.

Sheff's body, already slightly aroused, vaulted into unbridled lust. "So many nights I dreamed of you," he murmured as she kissed his throat. "Every night since we parted."

"I can't believe you were celibate the whole time." She licked his flesh, and he shivered.

"It took no effort. The only woman I wanted was too far away. I became very well acquainted with my hand, I must say."

Jo laughed, and Sheff unfastened her dressing gown. She shrugged it off with his help, then set it atop the bed. She wore a thin night rail, which he drew over her head and sent to join the dressing gown. Then he swept her into his arms and carried her the very short distance to the bed.

He set her atop the coverlet, then removed his nightshirt and let it fall to the floor. She was already pulling back the bedclothes and sliding between them. She held them open for him to join her.

Eyes locked, they caressed each other, their hands exploring. He cupped her breast, feeling the difference in its firmness since he'd held her last. She was going to have their child. He would be a father. He'd never known how much he wanted that. And perchance he *hadn't* wanted it before. But with Jo, he wanted everything.

Sheff kissed her, and the touch of her lips against his felt like he'd come home. She cupped his face as she kissed him back and moved her body to his. Sliding her foot up his calf, she hooked her leg over his thigh.

Why had he stayed away from her for so long? He pushed away thoughts of the weeks they could have spent together and focused on this moment. She moaned into the kiss as he rolled her nipple between his thumb and forefinger. Then he drew his hand down her side and over her hip, bringing his fingertips to her sex.

She moaned against his lips as he stroked her clitoris. Her hips moved, and he rose over her, pushing her back onto the bed. She wrapped her legs around him.

She pulled her lips from his. "I want you now, Sheff. Please don't wait. I need to be yours."

He kissed her cheek, her temple, her forehead. "You are mine. Now and forever." He positioned his cock at her opening. Her hand curled around his shaft, guiding him into her wet heat.

Closing his eyes, he rested there for a moment and reveled in the overwhelming joy of loving her and being loved in return.

"You don't need to worry about pulling out," she whispered.

He could tell she was smiling when she spoke, and he laughed. "I suppose not." He opened his eyes and looked down at her. "How careful should I be?"

"I don't think you need to worry. I did ask Persephone about that, and she confided in me that she and Wellesbourne did not curtail their activities until she became too uncomfortable. And then they 'modified' things, whatever that means. I'm confident we'll learn as we go."

"Did you tell your friends about the babe?"

"I did. My mother wasn't in London, and I needed advice." She put her hand to his cheek. "I didn't want you to think I'd entrapped you in a marriage you didn't want."

"My darling, I would never have thought that. Your thoughts on marriage were not different from mine, and aside from that, I would not believe you are capable of that sort of manipulation." He began to move, withdrawing, then sliding back into her sheath. "Rather, I would expect you to declare what you want, which you did."

"Eventually. Like you, I wish I hadn't hesitated. Think of all the time we wasted."

Sheff continued to move—and she was moving with him —which was causing his brain to lose focus. "Not that much in the great scheme. All that matters is we are together now." He drove deep into her, making her gasp and her eyes narrow with desire. "Quite literally."

Jo clasped her legs around him more tightly and drew his head down for a long, torrid kiss. Sheff lost himself in a haze of emotion and pleasure. He couldn't remember an experience like this because he'd never had one.

Their bodies rocked and glided together, rushing toward that peak of rapturous fulfillment. Jo clutched his back, her fingers digging deliciously into his flesh as her muscles clenched around him. He felt her orgasm grip her body and thrust faster and deeper to catch his own. He cried out amidst her moans and whimpers, holding her to him.

They remained like that, entangled together, for quite some time, their bodies settling into their normal rhythm. Yes, this was normal—Jo in his arms. He could hardly believe it.

He pulled out of her at last but still held her close. One of her legs was still wrapped loosely around his thigh. "Are you happy?" he asked softly.

She nodded. "More than I ever imagined I could be." A gentle furrow settled into her brow. "I am anxious about becoming a countess."

"Society will accept you," Sheff said firmly. "I will make them."

Laughing, she brushed his hair back from his forehead. "While I appreciate your primal instincts, I don't think you can force *everyone.*"

"I suppose not. But the cut direct goes both ways. I will not forget the people who treated you poorly when you were my pretend betrothed. When you are my wife, anyone who is less than welcoming and kind will simply be ignored."

"That sounds like a good plan, though I still don't want to be at the forefront of Society. Are you all right with that?"

"I am glorious with whatever you want. If you'd prefer to live in a cottage in the middle of nowhere, I would gladly do that."

"But you have responsibilities," she said. "Or, you will, someday when you inherit the dukedom."

"Yes, and I do think my father is going to want me to take on more responsibility. He has made some changes to his life since spending time with me in Weston. It was a revelatory period. He explained some things to me that I had not known, such as the true reason behind the strife in my parents' marriage."

Jo came onto her side and snuggled against him, putting her palm on his chest. "I am most intrigued."

He met her gaze. "Would you believe that it isn't entirely my father's fault?" He went on to explain how his father had been in love with his mother, but that she'd rejected him and had an affair. But Jo did not appear surprised. And why should she be when his mother had been awful to her?

"You don't have trouble believing my mother shares the blame," Sheff remarked. "I confess I didn't either once I heard it. I'm a bit annoyed with myself that I hadn't determined that before."

"I know about her affair," Jo said. Now Sheff was surprised. "My mother finally explained how she came to know your mother. She had an affair with my father."

Sheff bolted up into a sitting position, his eyes wide. "Oh, God. That means Ellis is your half sister."

Jo also jerked upright. "I suspected that may be the case. But you know it to be true?"

"Yes. My father told me she is my mother's daughter and is the result of her affair. However, my father didn't know the identity of Ellis's father. Now, I do." He looked to Jo in distress. "What are we to do with this information?"

She took his hand. "I don't know. It's certainly strange for us to know the entire truth when no one else does. My mother was aware of the affair, but only suspected your mother had a child. My father knows nothing of a child. We have all the pieces of the puzzle. But I don't want to tell Ellis about her parentage. Shouldn't that come from her parents?"

"My mother won't say anything." Now that Sheff knew the truth about her, he was incredibly angry. "I loathe the way she's treated my father and Ellis. I don't think I can be around her without saying so, without informing her that I know the truth."

"Will you tell Min?" Jo asked.

"The duke said he would speak to her the way he did me, but I don't know when that will happen."

"He hadn't told her as of yesterday," Jo said. "I saw her, and I think she would have said something."

"Though it will be hard to keep this secret, I think we must—at least until we can inform all parties." Sheff relaxed. "I'm so glad I have you. This would be far more burdensome on my own."

She stroked her thumb along his hand. "I feel the same. Now, where are we going tomorrow? London or Weston?"

"Where do you want to get married? Because that is the very next thing we are doing." He lifted her hand and kissed her palm.

"I would have said London, but my mother is in Weston and our friends will be, so I think I'd like to have the wedding there. But we'll need to send for my father. Can you arrange for his transportation to Weston as soon as possible? He must be at the wedding."

Sheff nodded. "Of course. I'll dispatch a letter to my secretary in the morning, and he can handle the arrangements. I will purchase a special license, which should not be a problem, particularly since I have been in residence in Weston for several weeks."

Jo gave him a sheepish look. "I'm afraid I didn't pack most of my new clothing—some of which I haven't even worn yet. I do have a gown that would be nice for the wedding."

"Then I shall instruct my secretary to coordinate the delivery of your clothing along with your father. Can your housekeeper organize everything?"

"I can write a letter to her if you could also dispatch that in the morning." She laughed. "We are suddenly very busy."

"Because we have a future waiting for us, and we are eager to start it!" He grinned at her, love overflowing from every part of him. "Wellesbourne told me that when you realize you are in love, you can't wait for the happily ever after to begin. Or something like that. In fact, another gentleman told me the same thing. Now, I understand, and I wholeheartedly concur."

"I think we started a while ago when you invited me into your room," Jo said with a sly smile. "Shall we continue?" She took his hand and put it on her breast.

Sheff narrowed his eyes. "Yes, please." He gathered her to him with a growl, settling her on his lap. "I can't believe how much I love you. Even more now than when you walked through that door."

"And I love you. More now than when you asked me to marry you. I expect to love you more still when we wake in the morning."

"That assumes we will sleep." He waggled his brows at her.

She looked at him in horror. "We *must* sleep. I was exhausted after the journey today, and some idiot next door to my room kept me from falling asleep. The babe is absolutely draining."

Sheff grimaced. "Hell, I wasn't thinking." He lifted her from her lap and guided her down onto the mattress. "Sleep, now."

"In a while. I'm not quite as exhausted as I was earlier." She gave him a sultry look. "You're going to have to tire me out, I think."

Sheff smiled down at her. "I will do whatever you need, my love."

CHAPTER 19

The garden drawing room—so called because it was one of two drawing rooms and opened onto the garden—at the Grove was full of Jo's family and friends following her wedding to Sheff. After dashing to the retiring room, which had become a regular occurrence in recent days, and would apparently only become more persistent according to her mother and Persephone, Jo now stood just inside the doorway. She wanted to take a moment to survey all the people she cared about most and cherish that they were all here to celebrate her most special day.

Good heavens, but pregnancy had turned her into a nostalgic sentimentalist.

And she didn't mind. She glanced at her left hand, thinking Sheff's grandmother's ring still felt odd, but it also felt right. Jo had returned the ring to Min after the fake betrothal had ended, then Min had brought it with her to Weston, much to Jo's surprise and delight.

Sheff had made a show of putting it on her finger in front of Min and Ellis, who were there. He'd even dropped to his knee again.

Being with Ellis was difficult. Jo and Sheff wanted nothing more than to tell her the truth, to reveal her parentage. But they were resolved in their decision to wait until all parties could be informed. That meant that Min didn't know the truth yet either.

Upon arriving in Weston, Jo had told her mother that Ellis was, definitively, Jo's half sister. Her mother was not surprised and immediately suggested they not tell her father when he arrived in Weston. He would go straight to Ellis, and they'd agreed that might not be the best way for her to learn about her parentage. Finding out she was the duchess's daughter would affect her greatly, and they'd reasoned it was best to wait until Sheff had spoken with his father. Jo ached to tell her father about his other daughter—and to recognize Ellis as her sister—but knew the timing was not yet right. It would be soon.

Sheff had agreed with this plan. Then he'd just kept telling Jo not to fret, that this time was for them, to celebrate their love and, today, their marriage. It had been a very joyous week. Jo could not remember ever being this happy.

"Do your cheeks ache yet?" Jo's mother asked as she approached her.

"Not yet, but I'm sure they will." Jo grinned. "Can one overdose on happiness?"

"I never thought so, but I don't know that I've ever achieved your level of joy." She kissed Jo's cheek. "Your love for Sheff appears to exceed anything I felt for your father."

"What about Marcel?" Jo glanced toward her mother's lover, a lithe gentleman with gray-and-sable hair who stood across the room speaking with Wellesbourne and Droxford.

Her mother's lips curved into a small smile. "I do love him, but I am not sure it is the same all-consuming passion you seem to have for Sheff. And, more importantly, that he has for you. I've never seen a man more smitten. It makes me want to roll my eyes, quite frankly."

Jo laughed. "I might feel the same if I were not the recipient."

Sobering, her mother said, "Marcel and I are returning to London tomorrow."

Jo pivoted to face her. "You are? I thought you were staying until the end of the month."

"Or as long as I could stand it. I am past my ability to withstand another week in this sleepy enclave." She shuddered. "Honestly, I would have left days ago, but you arrived and announced you were marrying as soon as possible, and I had to stay." Her expression softened. "I *wanted* to stay. But now I want to go home."

"What does this mean for future forays to Weston?" Jo asked wryly.

Her mother's eyes narrowed slightly. "It means I told Marcel that if he desires a short respite, and I mean a fortnight or less, at the seaside, we will go to Brighton. It's much closer to London, and I won't feel so trapped."

"Did he find that reasonable?" Jo asked.

"More than." Her eyes gleamed with mirth. "He then confessed he didn't like it here either."

Jo laughed. "This is why the two of you are so suited."

"Bizarrely, we've invited your father to ride back to London with us."

"That's surprising."

Her mother shrugged. "It was Marcel's idea. I think he enjoys provoking Rowland, but your father isn't jealous. He has never possessed those tendencies."

"What are you both whispering about?" Sheff asked as he walked up next to Jo and slipped his arm around her waist.

Jo pressed herself against him. "Mama and Marcel are

returning to London tomorrow. And they're taking my father with them."

Sheff's brows rose. "That's a bold move."

"Thankfully, it's only two days of travel. Though, I may regret my choice by tomorrow morning." Jo's mother looked from Jo to Sheff and back again. "When will you be going to London?"

"In a week or so, after we enjoy a honeymoon." He pressed a kiss to Jo's temple. "We are anxious to speak to the duke as soon as possible as to how we should proceed with regard to Ellis. I believe the duchess has gone to Beacon Park, so she may not be a part of any conversation."

"That may be for the best," Jo's mother said, making a slight face. "I don't think she'll enjoy having this history dredged up."

"No," Sheff agreed. "But it isn't about her or her feelings. This is about Ellis and making sure she is supported."

Jo's mother's gaze fixed on Jo with concern. "Have you considered it may be better not to tell her or your father? Perhaps it's best to just let the past alone."

"Ellis's parentage is not the past," Jo argued. "It's who she is. How can Sheff and I keep the truth from her? I would be so angry if I were in her place."

Sheff squeezed Jo's waist. "I agree. She needs to know, and we'll find the best way to tell her."

"I'll support you in whatever you decide." Jo's mother glanced toward Jo's father, who was sitting with a few of their friends—ironically including Ellis—regaling them with some tale that had them all laughing. "Now, if you'll excuse me, I need to collect Marcel, as we should be on our way soon."

Jo leaned over and kissed her mother's cheek. "I'll see you when we return to London."

"Yes, and do let me know where I can find you, because I know you're not moving into the Albany."

Laughing, Jo shook her head. The Albany was for bachelors. For now, they were going to stay at Henlow House since the duchess was not in residence. Sheff had already instructed his secretary to look for appropriate properties that they might call home.

A short while later, after Jo's mother and Marcel had left and Jo's father had retreated upstairs, Jo and Sheff were alone with their friends. Wellesbourne wasted no time lifting a glass to toast the newly married couple.

"To Sheff, whom we shall all endlessly tease about *leg shackling* himself, and to Jo, the only woman cunning enough to snare the roguiest rogue among us."

Everyone raised their glasses amid calls of "Hear, hear."

After drinking, Sheff, who sat very close to his wife on a small settee, raised his glass once more. "To the last remaining rogue, our dear Evan Price. Let's see how long you last." Sheff laughed, and once more, "Hear, hear," filled the room.

Price didn't drink but looked upon them all with superiority. "I am quite content as the remaining rogue. And as I am a couple of years younger than the rest of you rogues, I'm happy to say that I will last quite some time. I do not have parents harassing me to wed, nor am I on the hunt. Yet."

"Well, I am," Min said, surprising everyone into silence. "I shall give the Marriage Mart one last try in October for the Season in Bath. If I don't find a sufficiently nonroguish husband then, I shall cast myself into spinsterhood." She glanced at Ellis, who sat in the chair next to hers. "You will find Ellis and me running a school for girls or collecting cats or writing horrid novels under the name Euphemia Brightly."

"Perhaps all those things," Ellis said with a smile.

"Why not?" Min tapped her glass to Ellis's, and everyone drank.

"I think we must all go to Bath for the Season," Gwen suggested, looking around the room. "We can support Min."

"I would like that," Jo murmured to Sheff.

"Then that's where we will be," he said with a smile.

"Pandora will be there, of course," Persephone said. "Since she lives there with our aunt. I mention her because she was not able to finish Jo's embroidered copy of the rogue rules before today. But now, she can give it to you in person." Persephone smiled at Jo.

"She's making one for me?" Jo asked in surprise. The warmth and love of friendship rushed through her, and she was incredibly grateful to Gwen for inviting her into their set. "I was not part of the group when the rules were formed."

"You are part of the group now," Persephone assured her. "And I think we can all agree that you, out of us all, need a copy of those rules where Sheff can see them." She winked at Sheff, who laughed.

"My roguing days are over," Sheff declared.

"I might like you to be a rogue once in a while," Jo said with a slight shrug, and everyone laughed.

They visited awhile longer before their friends began to filter out—though Min and Ellis were merely retreating upstairs to their sitting room. At last, it was just Jo and Sheff in the drawing room. Jo kicked off her slippers and sat down sideways on a settee, putting her feet up.

Sheff slid onto the settee and put her feet on his lap. "That was lovely."

Jo smiled, feeling a warm satisfaction. "It was, wasn't it?"

"And you planned the entire thing," he said proudly.

"I was happy to organize things myself, and Mrs. Ingram was most helpful. She also apologized to me about twenty times for assuming you had been intimate with that woman at the duke's party."

Sheff chuckled. "She apologized to me probably fifty times." He started to massage one of Jo's feet, and she moaned softly. "She also told me that I am lucky to have you as my countess."

"That's nice to hear." Jo was nervous about returning to London and hearing differing opinions.

"Don't worry." Sheff gave her foot a comforting squeeze. "Everything will be fine back in town."

"I can't help thinking about it. I never imagined I'd be a countess." Or a duchess someday. Jo wouldn't think about that at all. "It's overwhelming, and you can't disagree with that."

"No, I can't." He moved to massage her other foot. "But I am here by your side. I will support you and love you every step of the way."

"I know." She wiggled her toes, and he lifted her foot to press a kiss to the inner arch. She could feel the softness of his lips through the silk of her stocking. "I keep meaning to give your five hundred pounds back to you. Seems rude of me to keep it."

He stared at her, aghast. "Why? We had an agreement, and you fulfilled your side of the bargain."

Jo laughed. "It failed. We did not go our separate ways at all."

"Well, it feels like a tremendous success to me. I insist you do whatever you like with the money."

"Anything at all?" she asked.

"Anything at all."

"Since becoming a book publisher would likely be frowned upon with my new title, I have been thinking about starting a library. I would be the patroness. But I would like for it to be in East London and provide a certain number of subscriptions for little or even no charge. I might also employ someone to teach people to read." She waved her hand. "These are all just rambling thoughts for now."

"They are *excellent* thoughts, and I wholly support them." Sheff moved his hand up her calf. "Only tell me how I can help."

"I will." She met his gaze and could see that his thoughts had taken on a decidedly lurid bent. "Should we go upstairs?"

"I suppose that would be best." Sheff removed her feet from his lap and stood. Then he gathered her into his arms, prompting her to gasp as she curled her arms around his neck. "Come, my lady wife."

Jo put her mouth to his ear and whispered, "Only if you make me."

His eyes met hers with wicked promise. "I accept your challenge."

*J*o walked nervously into Henlow House when they arrived from Weston. Though she'd been here once before—for the betrothal ball—it felt quite different now that she knew she would live here, at least temporarily.

Percy, the butler, greeted them. He bowed to Jo, so that she could see the top of his head was quite shiny. "We are delighted to welcome you to Henlow House, my lady."

Jo was still growing used to hearing that. She glanced over at Sheff beside her, who gave her an encouraging smile.

Retainers began filing into the hall, and the next half hour was spent meeting each one, including the maid who'd been assigned to assist Jo. The idea of a ladies' maid was completely foreign, but Jo understood that she would have better success if she assumed all the trappings of being a countess. If she eschewed a maid, people would find out, and it would not help her standing.

When they'd finished, the butler informed them that the duke was awaiting their arrival in the study. Sheff indicated which way to go.

"I've been to the study," Jo said. "Remember the betrothal ball when I found you there?"

"I do indeed. This will be the first time I share that space with my father since I had his valet and a footman practically carry him upstairs. I do wonder if my days of rescuing him are over. I hope so."

She smiled at him as she took his arm. "I hope so too."

He sent her a mischievous look. "That was a very arousing interlude we had in the study. I was desperate to kiss you that night. Every night since I proposed to you, really. No, before that. I think I wanted to kiss you the night I had to drag my father from the Siren's Call. That was the first time I realized I was attracted to you."

She snapped her gaze to his. "Really? That was when I first felt attracted to *you*."

Sheff laughed. "There must have been some magic in the air." He sobered, but his eyes still held a glow of mirth. "Do not tell my father, or he will try to take credit."

"Never," Jo whispered as they arrived at the study.

"Come in!" The duke beckoned, grinning. "Welcome, Lady Shefford. You have already brightened the room, and I can see you have completely transformed my son."

"For the better, I hope," she said.

There was an awkward beat as the duke moved toward her. He hesitated. "Is it permissible to hug you?"

"Yes." Jo found she could not discount the irony of embracing this man who'd been a one-time lover of her mother's. She would put that from her mind going forward.

The duke stepped back and clapped Sheff on the shoulder.

"We've something to tell you," Sheff said. "Let us sit." He guided Jo to a settee, and the duke took a chair opposite them.

"I think I know," he said shrewdly. "You're expecting a child."

Jo exchanged a look with Sheff and held back a laugh. "Well, yes," Sheff said with a charming lopsided smile. "But that is not what we wanted to discuss."

The duke slapped his thigh. "I was joking!" He laughed, then shook his head. "Well done, my boy. I knew you'd provide an heir. You just needed to do so in your own time." He did not seem to care that the child had obviously been conceived prior to their marriage.

Jo hoped he wouldn't say anything, but doubted he would. The same could not be said of her father, and for that reason, they had not yet told him she was carrying.

"The conversation we need to have does concern a child, though she is now a grown woman," Sheff said. He turned to Jo. "You tell him, my love. She's your relation."

Deep lines were etched into the duke's brow, but he didn't say anything. He watched Jo expectantly.

"My mother told me of the duchess's affair," Jo said gently. "She knew of it because the liaison was with my father."

The duke's eyes rounded. "Damn me. I'd no idea. That makes Ellis your sister. Half sister, anyway."

"Yes," Jo said, smoothing her hands over her lap. "We did not tell her or my father when we were together in Weston. We wanted to talk with you first."

"About how best to proceed," Sheff added. "Mother is going to be furious to have all this brought up. But Jo and I feel strongly that Ellis needs to hear the truth."

"I agree." The duke's expression grew sad for a moment. "I have been thinking a great deal about how I've allowed your mother to treat Ellis. I should not have permitted it. The duchess now knows she is no longer welcome here at

Henlow House, and she's to use the dower house at Beacon Park when she is in residence there."

"I can only imagine how that conversation went," Sheff murmured.

"Not well." The duke straightened. "But it was long overdue. She has taken a house in Bath for the Season, but then you probably know that Min has decided to participate in the Marriage Mart there."

"Yes, we are going to join her," Sheff said. "We think that will be the best time to tell Ellis about her parentage. And Min, for she will need to know too." He looked over at Jo, who gave him an encouraging nod. Then he returned his attention to the duke. "We also think you must be the one to tell Ellis. Since you are already planning to be in Bath with Mrs. Welbeck, I thought it the best solution."

The duke sucked in a breath. He turned his head and stared toward the window, his features drawn into a frown. "I want to say there is someone better, but who? It can't be your mother." He looked to Jo. "And your father—her father —doesn't know."

"No, and I'm not entirely sure who should tell him," Jo said. "We did not want him to know until Ellis does, for he will go directly to her and spill the secret."

"Will he come to Bath?" the duke asked. "I could tell them together—with Min. I think Ellis will be glad for the support."

"My father would be delighted to visit Bath, especially during the Season," Jo replied with a chuckle. "He can come with us."

Sheff looked toward her. "Then we'll send him home at some point, yes?"

"Of course. Or we can lodge him in a hotel," Jo said, patting Sheff's leg. Her father was lovely, but sharing a residence with him had been trying at times due to his persistent gregariousness.

Sheff grinned. "Brilliant idea."

"This will be an interesting respite in Bath," the duke said with a sardonic arch of his brow. "Your mother will not be pleased that I am there with Mrs. Welbeck, and she will be livid when I tell Ellis that she is her mother."

"We will be there to support Ellis—and you," Sheff said.

The duke nodded. "Thank you, my boy. You have been a true beacon of support and guidance. For longer than you realize." He met his son's gaze with an intent stare. "I owe you a great deal."

"Just tell me I don't have to rescue you ever again."

"You do not. At least, not because of my poor behavior." He stood. "I'll leave you to acclimate yourself. I'm so happy for you both. My only regret was missing the wedding. But I daresay you didn't miss me," he added with a self-deprecating laugh.

"Actually, I did," Sheff said. Jo moved closer against his side.

"Well, this is a day of surprises," the duke said softly. Then he whistled as he left the study.

Sheff pivoted toward Jo and put his arms around her. "That went well."

"I think so. But let us not speak of travel any longer. I am exhausted."

"Shall I carry you up to our chamber, my love?" Sheff asked before kissing her cheek.

"I beg your pardon, my lord," Percy said from the doorway. "You said you wanted the evening newspaper as soon as it arrived." He came forward with a tray bearing the *Globe*.

Sheff plucked it from the tray. "Thank you, Percy."

The butler departed, and Jo gave Sheff a quizzical look. "Why did you want the newspaper?"

He handed it to her. "There should be a matter of import inside. On the advertisement page."

Pursing her lips, Jo took the newspaper and opened it on her lap. At the very top of the advertisement page was what looked like a letter—in very small print. "Goodness, a great many people will not be able to read this."

"But you can, I hope," Sheff said, sounding eager.

"Shall I read it aloud?" Jo asked, thinking he was acting most peculiar.

"If you like."

Dearest Citizens,

I am pleased to announce my marriage to Miss Josephine Harker, the new Countess of Shefford.

Jo shot her husband a look of shock. He only shrugged in response, so she went back to reading.

She is charming, brilliant, kind-hearted, and above all, the very best of women. I am privileged to have her as my wife. I am especially fortunate that she accepted me given my past behavior as a rogue. I am pleased to share that those days are behind me. The only woman who interests me is my darling wife, and I will no longer be paying any attention to anyone else. So don't even try to ensnare me. I am completely, unabashedly, and eagerly the possession of Lady Shefford. I love her with all my heart.

-The Earl of Shefford

Jo set the paper down and gaped at him. "When did you do that?"

"I sent it from Weston a few days ago. It was Mrs. Ingram's suggestion. After she assumed I was being intimate with that woman at the party and since that woman and the others in the garden presumed to think I wanted their attention, I thought I should inform people of where my affections lie."

"Mrs. Ingram said to publish a notice in the newspaper?" Jo was aghast.

"She was joking, but I thought it a rather brilliant idea."

Jo groaned. "Now I will most certainly be the center of gossip."

Sheff tossed the paper to the floor. Then he pulled Jo onto his lap. "I wanted people to know that I am only interested in you. I only want you. I only love *you*. Now, there can be no question."

"You are a terrible romantic," Jo said, rolling her eyes. "But I love you anyway."

"Good, because I fear I am only going to grow more sentimental and more possessive. Will that be a problem?"

Jo sighed. "I suppose not. You must do as you like."

"I like you," he said with a suggestive leer. "Very much. What shall we do about that?"

"I believe it's time you showed me to our chamber, my lord."

"With pleasure, my lady." Sheff swept her into his arms, and Jo decided that being a countess—his countess—was exactly what she wanted.

Don't miss the next book in the Rogue Rules series: *Until the Rake Surrenders*!
After Evan Price is injured in an accident, Lady Minerva Halifax nurses him back to health, and they forge a surprisingly deep bond...until Min returns to the Marriage Mart and Evan becomes the most desired bachelor in Bath. Were the sparks between them real, or is Evan the worst scoundrel of them all?

Would you like to know when my next book is available and to hear about sales and deals? **Sign up for my VIP newsletter** which is the only place you can get bonus books and material such as the short prequel to the Phoenix Club series, INVITATION, and the exciting prequel to Legendary Rogues, THE LEGEND OF A ROGUE.

Join me on social media!

Facebook: https://facebook.com/DarcyBurkeFans
Instagram at <u>darcyburkeauthor</u>
Pinterest at <u>darcyburkewrite</u>

And follow me on Bookbub to receive updates on pre-orders, new releases, and deals!

Need more Regency romance? Check out my other historical series:

The Phoenix Club

Society's most exclusive invitation...

Welcome to the Phoenix Club, where London's most audacious, disreputable, and intriguing ladies and gentlemen find scandal, redemption, and second chances.

Matchmaking Chronicles

The course of true love never runs smooth. Sometimes a little matchmaking is required. When couples meet at a house party, provocative flirtation, secret rendezvous, and falling in love abound!

The Untouchables

Swoon over twelve of Society's most eligible and elusive

bachelor peers and the bluestockings, wallflowers, and outcasts who bring them to their knees!

The Untouchables: The Spitfire Society

Meet the smart, independent women who've decided they don't need Society's rules, their families' expectations, or, most importantly, a husband. But just because they don't need a man doesn't mean they might not *want* one…

The Untouchables: The Pretenders

Set in the captivating world of The Untouchables, follow the saga of a trio of siblings who excel at being something they're not. Can a dauntless Bow Street Runner, a devastated viscount, and a disillusioned Society miss unravel their secrets?

Marrywell Brides

Come to Marrywell, England where the annual May Day Matchmaking Festival has been bringing hopeful romantics together for hundreds of years. The dukes and rogues of the Regency will meet their matches with spirited and captivating ladies who may very well steal their hearts.

Wicked Dukes Club

Six books written by me and my BFF, NYT Bestselling Author Erica Ridley. Meet the unforgettable men of London's most notorious tavern, The Wicked Duke. Seductively handsome, with charm and wit to spare, one night with these rakes and rogues will never be enough…

Love is All Around

Heartwarming Regency-set retellings of classic Christmas stories (written after the Regency!) featuring a cozy village, three siblings, and the best gift of all: love.

Secrets and Scandals
Six epic stories set in London's glittering ballrooms and England's lush countryside.

Legendary Rogues
Five intrepid heroines and adventurous heroes embark on exciting quests across the Georgian Highlands and Regency England and Wales!

If you like contemporary romance, I hope you'll check out my **Ribbon Ridge** series available from Avon Impulse, and the continuation of Ribbon Ridge in **So Hot**.

I hope you'll consider leaving a review at your favorite online vendor or networking site!

I appreciate my readers so much. Thank you, thank you, *thank you.*

ALSO BY DARCY BURKE

Historical Romance

Rogue Rules
If the Duke Dares

Because the Baron Broods

When the Viscount Seduces

As the Earl Likes

Until the Rake Surrenders

Since the Marquess Demands

What the Scoundrel Desires

How the Devil Sins

The Phoenix Club
Improper

Impassioned

Intolerable

Indecent

Impossible

Irresistible

Impeccable

Insatiable

Marrywell Brides
Beguiling the Duke

Romancing the Heiress

Matching the Marquess

The Matchmaking Chronicles

Yule Be My Duke

The Rigid Duke

The Bachelor Earl (also prequel to *The Untouchables*)

The Runaway Viscount

The Make-Believe Widow

The Untouchables

The Bachelor Earl (prequel)

The Forbidden Duke

The Duke of Daring

The Duke of Deception

The Duke of Desire

The Duke of Defiance

The Duke of Danger

The Duke of Ice

The Duke of Ruin

The Duke of Lies

The Duke of Seduction

The Duke of Kisses

The Duke of Distraction

The Untouchables: The Spitfire Society

Never Have I Ever with a Duke

A Duke is Never Enough

A Duke Will Never Do

The Untouchables: The Pretenders

A Secret Surrender

A Scandalous Bargain

A Rogue to Ruin

Love is All Around
(A Regency Holiday Trilogy)
The Red Hot Earl
The Gift of the Marquess
Joy to the Duke

Wicked Dukes Club
One Night for Seduction by Erica Ridley
One Night of Surrender by Darcy Burke
One Night of Passion by Erica Ridley
One Night of Scandal by Darcy Burke
One Night to Remember by Erica Ridley
One Night of Temptation by Darcy Burke

Secrets and Scandals
Her Wicked Ways
His Wicked Heart
To Seduce a Scoundrel
To Love a Thief (a novella)
Never Love a Scoundrel
Scoundrel Ever After

Legendary Rogues
Lady of Desire
Romancing the Earl
Lord of Fortune
Captivating the Scoundrel

Historical Mystery

<u>*Raven & Wren*</u>

A Whisper of Death

A Whisper at Midnight

A Whisper and a Curse

Contemporary Romance

Ribbon Ridge

Where the Heart Is (a prequel novella)

Only in My Dreams

Yours to Hold

When Love Happens

The Idea of You

When We Kiss

You're Still the One

Ribbon Ridge: So Hot

So Good

So Right

So Wrong

ABOUT THE AUTHOR

Darcy Burke is the USA Today Bestselling Author of sexy, emotional historical and contemporary romance. Darcy wrote her first book at age 11, a happily ever after about a swan addicted to magic and the female swan who loved him, with exceedingly poor illustrations. Join her Reader Club newsletter for the latest updates from Darcy.

A native Oregonian, Darcy lives on the edge of wine country with her guitar-strumming husband, incredibly talented artist daughter, and imaginative, Japanese-speaking son who will almost certainly out-write her one day (that may be tomorrow). They're a crazy cat family with two Bengal cats, a small, fame-seeking cat named after a fruit, an older rescue Maine Coon with attitude to spare, an adorable former stray who wandered onto their deck and into their hearts, and two bonded boys who used to belong to (separate) neighbors but chose them instead. You can find Darcy in her comfy writing chair balancing her laptop and a cat or three, attempting yoga, folding laundry (which she loves), or wildlife spotting and playing games with her family. She loves traveling to the UK and visiting her cousins in Denmark. Visit Darcy online at www.darcyburke.com and follow her on social media.

facebook.com/DarcyBurkeFans

instagram.com/darcyburkeauthor

pinterest.com/darcyburkewrites

goodreads.com/darcyburke

bookbub.com/authors/darcy-burke

amazon.com/author/darcyburke

threads.net/@darcyburkeauthor

tiktok.com/@darcyburkeauthor